PRAISE FOR
BESTSE...
RAEA~~~~ ~~AYNE

'Emotional and deeply satisfying. I savoured every page.'
Sunday Times bestselling author Sarah Morgan
on The Sea Glass Cottage

'[Thayne] is a rising star in the romance world. Her books
are wonderfully romantic, feel-good reads that end
with me sighing over the last pages.'
—#1 *New York Times* bestselling author
Debbie Macomber

'RaeAnne Thayne is quickly becoming one of my
favorite authors…. Once you start reading,
you aren't going to be able to stop.'
—*Fresh Fiction*

'RaeAnne has a knack for capturing those
emotions that come from the heart.'
—*RT Book Reviews*

'Tiny Haven Point springs to vivid life in Thayne's capable
hands as she spins another sweet, heartfelt story.'
—*Library Journal* on *Redemption Bay*

Summer at Lake Haven

RaeAnne Thayne

MILLS & BOON

Mills & Boon
An imprint of HarperCollins*Publishers* Ltd
1 London Bridge Street
London SE1 9GF

This paperback edition 2020

1
First published in Great Britain by
Mills & Boon, an imprint of HarperCollins*Publishers* Ltd 2020

A catalogue record for this book is available from the British Library.

ISBN: 978-1-84845-812-3

MIX
Paper from
responsible sources
FSC FSC™ C007454

www.fsc.org

This book is produced from independently certified FSC™ paper to ensure responsible forest management.

For more information visit: www.harpercollins.co.uk/green

Printed and bound in Great Britain by
CPI Group (UK) Ltd, Croydon, CRO 4YY

To my wonderful readers,
who have made writing each
Haven Point book a joy.
Thank you!

Summer at
Lake Haven

CHAPTER ONE

TWO STRANGE CHILDREN were playing on her dock.

Frowning with concern, Samantha Fremont looked out the window of the house she had lived in all of her twenty-eight years, on the shore of Lake Haven in the small, picturesque town of Haven Point, Idaho.

She didn't recognize them. Who were they and what were they doing on her property? From here, she could see the trespassers looked to be a girl of about eight and a boy a few years younger. They were dressed in summer wear that even from here Sam could tell was costly, even designer quality. A sundress for the girl of a pale peach cotton dotted with white flowers, and khaki shorts and a blue striped shirt for the boy.

She looked out at the water and then back at the dock. The children were still there. Not a mirage, then, induced by a combination of too much work and too much time spent hunched over her sewing machine or looking at fashion magazines.

Most likely, they were renting the house next door and didn't realize the dock stretching twenty feet out into Lake Haven belonged to her house, not theirs.

Her mother would have had a fit. Linda had hated that the house next door had been turned into a vacation rental after the previous owner, a kindly older woman, passed away. She had complained to anyone who would listen about the noise level, strange people coming and going at all hours of the day and night, the lack of respect she claimed the short-term tenants showed for the established neighborhood.

If she had been here to see those two children out on the dock without any sign of supervision, Linda would have marched out there, grabbed them both firmly by the hand and trotted off in search of their absentee parents. Once she found them, she probably would have spent the next half hour haranguing said parents about the importance of teaching children to respect the property of others and the dangers inherent in allowing children to play next to a large body of water without adequate supervision.

But her mother wasn't here anymore.

The little spasm of hurt in her chest was as familiar to her now as her favorite pair of scissors. For all her mother's crankiness, the house didn't feel the same without her. Five months had passed since Linda Fremont died of a massive heart attack in her sleep. Five months without her tart tongue or her pessimism or her dire prognostications.

Sam wouldn't have believed it possible but she still missed her mother.

Betsey whined and she looked at the large pen where three puppies were crawling all over the little Yorkie/shih tzu cross lying on her side.

Her mother would have had a fit about the dog, too. Despite pleading, cajoling and, okay, even a few outright tantrums, Sam had never been allowed to have a dog. Or a pet of any sort, really. Linda would never budge.

Dogs were too much of a bother, her mother had always said, and cats were too sneaky. As Sam wasn't a fan of reptiles or rodents, she had contented herself as a child with pretending her stuffed animals were real or that her friends' dogs were really hers.

Months after her mother's death she had still been lost and grieving in that weird irrational place where the world didn't seem quite right when she had made an after-work visit to the grocery store for more TV dinners. Outside, she encountered a young couple who looked like ski bums holding up a sign claiming they had a dog for sale.

"Betsey is the sweetest thing," the woman, little older than a teenager, had assured her. "We love her and it will break our hearts to lose her. It's just that now the ski season is over, we have new jobs on the Big Island and it's a real pain to take a dog over there."

"Plus, you know, we're really not pet people," the young man had said in an apologetic voice, his eyes sorrowful beneath his dreadlocks.

Sam had fought the overpowering urge to tell him that since they had taken on the responsibility for a dog that made them pet people.

Before she could find herself channeling her mother, Sam had taken one look at that cute little furry face, with its big brown eyes and floppy ears, and had felt a sharp tug in the vicinity of her heart.

You could take her, a seductive voice had whispered. *What's stopping you?*

Her mother was gone. She was alone in the house. She was an adult running her own boutique. Surely she could have a dog now. What was the harm?

"Betsey is totally house-trained and hardly ever barks," the woman had pushed, obviously sensing blood in the water. "We'll throw in her crate, her toys, a bag of her favorite treats and a whole container of food. All we're asking is two hundred dollars to help us out with gas money."

Sam had been such a sucker. Looking back, she could see exactly how stupid she had been. She might as well have had Soft Touch tattooed on her forehead. For one thing, how would gas money help them get to the Big Island? For another, they had been entirely too eager to get rid of the dog, especially if she was as perfect as they claimed. Sam had been blinded by her own long-buried childhood desire for a pet and hadn't for a moment pondered why they were selling this cute pup outside the supermarket.

She wasn't sure if she had been lured more by their words, by the dog's extraordinary cuteness or her dread at returning to this empty house night after night. Whatever the reason, she had handed over all the cash in her wallet down to her last dollar, scooped up the little dog and her small assortment of supplies and headed home with a feeling of deep exhilaration.

Samantha didn't have to try hard to imagine how her mother would have rolled her eyes with a chorus of *I told you so*'s the next day, after she took the dog to her friend, veterinarian Dr. Dani Morales, to have her checked out and learned the little dog wasn't simply chubby, she was expecting puppies.

That was six weeks ago. Now, instead of living out her grandiose image of having one sweet-natured, quiet little lapdog who would sit at her feet while she sewed, she had one exhausted, stressed-out mama dog and three very active, very demanding, month-old puppies.

She sighed, turning her attention away from the puppies and back to the children on her dock. Where were the parents? She couldn't see a single adult in sight.

She was scanning the area when she suddenly heard a splash and then a scream. When she jerked her gaze back to the dock, she saw the boy in the water and the older girl, likely his sister, belly down on the dock, frantically trying to pull him back up.

It wasn't deep there, only about four feet or so, but would still be over a little boy's head. Sam yanked open the door of her sunroom and raced to the dock. At her arrival, the girl looked at her with mingled terror and relief.

"My brother's fallen in," she exclaimed in what Sam noticed was a British accent. "Please. Can you help him? Don't let him drown!"

Sam was already shucking her shoes and taking off her baggy sweater. She wore yoga pants and a workout tank underneath, her favorite sewing clothes.

The boy hadn't resurfaced, she realized as panic now washed over her, thick and greasy. Where were his blasted parents?

She didn't want to go in the water. If she could, she tried to avoid it at all costs. She *could* swim, she just didn't like to. It all traced back to a time when she had nearly drowned herself when she was four or five at this very same dock, trying to follow her father, who was getting into a fishing boat and hadn't noticed when she wandered out of the house to join him.

Inky water closing over her head, the instinctive gasping for air, the cold fear. It was probably her earliest memory.

She had overcome it, for the most part. She lived on the lake, after all, and loved it most of the time. Once in a great while, the old phobias came back.

None of that mattered right now. A child needed her.

Without giving herself time to think further about it, she jumped off the dock near the area where she thought she had seen the boy go into the water.

Though it was early June, the lake was icy with run-off from the mountains surrounding Haven Point. In her opinion, it should be against the law for anyone to swim in Lake Haven until at least August. By then, the summer sun had time to warm the water a little, at least in the shallows.

She ignored the cold, focusing only on trying to feel around for the child. The boy resurfaced finally about three feet away, slapping his arms wildly and gasping for air.

She pushed from the muddy floor and grabbed hold of him.

"Calm down. You're okay. I've got you now. We'll get you out."

"Cold. S-s-so cold."

He had a British accent, as well, she heard through his chattering teeth.

"I know. We'll get you warm soon enough. I'm Sam, by the way. Samantha."

"T-Thomas."

Though the shallow lake bottom here was muddy, making it difficult for her feet to find purchase, she managed to feel around with her bare feet until she found a rock, then stood on that and hefted the boy onto the dock, where his sister waited. A moment later, Sam pulled herself after him and flopped onto the wooden dock, shivering in the June sunshine while adrenaline still surged through her.

"Here you go. Safe and sound. See?"

"Thank you, ma'am." The girl said the word like "mum" as Samantha wrapped her sweater around the boy.

"You're very welcome," she answered.

"Thomas can be a bother but I would miss him. So would our father and Nana and Grandfather."

She couldn't help noticing the girl didn't mention anything about their mother missing them. What was that about? Did they have a mother? She had to wonder. Before she could ask, a man hurried out of the house next door toward the children.

A gorgeous man.

He had startling blue eyes and dark hair that looked tousled, as if he had only recently dragged a hand through it. He wore a blue Oxford shirt with the sleeves rolled up and one button on the collar undone. She had a wild, completely irrational urge to straighten his hair and fasten his button.

She coughed a little, telling herself the sudden tightness in her throat must be a delayed reaction from the cold water.

The man took in the scene at a glance. "Thomas. Did you fall in?"

"I did. And then the nice lady helped me out," the boy said, his teeth still chattering.

His father hardly gave her a look. "What are you two doing out here? I thought you were unpacking your things in your rooms."

"We finished and decided to go exploring," the girl said apologetically. "You were on your mobile so we didn't want to bother you and Mrs. Gilbert was having a rest. And then Thomas was looking at a fish in the water. We thought it might be one of your salmon. He bent down a little too far and lost his balance. Next thing we knew, he was in the lake. He didn't come up and then this very kind woman came and helped him out."

The man finally turned his gaze to her, and Sam was suddenly intensely conscious that she was now wearing dripping wet yoga pants and a thin workout tank. She felt exposed, vulnerable, as if she'd walked into Serrano's, her favorite restaurant in town, wearing only a bikini.

"Is that what happened?"

She couldn't tell what he was thinking. She gave a modest shrug. "I was watching from the window and saw him go into the water."

"I don't know what to say, Ms...."

"Fremont. Samantha Fremont. I live just...there."

She gestured back toward her house, feeling breathless and silly. Oh, good grief. This was ridiculous. So he had brilliant blue eyes and a rumpled air she found irresistible. The last thing she needed in her life right now was a man. Any man, especially a good-looking man with an accent and two adorable children.

"Hello. I'm Ian Summerhill and these wild creatures are my offspring, Amelia and Thomas."

At his introduction, a few of the pieces began to fall into place and she made a connection she should have earlier. "Summerhill. Are you any relation to Gemma Summerhill?"

"She's our aunt," Amelia exclaimed.

"You know Gemma?" Ian Summerhill asked.

"Yes. We're friends. I'm actually making her wedding dress."

Why on earth had Gemma never mentioned her gorgeous brother was coming to town for the wedding and bringing along his extraordinarily cute children?

Also, where again was the children's mother?

"We're here all summer," Thomas declared. His teeth had largely stopped chattering in the June sunshine and his hair had even started to dry, the dark locks turning blond.

"We're having an American adventure before Aunt Gemma's wedding." Amelia sounded less than enthused at that particular prospect.

"How fun for you. Welcome to Haven Point," Sam said,

eager suddenly to escape. She was growing increasingly aware that she was drenched and wearing skintight clothing…and also that she hadn't been around a good-looking man in a very long time.

"I hope you have a lovely stay. I'm sure we'll see each other around."

"No doubt, especially if you're friends with Gemma."

That did make things awkward, considering she had to deliver bad news.

"I should tell you the dock actually belongs to me. The property line is just there, on the far side of the dock."

"That's impossible." He frowned. "The real estate agent assured me we had dock access. I've rented a boat for the summer for my work."

Oh, her mother would have loved telling off him *and* whatever unscrupulous real estate agent had lied to him about the dock access.

"I'm afraid it's not only possible but reality. The dock is our property. You were misled. But I'm sure we can work something out, if it's that important to you." She didn't want to be a jerk about it, especially not to Gemma's family. She wasn't using the dock. In fact, it hadn't been used since Sam's father died, though her mother continued to make sure it was maintained properly as if it were some kind of shrine to Lyle Fremont's memory.

Her new neighbor looked at the dock, then back at her, his blue eyes as troubled as the lake on a stormy afternoon. "It is. It's vital. I must have water access during our stay."

If that's the case, maybe you should have nailed down ownership of the dock before you rented the property. Again, she could hear her mother's crankiness coming through her thoughts and swallowed down the words.

"Can I dry off first?" she asked, a little annoyed at his

urgency. It was only a dock, for heaven's sake. There was a marina only a five-minute drive from here where he could moor any boat he had rented during his stay.

"How much?"

She blinked. "Excuse me?"

"How much would it take for me to secure permission to use the dock for the summer? I don't want to have to go to Serenity Harbor or down to the marina every time I need to go out on the water, if I can avoid it."

A gust of wind blew across the lake and Sam shivered as it knuckled beneath her wet clothes with icy fingers. She had a sudden crazy impulse to snap back that no amount would be enough. She had jumped into the icy waters of Lake Haven to rescue his child and was still shivering from it, hadn't she? And now he was insulting her by implying she was crass and greedy enough to let him do anything he wanted if he paid her enough money.

She could imagine her mother's reaction too easily. After a lifetime, it was hard to shut her out. Linda would have never allowed him to use the dock. Or if she did, she might have tried to bilk entirely too much money for it.

Over the past few months as she tried to adjust to life without her mom, Samantha had become fairly good at imagining what Linda might have done in any given situation…and then doing exactly the opposite.

She swallowed her annoyance at her neighbor. Maybe he was jet-lagged or something. Or maybe it was a cultural thing, that he didn't understand how rude his implication was that he could buy his way past any hurdle.

"Go ahead and use the dock." She forced a smile. "It's fine. I don't have a boat and don't expect to get one any time soon, so it will only be unused all summer." As it's been unused for every summer since she was seven years old.

Eyebrows furrowed, he studied her as if trying to figure out her game. She wanted to tell him that sometimes a generous act was simply that. Generous, with no strings attached or hidden motivations.

"Thank you," he said. "That's very gracious of you."

"Your sister is my friend, Mr. Summerhill. It's the least I can do for Gemma."

Something in her brisk tone must have alerted him to her annoyance. He opened his mouth as if to apologize but before he could, a woman in her late sixties hurried out of the house next door. She was tall and thin to the point of gauntness, with large glasses and short-cropped hair, but her face still somehow emanated a kindness that made her plain features warm and attractive.

"Oh, good gracious. There you are. We were all supposed to be having a kip from the long flight. I close my eyes for five minutes and the two of you escape. And it looks like someone had a dunking, as well. Oh, Thomas. What have you done now?"

"I was looking for salmon and I leaned over too far and lost my balance."

"Oh, dear. I'm sorry, m'…sir," she said to Ian.

"We're the ones who are sorry, Mrs. Gilbert," the girl said, though she didn't look particularly repentant.

"Sorry, Mrs. Gilbert," the boy said. Samantha was relieved to see his teeth had finally stopped chattering. She wished her own would, but he had been wrapped in her sweater while she was still barely dressed.

"No harm done, thanks to Ms. Fremont here." The woman's employer gave Samantha a stiff smile.

"Bless you, then," Mrs. Gilbert said, her eyes bright

and so warm that Samantha immediately liked her. "Let's get you into some dry clothes, young man. Come along. You, too, Amelia."

They waved at Sam and then followed after the woman like ducklings, leaving her alone with their father.

She almost wished she had snatched her sweater back from Thomas before he left her alone with a man who was entirely too good-looking for her peace of mind.

It was a very good thing she had decided she was swearing off men for now or she would definitely make a fool of herself over someone like Ian Summerhill.

AFTER LETTY AND the children headed for their rental house, Ian was uncomfortably aware that he was alone with Samantha Fremont, in her thin, soaked clothing and her wet hair whose true color he couldn't really tell.

Something told him it was probably not wise to spend much time on his own with her. How unfortunate for him that his new next-door neighbor was so lovely. Soft, pretty, curvy.

"Thank you again for rescuing my son," he said, trying not to notice how her clothing clung to those curves. "He can be a bit of a rascal at times but I'm rather fond of him."

"You're welcome." She didn't appear to like him very much, though he couldn't quite figure out why.

"Thank you also for your offer to allow the use of your dock. It's very generous of you. Are you quite certain you don't mind? We're here until after Gemma's wedding."

"It's fine."

Yes. She definitely didn't like him.

Usually that wouldn't have bothered him but the woman was Gemma's friend, he would be living next to her for the next few weeks and she was doing him the tremendous favor of allowing use of a dock to which he wasn't entitled, contrary to his short-term rental agreement. He would be having a word with the estate agent who had helped him find the place.

"I'm sorry if I came across as too vehement earlier. I'm a professor, you see, of marine biology," he felt compelled to explain. "While we're here, I'm studying the particular subspecies of kokanee salmon that live in Lake Haven, which is remarkably similar genetically to a subspecies in England."

"Funny. I would have thought you were here for your sister's wedding."

Ian felt his cheeks flush with embarrassment. "You're correct. That is the main reason for our trip. In this instance, I'm fortunate to be able to combine work with pleasure. The salmon here in Lake Haven breed in chalk streams similar to a unique strain we have in Dorset and have evolved similarly. I've been interested in comparing the two subspecies for years, long before Gemma moved to this area to work for Caine Tech. It seems a dream come true to actually be able to study them in person."

He sounded an utter idiot. Get him around a beautiful woman and he completely lost his brain. Why would he possibly think she might be interested in salmon, unique or otherwise?

She gave a smile that looked forced. "How fortuitous that your sister's wedding allowed you the chance to tick an item off a bucket list. I hope you enjoy your stay here in Haven Point. Will you excuse me now? I need to find some dry clothes."

"Yes. Of course. Forgive me for keeping you. I'm sure we'll run into each other again."

"No doubt," she said. "Good afternoon."

He nodded and she turned to hurry back to her house.

Ian watched her go for a moment before he turned back to the lake with its infinite mysteries.

Clouds were gathering among the peaks of the steep mountains on the other side of the lake. Rain clouds, if he wasn't mistaken. He had heard there were often thundershowers in these mountain lakes during the afternoons.

He couldn't wait to discover the idiosyncrasies of this lake. He had been intrigued by the area for years, more so since Gemma came here to make a new start.

He found it every bit as beautiful as his sister had described, a pure, vivid blue surrounded by mountains and pine forests. Already he could feel some of the tension that had taken up permanent residence in his spine over the past three years began to ease.

He and his children both needed this. Thomas and Amelia were extraordinarily resilient but they had still struggled since their mother's death. Amelia was prone to tantrums and random fits of anger and Thomas had become much more clingy.

He had struggled, as well, Ian acknowledged, mainly to come to terms with his own failures.

When this holiday was over, Ian would have to put away his biology studies to turn his attention toward his responsibilities to his family. He knew what awaited him. While he dreaded some of it, he knew it was past time. His father had given him time during Susan's illness and the past year while they all grieved, but Ian knew Henry couldn't wait any longer.

He had one last glorious month of freedom.

Gemma's wedding had given the perfect excuse to come to a place that fascinated him, to spend more time with his children as they worked on their journey toward healing and to immerse himself in his research.

He had plenty to focus on while he was in Haven Point. He absolutely did not need the distraction of a soft, curvy woman with hazel eyes and a smile that left him light-headed.

CHAPTER TWO

WITHOUT A DOUBT, this was Samantha's happy place.

Some people enjoyed the adrenaline rush of a perfect run while downhill skiing. Others found most contentment while curled up in a comfortable chair with a good book and a mug of hot cocoa. Still others thrived as maestros in their own kitchen or while walking a mountain trail at sunrise.

For Samantha, it was right here in the workroom of her boutique, with a mouth full of pins and her hands holding up a length of gorgeous fabric.

Sam walked around Gemma Summerhill, who stood on a stool. Gemma had the perfect build to show off her creation. She was slim, tall, with dark hair and the vivid blue eyes she shared with her brother.

Samantha caught herself. She had told herself she wouldn't spend another moment thinking about Ian Summerhill. After a restless night with heated dreams that featured a handsome man with those same blue eyes saying tantalizing things to her with a British accent, Samantha had resolved to put the man completely out of her head.

"Are you doing all right?" she asked his sister. "I only need a moment longer."

Gemma, arms in the air, nodded. "For a dress this perfect, I'll stand here all day. I can't believe you've made so much progress in only a few weeks."

"It's really exquisite, Sam. One of the best dresses you've ever designed." Her best friend, Katrina Bailey Callahan, sat in the corner, watching the proceedings. She was there for moral support for Gemma but had also agreed to help Sam if she needed it.

Sam had started out helping her mother with fittings. By the time Linda died, their roles had reversed and her mother had played the role of an assistant. Linda had always been the one to help her with fittings. It still seemed odd not to have her there.

She was grateful for Katrina's help. While she had employees working out in the boutique area who could help her, including her assistant manager, Rachel Muñoz, she was shorthanded today and didn't want to take her staff away from the showroom while she focused on the custom design work. She would repay Kat with lunch sometime soon, or maybe an hour or two of babysitting for Kat's children, Milo and Gabriela.

"What about your own wedding dress?" Gemma asked.

Katrina made a face, considering. "Okay, you're right. My dress was divine, the most gorgeous dress in the world. But yours is definitely a close second."

"We will have to agree to disagree on that," Gemma said, looking so pleased at her reflection in the mirror that Sam had to smile through her pins.

She loved helping a bride feel her very best on her wedding day. It was one of the best feelings in the world.

"I'm so grateful you could find the time to make a dress for me," Gemma added to Sam. "I know how crowded your schedule is."

She pinned the last hem. "Never too busy for you," she vowed, and meant the words.

She had adored Gemma since the other woman came to

Haven Point. She was funny, kind, compassionate. Somehow Gemma had managed to slip seamlessly into the fabric of life in this small Idaho town on the shores of a stunning lake.

"Ah. You're the sweetest." Gemma looked genuinely touched. "Are you certain you'll be able to finish in time?"

"It shouldn't be a problem. There's not that much left to do. I've blocked all my spare sewing time for the next few weeks and intend to put my whole energy toward it."

"You're a doll. Thank you."

"I'm honored you're letting me do this for you."

"Don't be silly. When one of the most amazing clothing designers I've ever met is my dear friend, I would be crazy not to ask her to design my wedding gown."

Samantha glowed, not only at the praise of her work but because Gemma considered her a friend.

"Samantha is the best designer in the entire state of Idaho," Kat said loyally.

All right, that might be hyperbole but she wasn't about to argue. Sam *did* know she was extraordinarily lucky to be here in a town she loved, doing work she loved and surrounded by dear friends.

"I'm a seamstress," she felt compelled to clarify. "I'm not really a designer."

Katrina made a scoffing sort of noise. "Oh, stop it. The only one in this room who doesn't consider you a designer is standing there with a pincushion on her wrist."

Samantha fought down her instinctive impulse to disagree, to point out the many designs she had tried that were flops.

Of course Katrina would praise her work. She was Sam's best friend and had been since they were in grade school. Kat was contractually obligated to give her positive strokes, right? If she wasn't her best friend, would she still like Sam's designs?

She knew that was the negative voice in her head that still spoke in her mother's voice. Would it ever leave her?

She felt the twinge of guilt mingled with grief that had become painfully familiar to her since her mother died.

"I met your brother yesterday," she told Gemma to distract herself from it. As she spoke, she was careful not to meet Katrina's gaze this time. Her friend knew her entirely too well and might begin to guess at the whirl of conflicting emotions the man had stirred in her during their brief encounter.

Gemma's eyes lit up. "That's right. I forgot he decided to rent a house near yours. Did you meet the children, as well?"

"Yes. Actually, I fished Thomas out of the lake when he fell off my dock."

"Did you?" Katrina looked shocked, knowing full well her aversion to the water.

"Oh, thank you," Gemma exclaimed. "He might be a bit of a rascal but I'm fairly fond of him."

Samantha shrugged. "It wasn't deep water. He might have even been able to pull himself back on the dock or at least hold on to it to get to shore, but I think the cold water knocked the air out of him. I'm glad I was there. It was an accident. Amelia said he was looking at fish and lost his balance."

Gemma shook her head. "That boy is going to be the death of poor Mrs. Gilbert, their nanny. He's even more of a handful than Ian was at that age."

Samantha had a difficult time imagining Ian Summerhill as a mischievous, troublesome boy. He seemed too stiff for that. Her mind chose that moment to replay one of those heated dreams she'd had about him and she felt her cheeks flush, hoping neither Kat nor Gemma noticed.

"I didn't realize your family was coming to town for the wedding," Katrina said. "Silly me. I should have realized. How long are they staying?"

"My parents don't arrive until the week before the wedding but my brother and his children came to the area a bit early."

"Amelia said they're having an American adventure."

Gemma smiled as Sam moved to the other side to finish pinning up the train.

"Ian likely won't appreciate me spilling his secrets but my brother has been obsessed with the Wild Wild West since he was a boy watching reruns of old Westerns on the telly. Both my brothers loved them. Father, too. He bought them matching cowboy pajamas."

She tried again to picture Ian as a boy of Thomas's age, hair still dark and tousled, eyes still that bright blue, wearing cowboy pj's and watching old-time heroes riding through the mountains in search of the bad guys who had betrayed them.

It was an entirely too endearing image. She didn't want to feel fondly toward him. She didn't have time to think about him at all.

She was the one who brought up his name, Sam reminded herself. This whole conversation was entirely her fault.

"How old are the children?" Katrina asked. As an elementary school teacher and mother of two adopted children, she always focused on children first.

"Amelia is eight and Ian is six. They're lovely children, despite everything they've been through."

"What have they been through?" Kat asked with a concerned frown.

"It's very sad actually. Their mother died a year ago of cancer."

"Oh," Sam exclaimed, letting go of the material. "Oh. Those poor dears."

"She was sick for a year before that. I think they're all still figuring out how to go on."

That must be the reason for the shadows she thought she had seen in his eyes.

Sunlight filtered in through her high windows, making the dress glow as Sam quickly finished.

"I won't lie. I had my own issues with Susan before she grew ill, but I would never say she wasn't a loving mother. The children miss her very much. They're all a little lost, if you want the truth. I'm hoping this time together in Haven Point helps them find their way a little. It certainly worked its magic on me."

Sam didn't know Gemma's entire story but she knew enough to be certain her friend very much deserved her happy ending with a good man like Josh Bailey, Katrina's cousin.

She had dated Josh herself a few times. He was nice, gentlemanly, funny. For a week or two, she had even thought she might be falling for him.

Of course, she could say that about a dozen guys in Lake Haven County.

Sam shoved a pin in a little too hard, poking her finger in the process. She told herself that was the reason she had winced, not the reminder of her own years of stupidity.

"I'm sorry I didn't think to mention they were renting the house near you," Gemma said.

"It's fine," she answered. "You have a few things on your mind."

"I do, but I would've told you to watch out for them. It's just that I didn't know until last minute which house he would choose. There were two or three rental properties in the offing."

And she had been lucky enough to win the Ian Summerhill lottery apparently.

"I'm thrilled he'll be close so you can keep an eye on him."

She did not want to keep her eyes or anything else on the man. Okay, it wasn't precisely a hardship, but she knew her own weaknesses and one of those was any gorgeous man with a tragic backstory. She tended to find them impossible to resist.

Not this time. She was entirely too busy to obsess over her new neighbor.

"I'll look forward to getting to know them," she said. It wasn't precisely a lie. The children were adorable.

When the fitting was over, Gemma hugged her one more time, almost weeping over the beauty of the gown. "Genius. I'll say it one more time. You're brilliant."

Samantha laughed roughly. "We both know that's not true but thank you for saying so."

"I'm sorry I can't come to the Helping Hands meeting today."

"Oh, no. I'm sorry you'll miss it," Sam said.

"I am, too. After you called me to let me know the dress was ready for the next fitting, this seemed the perfect afternoon to take care of a few other wedding details. I've plans to meet with the caterer this afternoon in Shelter Springs. This wedding planning is not for the faint of heart!"

"Too bad you couldn't do what Bowie and I did," Katrina said with a grin. "We eloped to a private island in the Caribbean."

It wasn't precisely the entire story. The private island was correct but they hadn't really eloped. The wedding had been more of a destination event off the coast of Colombia. All the Baileys and their significant others had flown over for it. Sam had been there, too, along with her mother, who had complained the entire time about the heat, the food, the ridiculous expense that could have been spent on other things.

While there were a few moments when Samantha might have been envious, she would never begrudge Katrina her happiness. She and Bowie were ridiculously happy together and were doing an amazing job raising two special-needs children, Bo's younger brother whom they had adopted and who had been diagnosed with autism, and a young girl from Colombia with Down syndrome who had found her way into Katrina's heart before she ever met Bowie.

"I will say a private island destination wedding sounds heavenly. It really does. But I'm afraid it's too late now. For one thing, Josh's family would kill me if I did that. For another, Eliza has been working for weeks to have Snow Angel Cove ready for the wedding. And finally, my brother and his children are here now and my parents will be here soon."

"I think you're stuck at this point."

Gemma gave a good-natured smile. "Ah, well. Might as well make the best of it."

"It will be wonderful," Sam said. "What's more romantic than getting married on the shores of the lake at sunset at Snow Angel Cove, one of the most gorgeous spots on Lake Haven?"

"True enough. Thank you for reminding me."

Gemma kissed her on the cheek, then picked up her purse. "I really do have to go. Thank you again for *everything*. I mean that. I adore you both."

When she left, Gemma seemed to take all the energy of the room with her, leaving Samantha suddenly exhausted. She wanted to flop to the ground right there on the floor of her workroom and close her eyes for five minutes.

"It really is an exquisite gown," Katrina said when the room was quiet once more. "I especially love the neckline that highlights her gorgeous shoulders and collarbones."

"I agree. That's my favorite part, too. She's going to be a beautiful bride."

Gemma was only the latest in a string of beautiful brides Sam had helped to shine on their special day.

"Are you okay?"

She looked up quickly, wondering if Kat had heard that wistful note in her voice she hadn't meant to reveal. "Sure. Terrific. Why do you ask?"

"I don't know. You seem a little down. Is it because your mom's birthday is coming up?"

She had almost forgotten Linda's birthday would have been the following week. Her mother had never much wanted to celebrate her birthday. She supposed it was the mark of a true friend that Kat had remembered, anyway.

"That must be it," she lied.

Katrina gave her a hug. "I'm sorry. I know how much you miss her."

"It's just different, you know?"

"I can't imagine how hard you must find it now that she's gone."

Charlene, Katrina's mother, was just about the exact opposite of Linda. She was funny and kind, supportive of all her children, no matter what they chose to do with their lives.

"I'm doing all right. To be honest, the past few months I've been so busy with the puppies and the wedding dress orders that I haven't had much time to think about how empty the house feels."

"Those puppies are so adorable. I still can't believe my mom is taking one when they're old enough to leave Betsey."

Charlene had fallen for the puppies and had been the first to claim one. She would be the perfect puppy mom to Oscar, the smallest of the litter. All the puppies had been placed, which was a relief. In a few short weeks, she hoped to have them ready for their forever homes.

"So. Gemma's brother. I'm imagining a sexy blond Jude Law type. Am I right?"

She pictured him for a moment, big, muscular, dark-haired with his collar button undone and his hair mussed. "No. He does have blue eyes but that's about the only resemblance. I gather he's a biology nerd. He's doing research on Lake Haven's salmon population."

"Maybe a summer romance with a handsome Brit who will be leaving in a few weeks is just what you need. That would certainly shake you out of your blues."

She frowned at her friend. "Ha. When would I have time for a fling, even if I wanted one? I'm working every waking moment either at the store or on my own projects at home. I've got orders for four wedding dresses to be created by the end of the summer and I've gone from never having responsibility for a pet to now having a dog with three puppies who need attention. All. The. Time."

Suddenly the weight of everything was too much. The sleepless nights working, the worry over the business, missing her mother. Gemma's upcoming wedding to the man of her dreams...who had for a very short time once been the man of Sam's.

The loneliness.

Everyone in her world had someone else to love. Everyone but her.

The tears came out of nowhere, bursting out before she could stop them.

Katrina gave her one astonished look, then hugged Sam hard, which only seemed to intensify her sobs. Though the gesture was comforting, kind, it only made her feel more stupid.

"You've got so much more on your plate. You've got Milo and Gabriela and Bowie. I have no right to feel so overwhelmed."

"You're dealing with a lot. And dealing with it on your own, without Linda there to help you out. I understand how tough that can be."

"Nothing like you have."

"You can't compare our lives, honey. My life is busy in my way, your life is busy in yours."

"I feel as if I'm running a hundred miles an hour and never catching up. I always have something I should be doing."

"That's the blessing and the curse of being good at what you do. People want your designs, which means more work and more stress but more job satisfaction, too."

"You're right. I know you're right."

She would be embarrassed about this in about an hour but right now it felt good to vent to her best friend. "If I could only design the dresses, that would be wonderful. But I have to manage the store, too. Payroll and inventory and employees who call in sick last-minute and need me to cover their shifts."

Katrina looked as if she wanted to say something but then closed her mouth.

"What?"

Her friend sighed. "If you don't want to run the store anymore, why do you have to? Your mom had a good life insurance policy. The house is paid off and so is the store. You now have the freedom to do something different, if you want. Sell Fremont Fashions. Then you can focus on your wedding gown designs, which is what you love."

The very idea sent her into a panic. What would Linda think about that? Her mother had loved running the boutique, though her taste in fashion had been questionable at best.

Fremont Fashions had been her mother's salvation in those dark days after her father's death. Linda had thrown herself into salvaging the store, building a clientele, handling all aspects of running a small business.

Selling the store to focus on her own love of designing dresses would feel like a betrayal of everything her mother had worked for.

"I could never do that."

"Why not? You have the talent, certainly. All you lack is the confidence."

And the contacts. And the skills. And the customers.

"You're a sweetheart," she said to Kat. "And you know I adore you. I'm just having a bad day. I'm sorry you bore the brunt of it."

"I'm not sorry. I'm glad I was here. You know I always have your back."

Her friends were the greatest blessing of her life and she didn't know what she would do without them. She would have been lost these past five months without the constant support of the Haven Point Helping Hands, the loosely organized group she belonged to whose goal was to try making their community better.

"Now," Katrina said, "tell me more about Gemma's brother. Any sparks?"

Sam could feel her face heat again and hoped Kat didn't notice. "Even if there were, it wouldn't matter. He could actually be Jude Law and I wouldn't have the time or the energy for romance right now."

"Do we need to take you to a doctor?" Kat asked with a wide-eyed look of astonishment.

"I don't have time for that, either. Once the puppies are gone and the summer wedding frenzy, er, season is over, I might be able to think about dating. But I'm afraid by then Gemma and Josh will be married and her cute brother, who, again, looks nothing like Jude Law, will once more be back in England with his cute kids."

"Then we'll have to find you someone else, won't we?"

Katrina looked so determined Sam didn't have the heart to tell her she hadn't been interested in dating since her mother died.

"We can talk about finding me the perfect man again in September," she said. "Now help me put away the dress, then we can walk across the street to the Helping Hands meeting."

"Who knows? Maybe we'll meet him on the way."

"Who? The perfect man? Or Gemma's brother?"

Katrina laughed. "Maybe this Ian Summerhill is both."

Sam knew that absolutely wasn't true, despite her unfortunate dreams—dreams she wasn't at all prepared to share with Katrina, who knew her entirely too well and knew her unfortunate tendency to think she was in love every time a man smiled at her.

"You should see it. It's seriously the most spectacular wedding gown in the entire history of wedding gowns."

"Is it?"

"Yes. The way she's done the neckline is a wonder. It's a work of art. And the sleeves are perfect. When I wear it, I feel like I should be starring in my own personal rom-com or something."

"What is a rom-com?" Thomas asked from across the table at the Shelter Springs restaurant where they had met Gemma for dinner.

"It's a movie," Gemma told him. "It stands for romantic comedy."

"Is there lots of kissing?" Amelia asked.

"Oh, yes," Gemma said with a dreamy smile. "Loads and loads of it."

He didn't want to think of his sister enjoying loads and loads of kissing with anyone, though he had to admit he liked her fiancé very much. Josh Bailey seemed a genuinely good man who obviously adored Gem.

"I want to see your wedding dress," Amelia said. "May I?"

"Of course. The glorious creation should be ready about a week before the wedding. Perhaps you could come with me to pick it up."

Ian had to smile at Gemma's enthusiasm. He couldn't remember seeing her work up any interest in clothing before. She always looked nice but seemed most happy in yoga clothes, yet here she was waxing almost poetic about a dress she would wear for one day.

"It's a good thing you like it," Ian said.

"I love it. But then, I knew I would. Samantha is amazing with a needle and thread."

"Sounds like it."

"How do you like living next to her? She mentioned that she met you all yesterday."

"I fell in the water," Thomas said. "Our neighbor helped me out."

"That's what I heard."

Ian tried not to picture his lovely neighbor dripping wet, tight clothing sticking to places he didn't want to notice.

"She seemed very nice but we spoke only for a handful of moments. I didn't have much opportunity to form a solid impression."

"When you have the chance to come to know her a little better, I have no doubt you will love her as much as I do. Truly, she's become a dear friend. She's funny and smart and so creative with that dress shop of hers."

As she continued gushing about her friend, Ian frowned as a sudden suspicion took root. He glanced at the children, who were now busy coloring pictures on the paper tablecloth with the crayons their server had provided.

"Tell me you're not trying your hand at matchmaking," he murmured in a low voice.

"Don't be silly," she protested, but the sudden pink that stole across his sister's cheeks was all the answer he needed.

"Gem. Don't."

"Who said anything about matchmaking? I only meant she will be the perfect neighbor to you and the children. She's lovely. Truly lovely."

"I'm sure she is."

He wasn't available for a summer fling with an American woman, no matter how lovely she might be. Surely his sister understood the myriad reasons for that. Anyway, even if circumstances were different and Ian wasn't buried under the weight of his impending responsibilities, he still wouldn't have an affair with Samantha Fremont.

Why would a soft and pretty woman like her have any interest in a stiff, rumpled British professor who knew more about the reproductive processes of Lake Haven kokanee salmon than he did about the kind of things that might interest a young, attractive woman?

There was a flurry near the table and Josh Bailey finally joined them.

"Sorry I'm late. We had some issues at the store trying to track down a large order that's gone astray and I lost track of time."

The owner of a chain of sporting goods stores might not be the man Ian expected Gemma to fall for but Josh utterly and completely adored Gemma. That made him perfect for her, as far as Ian was concerned.

"Did you find it?" Ian asked.

"Yes. In North Dakota, of all places. I've got it rerouted now and heading our way."

The waiter came to take their order. Ian thought Josh might need more time but he explained that he had eaten there many times before and always ordered the same thing: French dip with sweet potato fries.

"How are you settling into your new house?" Josh asked after the waiter left to give their order to the kitchen staff. "I'm still sorry you decided not to stay at my ranch. You know I have plenty of room."

"That's very kind of you to offer but I needed to be close to the water since that's the only way to get to Chalk Creek without hiking three miles over hard terrain. Thank you also for arranging a boat for me to use, by the way."

"Not a problem at all. It belongs to a friend of mine who owes me a favor. Since he's going to be gone all summer, he assured me it's no problem for you to use it. I'll try to bring it by tomorrow."

"I appreciate that."

"And we still need to go horseback riding, don't we?" Josh said to the children with his friendly smile. "Maybe we can go this weekend."

"Oh, please." Amelia looked thrilled at the possibility, happier than she'd been in ages.

His heart ached when he looked at his daughter. She and Susan had been close and he knew Amelia missed her mother dearly. He might have guessed she would inherit Susan's love of horses, too.

"Josh's horses have the sweetest natures. Every one of them," Gemma said. "A Western saddle takes a bit of getting used to but I don't doubt we could find a saddle for you that's similar enough to the one you're accustomed to using at home."

Some of Amelia's enthusiasm seemed to fade. "I only wish I had a friend to go riding with. I miss my friend Olivia terribly."

She had not let him forget that she wasn't happy about spending a month away from her friends, especially when they would be moving to Dorset at the end of the summer.

Oh, guilt. His old friend. He should be used to it by now as a parent. There was always something else, something better, he knew he ought to be doing. Every day he encountered some innovative parenting technique, some new superfood to add to their diet, a learning model he should be following.

"I'm quite certain you could find a friend here to ride with," Ian said. "We will be here almost a month. Perhaps you could connect with some other girls and we can arrange a riding date or something."

"I have friends with daughters around your age," Gemma said. "I'll talk to them about planning a few outings."

"Maybe."

Amelia did not look particularly enthusiastic at the idea of making a new friend. She used to be a friendly, open child. Since the onset of Susan's illness and then her death a year earlier, Amelia had become more introverted and nervous about new situations.

For the past year, Ian felt as if they had been simply going through the motions of their lives. He had been hoping this trip together to the States would help snap them all out of their doldrums.

Neither child was thrilled about leaving their friends in Oxford to move back to Dorset to be closer to his parents. Perhaps by the time the summer was over, they would feel better about the move.

Regardless, he was glad to see his sister so happy. For different reasons, they had all struggled with their older brother's death in a car accident just months before Susan's diagnosis. Ian suspected Gemma's grief was mingled with a certain guilt, considering she had been driving the car at the time and had also been coping with her own injuries.

The accident hadn't been her fault whatsoever. An inebriated lorry driver had plowed through a light and struck the passenger side of Gemma's car as she and David had been heading home after a party.

No one blamed her except Gemma herself.

He was delighted to see that her emotional scars seemed to be healing. Throughout the dinner, her happiness seemed to surround them all like a warm blanket. The dinner was pleasant and the company more so.

"Thank you for a lovely evening," he told her when they had all walked out to the car park and he'd loaded the children into the rental.

"I'm so glad you're here," Gemma said, giving him a tight embrace.

"As am I."

She looked to make the sure the children were inside the vehicle with the doors closed before she spoke in a low voice.

"How are you doing, Ian? Really doing, I mean. I don't want to hear platitudes. I want the truth."

The weight of responsibility pressed in on him. He had less than a month to savor this time with the children before he had to return to England, pack up their things and move to start the next phase of his life.

"Couldn't be better," he said, forcing his voice to be cheerful. "This part of the world is every bit as beautiful as you promised. I have my work and my children. I'm happy."

"Are you?"

He knew all she was asking. Gemma knew the whole ugly truth about his marriage.

"I'm happy," he repeated firmly. "We're on a grand adventure. I can't wait to dig into my research project, to go fishing on the lake, to take some hikes into the mountains. I'm here with my children. What else could I possibly need?"

She raised an eyebrow and he suspected he knew what she wanted to say. A woman. Particularly a woman like Samantha Fremont.

Why was it an unfortunate truism that those in love

couldn't rest unless everyone else in their circle shared their condition?

He couldn't tell his optimistic, deeply enamored sister that he was done with love. He had scars on his heart that covered everything good and right that might have once been there.

"Don't worry about me. This is the season of your life when you should be focused on you and Josh and the life you're building together."

"I can't help it. I believe worrying about my family is one of my superpowers."

He smiled a little and hugged her back. "Well, try to contain it, then. I don't need you to worry about me. I need you to think about your spectacular dress and how deliriously happy you'll be wearing it when you marry in only a few weeks."

"Don't worry. I am good at multitasking. I can do both of those things," she said, which made him smile.

He really did feel better here in Haven Point than he had in months. Years, even, as if he had set a large weight down when he drove past the town's welcome sign.

CHAPTER THREE

SUNDAY AFTERNOON AFTER CHURCH, Samantha was working away in her sewing room with the television set to a documentary about coral reefs she would likely never visit when her doorbell rang.

She waited for the chorus of yips and yaps that always heralded a new arrival at her home these days but was greeted by a frightening silence. With a jolt, she suddenly remembered she had put Betsey and the puppies outside in the large portable pet enclosure she had bought so they could play in the grass and enjoy the June sunshine.

Okay, that was only part of the reason. Mostly she needed a little peace and quiet to focus on her work. Gemma Summerhill's dress would be spectacular. Each time she worked on it, she fell in love a little more with the elegant lines. Kat was right. It was one of her best designs.

Back in the early days, her mother had really been the seamstress, though Sam felt as though she had always known how to sew. Her mother started her with her own sewing machine when she was still in grade school and she could remember sewing an elaborate doll wardrobe for her and for Katrina.

At first, she had started designing with things found around the house. Scraps of fabric her mother had discarded, a glue gun, hair scrunchies.

After she received her own sewing machine for Christmas along with some lengths of fabric and a basic doll dress pattern, Sam had learned to add her own flair to outfits.

Oh, she and Katrina used to have fun. She felt a pang, missing those times. They still got together as often as possible and both worked hard to maintain their friendship. But Katrina was so busy with her marriage and children with extra challenges. Sam didn't like to take her away from Bowie and the children too often strictly for girl time.

The doorbell rang again, yanking her out of her thoughts, and she winced as she jumped up. What an idiot. She had completely forgotten someone was there.

When are you going to get your head out of the clouds and focus on what's going on around you?

Her mother's voice was strong today. She sighed as she hurried to the front door and pulled it open.

The children from next door stood on her porch, their arms overflowing with familiar black-and-tan puppies.

"Hello, ma'am," the girl said politely. "Are these your puppies? They've wandered into our garden."

Wandered. Oh, no. She shot a look at the enclosure she had set up so carefully earlier that day, puzzled to see it looked completely intact.

How on earth had they escaped this time?

"Oh my goodness. You little rascals."

"Excuse me?" The girl looked affronted.

"Not you. I'm sorry. I was speaking about the puppies. They're very good escape artists. I'm not sure how they keep getting out. It doesn't matter what measures I take to prevent it, they immediately find another way to escape."

"I love puppies," the little boy, Thomas, said with a dreamy look, resting his cheek on Coco's head.

"They are adorable, aren't they? These particular puppies are very mischievous, though. They are always trying to explore."

"Can I put one down?" The girl, Amelia, had her hands full trying to contain them—the runt of the litter, Oscar, and his chubby older brother, Calvin.

"Yes. Of course. Here. Let me take one." She grabbed the larger of the puppies, who licked at her forearm as it wriggled to get away. "I need to find their mama, too."

"When we walked past on the way to your door, she was sound asleep in her pen," Thomas informed her.

"Perhaps she was enjoying having all that room to herself," Amelia suggested.

"No doubt you are correct. I imagine it can't be so easy to have puppies climbing on you all day long."

"I wouldn't mind," Thomas said cheerfully. "I love puppies."

He was adorable, she had to admit. She wanted to hug him like he was hugging the puppy.

"I do love them, too, especially when they stay where they're supposed to. Let's go see if we can figure out how they wriggled out this time."

She and the two children walked to the metal enclosure, supposedly held into place by stakes she had driven into the ground. They did indeed find Betsey stretched out inside by herself, looking perfectly content with the world.

She could see immediately how the puppies had escaped. Somehow they must have managed to burrow under one of the metal panels that was raised off the uneven ground only about three or four inches.

She should have noticed that one of the fence panels wasn't flush to the ground. If she hadn't been so distracted by her workload, she might have done a much better job of ensuring the pen was secure.

"Oh, you little rascals," she exclaimed again, shoving the panel farther down into the dirt.

The puppies were too smart for their own good and seemed to spur each other on to increasing levels of deviousness.

She set Coco inside the pen and the children did the same with the other two puppies.

"I love dogs. I wish we had one at home," Thomas said with a happy sigh as soon as he'd set his puppy down inside the enclosure. "We don't have one at home."

"No. But Grandfather and Nana have four," Amelia reminded him.

"Four. That's a lot of dogs."

"They're very cute. We play with them whenever we go to their house. I suppose we'll see them more, now that we're moving to be closer to them."

"Right now we live in Oxford," Thomas informed her. "That's in England."

Fitting, that a nerdy salmon researcher lived in a university town like Oxford. Why was he moving to be closer to his parents? For help with the children, now that his wife was gone?

"How are you enjoying your stay here in the States?"

Amelia pursed her lips as if considering how to answer. "I miss my friends, if you want the truth," she finally said. "My best friends are called Jane and Sarah and they're eight years old, same as I am."

"Eight is a very good age," Samantha said.

"I think twelve is the perfect age. My father says I can get my ears pierced when I'm twelve. I like your earrings very much."

Sam touched one of the dangles and sent it swinging. She had made these herself at McKenzie's store one time when the Helping Hands had tried their collective hand at beading.

"Thank you. Have you gone swimming or anything like that out in the lake while you've been here?"

"I wanted to. We waded a little the other day but the water was so cold we nearly froze!" Amelia looked aghast. "I thought it would be like going to Nice in the summer. We used to do that with our mum during holiday. Swimming in the ocean there was like having a bath."

"Only with about a hundred other people," Thomas said.

"Yes. And in a really big bathtub," Amelia agreed.

Lake Haven was always cold, since it was filled by snow runoff from the surrounding Redemption mountain range.

"That sounds nice. You must have enjoyed it very much."

Amelia nodded. "The beach was nice, I suppose, but spending time with Mum was the best part. She liked to build sandcastles with us and she always said ours was good enough to win a prize."

"Our mum died," Thomas offered, his voice small and sad.

These poor children, losing their mother at such a young age. Her heart ached for them and she wanted to cuddle them both close.

"How lovely, then, that you have such wonderful memories of the time you spent with her."

"Our mother was sick for an awfully long time. Months and months," Amelia said.

"I imagine that must have been very difficult for all of you."

"Yes." Amelia acknowledged her sympathy with a regal sort of nod and they stood for a moment, each lost in thought, until Coco waddled after a ball and ended up falling on her face, which made the children laugh.

Samantha loved how resilient children could be. Even when they were grieving and sad, they could often still manage to find moments of joy in the world around them.

She had tried to be strong after her beloved father died when she was around Amelia's age, as her mother told her she must be, but in her case the shock had been as powerful as the grief.

One day he had been there, the next he was gone.

At the time, Linda told her he had been sick, that he'd been sick a long time and they had kept it from her.

In her child's imagination, she had imagined cancer or a bad heart. Something tragic but understandable.

She could still remember learning the truth about a year after her father died. She had been hiding inside one of the circular racks of clothing in the shop with her dolls. That had been her happy place, where she could be alone, away from her mother's sometimes biting tongue. She used to love sitting inside the rack and playing surrounded by all the cool, soft fabrics of the dresses.

Two of her mother's customers from Shelter Springs, women she hadn't known well, had been looking through the rack, not knowing she was there. Shopping and gossiping were perennially two of the favorite pastimes of some of the women around Lake Haven.

One of the women had whispered something about her mother and the store and the ugly clothing Linda had started ordering in to stock the shelves, then they both had laughed unpleasantly.

"She's awful, isn't she? Is it any wonder her husband killed himself to get away from her?" the other one had said.

"Poor man," the other one had said.

Samantha hadn't known what they meant but knew by their tone it couldn't be good. She remembered feeling sick, hiding there inside the clothing rack, her stomach turning as if she needed to throw up. She hadn't wanted to reveal herself to those vile, ugly women, not wanting to let them know she was there at all or that she had heard what they said.

She stayed inside the rack until closing time, when her mother had finally dragged her out so they could go home and have dinner. She remembered barely touching her food that day and for several days afterward, those words running and running around in her head.

Killed himself. Her father had killed himself. He hadn't had cancer or the flu or some other terrible disease. He had chosen to leave her and her mother.

That moment had changed her fundamentally, though it had taken her years longer to fully understand.

Technically, Linda hadn't lied. Her father had indeed been sick for a long time, a deep clinical depression that he hadn't been able to overcome.

When she was a child, she didn't understand that. She had been hurt and angry, as any child would be. She had missed him dearly, especially as her mother's personality had undergone a dramatic shift after Lyle Fremont died. While Linda had always been sharp-tongued and impatient, her comments began to take on a cruel edge. Linda had become bitter and angry, had changed from a devoted, loving mother to someone impossible to please, who seemed to find fault in everything Sam did.

As an adult, Samantha had tried to be compassionate, imagining how her mother must have felt after her husband killed himself. Betrayed, abandoned. Alone with a needy child and a struggling business.

She was aware that her compassion and sense of responsibility had kept her in Haven Point long after she would have otherwise escaped.

"We will always miss our mother but we're managing," Amelia said now, her voice small and resigned, as if it was taking every ounce of her energy to stay brave in the face of such overwhelming sadness.

"We still have Father," Thomas said. "And Mrs. Gilbert, who looks after us. And Nana and Grandfather."

"How very wonderful it must feel to have so many people who love you," she said.

She would have adored that. After her father died, Samantha had been left with only her mother. Linda had been estranged from her family, something she never spoke about, and Lyle had been an only child whose parents died when he was still a young man.

Linda had been Sam's only relative. As far as Sam knew, she had been all her mother had, too. Perhaps if she hadn't been an only child, if there had been another sibling or two in the family, her mother's laser-sharp focus on her might have been diluted. Perhaps she wouldn't have had to bear the weight of her mother's expectations all on her own.

"I suppose you're right." Amelia studied the dogs, who had once more started clamoring over Betsey to nurse. "I still miss my mother."

"I understand. My mother died just after the new year. I miss her very much." Though, of course, it wasn't at all the same. She was nearly thirty.

To her astonishment Thomas slipped his hand in hers,

his palm a little moist and warm but still providing comfort beyond words. She stood for a moment, staring out at the lake, holding the hand of a six-year-old boy and fighting the unexpected urge to cry.

"I'm very sorry," he said.

"That's very kind of you," she managed through the lump in her throat.

"Was she a nice mother?" Amelia asked.

Samantha did not know how to answer that. No one would ever call Linda Fremont *nice*. Smart? Yes. Determined? Yes. *Nice* didn't really apply.

"She could be nice," she qualified. "What about your mother? What was she like?"

"She could be nice, too," Amelia answered, parroting Sam's own words.

"We're awfully sad she's dead. So is our father," Thomas said. "We miss her terribly."

"But we're not supposed to talk about her anymore," Amelia said.

Sam frowned. "Why on earth not?"

"Our dad said she's gone and it's time to move on with our lives."

Sam stared at her, appalled that any man would tell his children to move on while they were busy grieving the loss of their mother. Could he really be that cold and unfeeling that he wouldn't let the children discuss their memories of their mother?

Her mother had done the same. She hadn't wanted Samantha to talk about her father, as though ignoring her pain would ease it somehow. Instead, it had only made her feel worse, as if her father and all her memories of him had been wiped off the earth.

She wanted to march to the house next door and shake Ian Summerhill. His children were grieving for their mother. How could he have the gall to tell them it was time they forgot their pain and moved on with their lives?

"We should probably go," Amelia said, tugging her younger brother in a way that told Samantha she was very much the dominant sibling.

"Thank you for rescuing my puppies," she said with a smile.

"It was no trouble. They're very cute," Amelia said.

"I think they like us," Thomas said.

"Dogs are smart, you know," Samantha said. "They love to be with people who like them."

She sounded like much more of an expert than she was. Every scrap of knowledge she had learned about dogs had been obtained over the past few months from books, websites and trial and error with Betsey and the puppies.

"That must be why they like us and came right to us when we found them in the garden." Amelia looked pleased.

"I'm sure it was. They knew you would be kind to them," Samantha said. "You know, you are welcome to come visit Betsey and her puppies anytime you would like."

As she spoke, Samantha suddenly had an idea. She had been looking for someone to check in on the puppies once or twice a day, to refill their water should they need it and entertain them for a few moments. Amelia and Thomas were right next door. They would be perfect for the job.

Would an eight-year-old girl and six-year-old boy be responsible enough for that? Perhaps their nanny could supervise. Would they be willing?

She wanted to blurt out the question, then thought better of it. She couldn't possibly bring up the idea to the children before she'd had the chance to speak with their father about it.

Of course, that would mean having a conversation with the man and she wasn't sure she wanted to do that, especially if he were the sort of ogre who discouraged his children from grieving their mother.

"We had better go," the girl said after a moment. "We're not supposed to come here without permission and we're also not to go close to the lake again without Mrs. Gilbert or Father with us."

"A very good rule," Samantha said.

"We wouldn't have broken it except the puppies came to us," Thomas said. "We saw them from inside and couldn't allow them to wander far."

"Sometimes you have to break a few rules in life, especially when the stakes are high enough."

They looked shocked that a grown-up would ever dare say such a thing. Sam couldn't really blame them, as she was only now beginning to accept that herself. Still, she quickly changed the subject.

"Betsey and I are very grateful to you for rescuing her pups," Sam said with a smile. "Come over anytime, as long as it's okay with your father or Mrs. Gilbert."

"Thank you. Goodbye, ma'am."

"Goodbye," Thomas said, waving with one hand as his sister took the other and marched across the grass with him.

She watched them go back inside the house, charmed by them both.

Poor dears. Amelia and Thomas were sweet children who appeared hungry for emotional nurturing.

She certainly had experience with that. Perhaps that was why she was so drawn to them, considering she was something of an expert at yearning for something from a parent she could never have.

CHAPTER FOUR

HER OPPORTUNITY TO speak to Ian Summerhill about his children came sooner than she would have liked.

Later that night, she finally set aside her sewing machine and moved Gemma's dress to the wardrobe where she stored items she was working on, out of the dust and the elements.

Betsey whined softly and Samantha looked over to see the puppies were sleeping.

She was exhausted herself after sewing for ten hours straight and was only too ready to crash into her own bed, but she had learned in her limited time as a pet human that when animals needed attention, they needed attention.

Moving quietly so she didn't wake up the puppies, she scooped the little mama up from behind the gate in the doorway.

"You need to go out?" she whispered.

Unlike dogs Sam had read about in books, Betsey didn't communicate in some mysterious, almost-human way like tilting her head in approval or whining or giving any other indication that she understood Sam's question or had any interest in going outside.

She only gave Samantha a quizzical look and slumped in her arms.

Maybe if Samantha had been able to communicate a

little better with the dog, Betsey might have mentioned earlier in their relationship that she was expecting puppies.

She smiled, imagining what the conversation might be like. *It was a one-night stand that meant nothing, and the minute he found out about the buns in the oven, he took off to eat out of somebody else's bowl.*

Too late for true confessions, even if Betsey could talk.

"Let's go out. You might not need to but I could use a little walk around the yard."

As she always did at night, Samantha hooked the leash onto the little ten-pound dog, more for Betsey's protection than anything else. The dog didn't seem inclined to wander but she could easily slip away in the dark.

And then there was the wildlife to worry about. Larger creatures like moose or mountain lions or even bear could be spotted around the lake sometimes. More common were raccoons, porcupines or, heaven forbid, skunks.

With the dog on her leash, Sam walked outside into the quiet music of a June night. The gentle lap of the water against the dock, the leaves of the trees rustling in the breeze, the hoot of a nearby great horned owl she had seen around the neighborhood.

The night was sweet with the scent of pine and fir and that indefinable, distinctive smell of the lake in summer. Someone in the neighborhood must have cut their grass earlier, adding the delicious scent to the mix.

She drew in a deep breath, feeling some of the stress from a day hunched over a machine begin to ease from her shoulders.

No place on earth could possibly compare to Lake Haven for perfect summer evenings.

She loved this place. It was part of her. She briefly had dated an airplane pilot who had been appalled when she told him she had never traveled outside of the western United States. She hadn't had the heart to tell him she rarely even left Lake Haven County and had only been on an airplane twice, both times to attend a fabric trade show in Dallas.

Linda Fremont had not been one to take vacations. That would have required her to close the store or leave it in the hands of her employees, something she had rarely been willing to do.

Besides, they didn't need to go anywhere else, Linda would often say. Why should they, when they lived in such a beautiful place?

On this, her mother had a point. Still, the world was full of beautiful places. Staying here for her entire life felt a little like choosing to sew every pattern with only one color of fabric.

Where would she go, though? Her entire world existed around this lake.

This wasn't the night to figure that out, when she was mentally and physically exhausted from sewing all day.

Betsey quickly did her business but didn't seem in a hurry to go inside so Samantha decided to walk to the water.

Every muscle in her spine and shoulders ached from spending the day either hunched over a sewing machine or using needle and thread for the fine handwork on the wedding dress.

It really would be magnificent. She couldn't wait to see the finished product.

Yes, making wedding gowns was hard, challenging work but she loved every moment.

She felt strongly that every woman deserved to feel

beautiful on her wedding day. Samantha loved being able to do her part to provide that.

She was almost to the dock when she suddenly saw a beam of light coming from the house next door.

Betsey froze in the act of sniffing a tuft of grass, then hurried to hide behind Samantha as Ian Summerhill emerged from the darkness.

Everything inside her seemed to coil, like a bobbin too tightly wound. Her reaction was ridiculous. Okay, he was gorgeous. She couldn't deny it. The younger version of herself might have tried to flirt and tease and otherwise make a fool of herself.

A few years ago, she would have been entranced by the idea of a gorgeous Englishman living next door. Okay, let's be honest. She might have had the same reaction to him six months ago, before her mother died and all of her priorities in life shifted.

That was then. She was a different person now. She had four employees, numerous suppliers and dozens of customers who counted on her to keep the doors open at Fremont Fashions. She didn't have time to nurture a crush on every man who entered her orbit. Heck, she barely had time to shower these days, with all the custom orders she was taking for wedding dresses.

Anyway, if she were going to develop a crush on any man, it certainly wouldn't be for an unfeeling brute who wouldn't even let his children grieve for their mother.

Surely she had developed better taste than that, after all these years.

She sighed as the man came closer. He hadn't seen her yet and she was half tempted to slink into the shadows and skulk back to her house so she could avoid talking to him altogether.

But she needed to ask him about allowing the children to help her with the puppies. When would she find a better opportunity?

"Good evening," she said.

The flashlight's trajectory wobbled as he gave a little jolt of surprise. "Oh. Ms. Fremont. I didn't see you there."

Maybe because you were too busy being a jerk?

"Sorry to startle you," she lied. She would have liked the man to fall into the lake, but she supposed that wasn't very charitable.

This sudden fierce antagonism left her uncomfortable. She was basing her entire opinion on him because of one thing his daughter had said, that he had told them it was time to move on after their mother's death.

Why was she so upset about that? He was the children's father. It was his right to parent them as he saw best.

Was it because her mother had done the same thing to Sam when she was his children's age, refusing to let her talk about losing her father?

Or did it have more to do with her own struggle to move on from her mother's death?

Neither of those things concerned Ian Summerhill. He was her good friend's brother. She could at least treat him with politeness.

"Lovely evening, isn't it?" she tried.

"Yes. Beautiful." He looked at the stars spread above them for a moment, his features in profile, then turned back to her and held up what looked like a complicated fish finder. "Some of my equipment arrived and I wanted to load it onto the boat so I wouldn't forget in the morning. Sorry to disturb you. I won't be long."

"You're not bothering me." It was a lie, but she didn't need him to know that.

"Again, thank you for allowing me to use your dock for my research boat. It would have been far less convenient if I had to travel to the marina every time I wanted to use it."

She wanted to tell him she had given permission before discovering what an unfeeling father he was. Now that she knew, she wanted to rescind her approval.

That would be petty and unfair, though. Something her mother would have done. Just because she didn't like the man's parenting techniques was no reason to stand in the way of science.

"It's fine. Do what you need to do. Betsey and I will get out of your way."

"It is your dock," he said, his tone crisp, bordering on stiff. "I wouldn't want to chase you away from your own property. As I said, this shouldn't take long."

He walked around her, the flashlight moving again, and climbed from the dock to the large wooden boat there. A moment later, he climbed out again without the equipment.

"Is it safe there? That looks expensive. Haven Point is mostly safe from crime, but sometimes during the tourism season, we get some vandals and petty thieves."

"First of all, nobody but another fisheries biologist would want it. Second, there's a locker on board with a padlock. I stowed it in there."

"So it should be safe from any wandering salmon researcher looking to cause trouble."

"For now, anyway. I hope to get an early start in the morning and that's one less thing I'll have to haul aboard then."

She supposed it was the same concept as her sometimes loading her sewing projects into the car before she went to bed when she knew someone might be coming into the boutique for a fitting the next day.

"Well, good night. Sorry to bother you," he said in that same stiff tone, then surprised her by reaching down to pet Betsey, who immediately turned her face into his hand with adoration. Her dog liked him, which was enough to make Samantha question her own antagonism.

This was her chance, she reminded herself. What better opportunity would she find to talk to him about the children helping with the puppies? "I'm actually glad of the chance to speak with you."

In the moonlight, she could see one eyebrow raise. Why did the man have to be so blasted good-looking?

"Oh? Have you reconsidered giving permission for me to anchor the boat here?"

"No. Actually, it's about your children."

He frowned. "Have Amelia and Thomas been bothering you? I'm sorry. I've told them to stay on our rental property."

"No. They helped me today actually. You see, Betsey here has three puppies."

"I saw them out on the grass over here earlier in some sort of pen."

"I thought it was a nice idea to let them enjoy the outdoors on summer afternoons but they have become little escape artists and apparently they wandered into your garden. Thomas and Amelia were kind enough to bring them home for me."

"Is that right?"

"Yes. I'm very grateful to them. The puppies might be rascals but they're adorable rascals. I would have hated for them to go astray. That would make both me and Betsey sad, not to mention the new owners they'll be going to in a few weeks."

"I'm glad Thomas and Amelia could help."

"You should know, the children were wonderful with them. They knew how to hold them correctly and seemed to enjoy playing with them."

"I'm glad to hear it. We don't have a dog but my parents have four. The children have had some experience with them over the years and have been trying to persuade me for some time now that we should get a dog."

She wanted to tell him to go for it. Children need something to love them unconditionally.

Not that she knew that from experience or anything.

"I could tell they were comfortable around animals. Seeing them today actually gave me an idea."

"What sort of idea?" he asked, his voice wary.

At his tone, she almost lost her nerve, especially when he narrowed his gaze and studied her intently in the moonlight.

"I've been trying to find someone who might be available to check in on them during the day while I work, but so far it's been a challenge."

He gave her a look of confusion. "Forgive me, but I thought you were a seamstress. Aren't you making my sister's wedding gown?"

He made it sound like she was some kind of Victorian dressmaker far beneath his notice, toiling away in some sweatshop.

She tried not to bristle. "I sew wedding dresses at home on my own time. But during the day I run a small clothing boutique in downtown Haven Point. Fremont Fashions."

"Do you?"

He wasn't being supercilious on purpose, she suspected; it was only that British accent that made his words sound clipped and questioning and left her feeling defensive.

"It's small but thriving. Our business has increased substantially in the past few years." She didn't add that was because she had taken over the responsibility of ordering inventory. Now that the boutique actually offered clothing at reasonable prices that people weren't ashamed to be caught dead in, business had improved tremendously.

"We serve the clothing needs of women who want something a little more unique than they can find at the box stores in Shelter Springs," she went on. "I try to think about my clientele and order in clothing items that will be a good fit for a variety of lifestyles and budgets. Stylish and well-fitted, while still rugged enough for our varied climate."

She was rambling, she thought, and promptly clamped her teeth together.

"Sorry. That's not the point."

"What is the point?"

"My job keeps me very busy when I'm there. I've tried to take the puppies and Betsey to the shop with me so I can keep an eye on them. That worked for a few weeks but they've grown too big and too active for that now. I've taken to leaving them here and checking on them throughout the day when I can but even that isn't the best solution."

"Where would my children fit into this picture, Ms. Fremont?"

"Please call me Sam or Samantha. Everyone around here does. When you say Ms. Fremont in that stiff upper crust accent, you sound like something from a Jane Austen novel."

He gave a sharp, humorless laugh. "I am no Mr. Darcy, I can assure you."

"No kidding," she muttered under her breath. Unfortunately, she didn't say it far enough under her breath and unfortunately he heard her. He stiffened and she wanted to kick herself. This was *not* the way to go about asking a favor of the man.

"Anyway," she said quickly, "I was, er, wondering if you would allow the children to help me out with the puppies while you're here for the next few weeks."

"Help you in what way?"

"I need someone to check on them once or twice a day. Perhaps play with them for half an hour or so. If the weather is nice, they could take them outside to their pen, which I will make sure is completely secure from now on."

He said nothing, only continued to study her.

"I would be willing to pay them. Would ten dollars a day be sufficient?"

"You want to pay my children to keep an eye on your puppies." He said the words in the same disbelieving tone he might have used if she had suggested the children join the circus.

Of course he would dislike the idea. He was a cold-hearted jerk who obviously couldn't see how perfectly children and puppies meshed together. "I'm sorry. It was a stupid idea. Forget I said anything. You are here on vacation and so are the children. They don't need a job."

"Don't be so hasty. I was surprised, that's all. It's not a stupid idea. They would enjoy earning a little spending money for souvenirs and they do love dogs. My parents have four Jack Russell terriers. They're very smart."

"Amelia and Thomas told me how much they love visiting them. They also told me you don't have any pets."

"My late wife was allergic to cats and was afraid of dogs after an unfortunate episode in her childhood."

She wanted to ask what was stopping him from getting a dog now that his wife was gone but that seemed a crass question in light of their loss.

"If your parents had four dogs, that must have made Sunday dinners difficult when you visited their house," she said instead.

He gave a smile that looked strained. "Whenever Susan would visit, my parents kept their dogs locked in their bedroom or outside."

He spoke in such a stiff tone she had to wonder if even talking about his late wife was difficult for him. He must have loved her very much. Still, that was no excuse for discouraging the children from grieving over their mother.

She should say something. But how could she bring that up to him, especially when she was asking a favor of his children?

"It was a crazy idea. I just thought—I don't know—that they might enjoy playing with the puppies as much as the puppies would enjoy playing with them."

That seemed to give him pause. "Once or twice a day, you said?"

"Yes. And really, I wouldn't need them to do anything other than check on them and maybe throw a ball or something for a few minutes."

"It's not a crazy idea at all. Amelia is eight and Thomas six. They're certainly old enough to put out food and water for the puppies, if you should need that."

That almost sounded as if he was at least considering her request seriously. She was afraid to hope. "Does that mean you will let them help me?"

He gazed out at the water for a moment where the moonlight danced on the waves, then shifted back to her. "I think ten dollars a day is too much. What about five?"

"Five each, then."

He shrugged. "Fine. But we may be busy some days and they won't be able to check on them," he warned.

"Totally understandable. You're on vacation. If there's any day that doesn't work, just let me know or have your nanny let me know and I can easily come home myself. Sundays are my day off when the store is closed so I wouldn't need help on that day."

"And you know we're leaving to go home the Tuesday after Gemma's wedding."

She did a quick mental calculation of the dates. "Also fine. The puppies will be ready for their new homes right around then and I will no longer need the help."

"In that case, I believe they should be able to help you most days."

"Oh. Thank you!" Okay. Maybe he wasn't as bad as she had been thinking.

"I'm grateful for the suggestion, if you want the truth. They are in need of a project, I think. To be frank, they're not enjoying this trip to Idaho as much as I had hoped. They both miss their friends and say they're bored. I tried to get them interested in my research, but neither of them wants much to do with salmon."

"How odd of them," she said, trying to keep the dryness out of her voice.

He gave her a sidelong look, not missing it. "For your information, salmon are fascinating creatures. Kokanee, for instance, are the nonanadromous form of sockeye salmon. *Anadromous* means a creature that can live in both seawater and freshwater, which is incredibly rare in nature."

"Okay."

"Unlike the sockeye, which are born in a freshwater stream and then migrate to the ocean for most of their lives until they return to that same freshwater stream to spawn, kokanee spend their entire life landlocked, though they also go upstream using small rivers and tributaries to spawn."

"Right."

"They were likely originally in the old prehistoric lakes that covered this area and then became trapped when the waters receded, adapting to their new environment in fascinating ways. They spend on average about four years in the lake before they return upstream to spawn, in this case to Chalk Creek, which has a high level of calcium carbonate from erosion of the surrounding geography."

"Good to know."

"Unlike many other variants of kokanee that spawn in August and September, those in Lake Haven spawn in June. We're not sure why and that's what I would like to find out. That's what I'm here to research."

He suddenly looked embarrassed. "Sorry. I'm droning on. It's a bad habit when I talk about my work."

Oddly, she found she liked that particular chink in his armor. She tended to do the same when talking about her dress designs.

"We all have our passions, don't we?"

To her shock, she was almost certain his gaze flickered to her mouth.

"Yes," he murmured. "We do."

Glittery heat suddenly flared in her stomach, as if he had pressed his finger to her skin instead of just a look.

Where had *that* come from?

She swallowed, reminding herself she still wasn't sure if she liked the man.

Her little dog tugged on her leash, yanking her back to her senses. She might be physically attracted to him but that didn't matter. She wasn't in the market for a fling with her sexy neighbor.

She chose to focus instead on her dog. "Betsey's passion is her puppies right now, as much as she likes the odd break from them, so I had better take her back to them. I'll be in touch in the morning with a key for the children."

"If you'd like, I could send Thomas and Amelia over first thing before you leave for your boutique."

His thoughtfulness startled her. "I thought you wanted to make an early start tomorrow."

"That should be a short trip. With the boat close by, I can leave before sunrise and will plan to be back so that I can have breakfast with the children."

Maybe she had judged him too hastily. She knew plenty of fathers who wouldn't put a priority on spending mealtime with their children, especially when it conflicted with work.

"Are you sure it's no trouble?"

"None at all. Would eight be early enough?"

"Yes. That's perfect. Thank you, Mr. Summerhill."

In the moonlight, she saw his mouth quirk into a smile. "Please. Call me Ian. When you say Mr. Summerhill in that tone, it sounds remarkably like you really mean Mr. Darcy."

She couldn't help smiling at his reference to her earlier words.

He was looking at her mouth again, she realized with no small amount of consternation. The moment stretched between them, heady and sweet. She wanted him to kiss her. Quite desperately actually.

Oh, this would never do.

Impatient with herself, she tugged on the dog's leash. "Come on, Betsey. We need to go."

The dog followed her reluctantly as Sam hurried back to the relative safety of her house.

She was still as flighty and flirty as she'd ever been, she thought with frustration as she closed the door tightly behind her. It took all her self-control to resist the temptation to look out so she could see if he was still standing by the dock.

A short time ago, she had been convinced the man was a horrible father who didn't deserve his two adorable children. After only a quick conversation, here she was wanting to make out with him in the moonlight.

What was *wrong* with her?

She didn't want to be that giddy, silly girl anymore. Starry-eyed Samantha, who fell in love at the drop of a hat and who started making wedding plans if a man so much as looked twice at her.

When she looked back at her past, she was mortified at how immature she had been. Sometimes she thought her mother had purposely encouraged her shallowness so Linda could ultimately control her better.

If she was focused on romance all the time, her latest crush, she didn't have time to think about how unhappy she was with her life and the choices she had made with it. She might have even become unhappy enough to decide she wanted something else, a life away from Lake Haven.

She sighed as she put the dog back into her pen with her puppies. Betsey immediately sniffed the sleeping puppies, making sure each was all right before curling up beside them.

The instinctive gesture somehow made a lump rise in Samantha's throat.

She swallowed it down. Her mother was gone and it was long past time she grew up.

IAN WATCHED SAMANTHA FREMONT return to her house, doing his best to tamp down his shocking, unexpected reaction to her.

What was it about the woman that left him feeling like a bumbling idiot?

There was something so appealing about her. She was lovely, yes, with her honey-gold hair and hazel eyes, but it went beyond the surface. There was a light to her, a soft energy that seemed to draw him inexorably closer.

Had he really babbled on about his research to her for a good ten minutes? She must think him an utter idiot.

He wasn't quite sure what had happened. He didn't usually have trouble talking with women. Yes, he could be a bit of an absentminded professor but he generally could at least be trusted to carry on a halfway coherent conversation with most people.

Not with Samantha Fremont. With her, he started spouting off about chalk streams and anadromous species. At least he hadn't gone off on sympatric speciation or predatory nonnative lake trout that could decimate a population.

With a heavy sigh, he headed back to the rental house where the children and Letty had settled in for bed hours ago.

What was wrong with him? He had wanted to kiss her for a few moments there, with an urgency that had left him feeling a little light-headed.

He wasn't sure why being in Samantha Fremont's presence left him so off-balance but he didn't like it. At all.

He had less than a month at Lake Haven to finish his research. He didn't have a moment to waste pining over his next-door neighbor, who would be only a memory in a month's time, when he had to leave this place, put away his work and focus on helping out his family.

CHAPTER FIVE

"MISS FREMONT WANTS us to take care of her puppies?" Amelia gaped at him. "And you told her we would? Are you joking?"

"I assure you, I'm not."

Amelia ought to know by now that his sense of humor wasn't nearly so well-defined.

"Did you hear that, Thomas? We can play with those darling puppies every single day!"

"Yes!" Thomas punched the air and slid off his chair to dance around the breakfast table.

"Here, now." Letty, oatmeal spoon in hand, looked alarmed at their energy. Ian winced. He probably should have spoken with his nanny/housekeeper first before springing the ideas on the children like that.

"When will we begin?" Thomas asked eagerly. "May we go see them today?"

"Yes. Actually, I told Ms. Fremont I would take you both over to her house this morning so that she could provide instructions on how to take care of them and what your responsibilities will entail." He gave them a serious look. "This isn't only about playing with the puppies, remember. It will take a great deal of work to make sure three puppies and their mother are looked after properly."

"We don't mind the work, do we, Thomas?" Amelia said, her features still dazed with joy.

"No, especially when it means we can play with puppies."

He should have found a dog for them before this. Ian fought down guilt as he watched their enthusiastic response to what was a very good idea from Samantha Fremont.

As was the case for too many other things, he had used Susan as an excuse not to move forward. They could have found a dog the moment she moved out and filed for divorce, when they were so lost and confused in the Oxford flat.

What would they have done with a dog, though, when Susan came back after her cancer diagnosis?

He could have figured something out. She had been desperate and in no state to put up a fight about having to live with an animal.

It didn't matter. He didn't have any real excuses now. Susan was gone, had been gone more than a year. It was time he and the children started figuring out their lives without her.

"If you can show responsibility as you help care for Ms. Fremont's puppies, perhaps we can discuss looking for a dog ourselves when we return to England."

Their eyes widened with delight.

"Do you mean it?" Thomas asked, as if he were afraid to hope.

"Yes. We will have to talk about it to determine what sort of dog, but I don't see why we can't, as long as you do an excellent job helping our neighbor with her puppies."

"Oh, we will," Amelia assured him. "We will take the best care ever of them. You'll see, Dad."

She rarely called him *Dad*. Susan had always encouraged the children to call them Mother and Father. He had always found that too formal and decided he liked Amelia veering away from the path her mother had set her on.

"Can we see them now?"

"Yes. Find your shoes, both of you, while I talk to Mrs. Gilbert a moment."

The children raced off, leaving him alone with the housekeeper, nanny and chauffeur who was worth far more than her weight in jewels. He and the children truly would have been lost without her, both before and after Susan's death.

He faced her warily, this woman who had raised him, David and Gemma as much as their own mother had. "I hope checking in on the puppies once or twice a day won't be too much of a bother. I should have talked to you about it first."

"I'm only surprised to hear of it, that's all."

"I'm sorry. I bumped into Ms. Fremont last night out on the dock and she proposed the idea of having the children look in on the puppies while she's at work. She has a clothing boutique in town. Did you know?"

"I did. She's a lovely girl, that Samantha Fremont. I met her the other day while you were out on your boat, when the children and I were outside playing. She's sewing your sister's wedding gown."

"I know."

Letty tilted her head and gave him an appraising look. "You know, maybe while you're here, you should go on a date or two. It might take your mind off everything."

He didn't have to ask what she meant. Letty was as much a trusted friend as an employee. She knew he regretted having to leave his work behind when they returned.

All their lives would change forever when this summer

was over. Letty understood how he dreaded packing up their things and moving to Summerhill.

"Thank you for the advice," he said stiffly.

"I'm only saying. You're handsome enough when you're not glowering like that. You're on the tall side but some women like that. You can be a bit too bookish but so far you have your own hair."

"A glowing endorsement if I've ever heard one." He tried not to laugh.

"Not to mention, you're the heir to an earldom. I'm told some women apparently favor that kind of thing."

He knew that only too well. Since his brother died, leaving him the only male heir of his father besides Thomas, Ian had struggled with a sudden unexpected and unwanted popularity among certain women who had been drawn to him only because he was a viscount now and would one day inherit several properties, farms and businesses.

He preferred not to think about any of it.

"Do you mind about the puppies?"

"Not at all. Not at all," she said as she cleared away the breakfast dishes. "As I said, I was just surprised, that's all. They're darling little things and the responsibility will be good for the children."

"Exactly what I thought."

"And they'll be glad of the distraction from their lessons."

"Thank you. You're a wonder."

"As I've been telling you for years now," she said with a cheeky smile that made him smile reluctantly in return.

"As this is the first visit, it may take a little longer than usual. Put your feet up and read a book for a few moments, why don't you?"

"Now that is the best idea I've heard all week," she said.

"When you're back, you can find me in the cozy sunroom, looking out at the water and reading my book. I only need a big floppy cat to make the scene perfect."

"Thank you, Letty."

He really didn't know what he would have done without her and considered himself the most fortunate of men that she had agreed to come out of retirement to help him and Susan after Amelia was born and later when Thomas came along. She had been about to retire for the second time when Susan had left him. Letty had stayed to help pick up the pieces, and though she had threatened to quit when he agreed to take Susan back after her diagnosis, she hadn't followed through.

She was a lifesaver, though he supposed he would have to figure out how to go on without her eventually. She was a few years away from seventy, after all. He wasn't sure she would be able to stay with them much longer.

On that less than cheerful note, he walked back through the house and found the children with their heads together, Amelia whispering something to her brother. She clamped her lips together tightly the moment she saw him.

What was that about? Ian wasn't sure he wanted to know.

"We should go. Ms. Fremont likely needs to be leaving soon to open her store."

The children didn't need to be told twice. They hurried for the door, obviously thrilled that they unexpectedly would be spending at least some portion of their family vacation playing with three cute puppies.

The morning was gorgeous, the mountain air cool enough for the children to need their jumpers. He loved these refreshing mornings. They reminded him of fishing trips he used to take with his father and David in Scotland, when they would rise before dawn and traipse through heather to the fishing spot his family had been coming to for generations.

Grief for his brother hit him out of nowhere, as it did at random moments. It had been three years and he still missed him with a fierce ache. He had so many vivid memories of their childhood, leading each other into trouble. Okay, usually it had been David doing the troublemaking and begging Ian to put away his book and join him.

Two years older, David had been smart, funny, brave, good-hearted. He would have made the perfect Earl of Amherst—unlike Ian, who had been perfectly content being the spare. David had been engaged when he died, two months away from marrying his longtime girlfriend. They had no children, alas. He mourned that, too, not only because it would have meant the child, if it were male, would become viscount instead of Ian and subsequently earl but, more, because he would have loved having any piece of his brother beyond his memories.

He pushed away the sadness, as he had become used to doing over the years, and followed after his children. The lake glistened in the sun, already more active than he had found it that morning when he left before daybreak. He could see a few fish jumping and several fishing boats slowly trolling.

The mountaintops across the way were still coated in snow with high clouds obscuring the highest peaks. He had only seen them out of the clouds a few times since their arrival.

Thomas reached the door first and pressed hard, a long, low sound that echoed through the morning.

Samantha Fremont opened her door before the boy

could ring it a second time. She looked cool, professional, wearing a lacy white blouse and a pale blue skirt.

She smiled a greeting for the children and Ian was uncomfortably aware of a curious twitch in his chest.

"Good morning, Amelia. Thomas. I'm so happy to see you. This must mean you've agreed to help me out with my puppies."

"We are. Dad just told us about it this morning." Amelia's voice seemed to vibrate with excitement, as if she couldn't contain it all inside.

"Oh, I'm so glad. I can't tell you what a big help this will be to me. Come in. You're just in time. I was about to prepare breakfast for the puppies. I'll do this before I leave every day so you won't have to worry about it, but it's fun to watch them eat."

She scooped food from a large storage container into a rectangular bowl, filled another one with water and then carried them into a small room where the puppies were contained by a gate.

The three little puppies, no more than a few pounds each, attacked the food like they were wild coyotes on a fresh carcass.

"They're so cute," Thomas said, enthralled.

Samantha stood next to Ian, the children in front of them, and he found himself painfully aware of her. She smelled delicious. He couldn't place the scent exactly. Berries and lemons with a sweeter note he couldn't quite identify. Whatever it was, he wanted to bury his face in her hair and simply inhale.

He held himself stiffly, doing his best to ignore the urge as they watched the puppies for a few moments. He was relieved when she finally headed toward her kitchen.

"Here's a key to my house." She held out a key on a

sparkly pink lanyard. Amelia reached for it, but before her hand could connect, Samantha held it out of her reach.

"Wait a minute. Before I give you my house key, I forgot to ask. Are you secretly a mysterious band of traveling house burglars who want to steal all my tiaras?"

Thomas and Amelia giggled.

"No, silly," Thomas said. "We're just two children."

"Your father's not a child."

She sent him a look under her lashes and Ian could feel his face heat. Hunger flared again and he wanted to wrap his arms around her and press her against the kitchen cabinets, kissing her until neither of them could think straight.

Where in the *hell* was this coming from? This wasn't him at all.

"He's not a burglar, either," Amelia assured her. "He's our dad and he's usually very nice."

"Unless you leave your toys on the floor for him to trip over," Thomas said thoughtfully.

"Or stay up late reading when you've promised to turn off the light," Amelia added.

"Good to know," Samantha said with a slanted smile in his direction that left him slightly dizzy.

"You can trust Amelia and Thomas," he said gruffly. "You won't find two nicer, kinder, more responsible children anywhere."

His words must have been the right ones. She gave him a startled look first, as if he had said something completely unexpected, which quickly turned into a blinding smile that made him feel as if his head was spinning.

"That's good enough for me, then." She handed over an index card covered in a neat, flowing script. "Here is everything I need you to do. As I said, I will feed them breakfast before I go so you won't have to worry about that.

I thought perhaps you could check on them once around noon and once more a little later, if you're around. If you're not, don't worry about it. Just text or call me so I can come home or send someone from the boutique."

"Should we take them outside?" Amelia asked.

"They would enjoy that very much. Perhaps on sunny days you can take them out to their pen in the afternoon so they can play in the grass."

"Would you like us to take them on walks?" Amelia asked eagerly.

"For now, they get enough exercise in here, playing with each other. If you'd like to walk them around the yard that would be fine but it isn't necessary. I should warn you that they're not very good on leashes yet. If you decide to do that, you can find leashes for them hanging inside the room where I keep the puppies."

"All right."

"Let's see. What else? They love to play with toys. Balls and sticks are their favorite."

"Got it," Amelia said.

"The gate on the door to their room opens by pushing the button on the top, then swinging it inside the room. If you have any questions at all, I've put my cell phone number on the card there. You can reach me throughout the day. Please don't hesitate to call me. It's no problem at all and I can be back here in ten minutes."

"I can't imagine they'll have any problems we can't handle but it's good to know how to contact you," Ian said.

She held out the card. "I'll give the instructions to you, Amelia. Though you may want to have your father take a picture with his phone, in case it gets lost somewhere."

"Good idea," Ian said. "I'll do that now."

He pulled out his mobile, snapped a picture, then handed

the note back to his daughter, aware of Samantha watching the entire process.

"Thank you so much for your help," she said when he was done. "I can't tell you how grateful I am."

"You're very welcome," Amelia said in a solemn voice. For all her seriousness, Ian could see how excited she was at the task ahead.

Samantha had to know what a treat this was for the children. It wasn't a burden at all but an experience they would treasure. He suspected their time playing with the three cute puppies might even become their most memorable part of the entire trip.

"Is there anything else we need to know?" Amelia asked with that same air of solemnity.

"I can't think of anything right now but if I do I'll let you know." She glanced at her watch. "I'm afraid I need to leave so that I can open my store on time. Again, if you have any questions at all, please call me."

Her smile encompassed all of them but Ian still wanted to burn it into his memory.

Letty's words seemed to ring in his head as he and the children walked back to their house, Amelia carrying the key as carefully as if she'd been asked to transport the crown jewels.

You know, maybe while you're here, you should go on a date or two. It might take your mind off things.

He couldn't deny he was tempted. Samantha was a hard woman to resist. He couldn't ask her out. He would only be here a few weeks and he would be busy with his research, the children and the wedding the entire time. What would be the point in dating someone he wouldn't see again after this summer?

Even as tempting as he was beginning to find the lovely, sweet, delicious-smelling Samantha Fremont.

"WHERE ARE YOU? I thought you were coming to the Helping Hands meeting today."

Sam frowned at her phone, glad McKenzie Kilpatrick couldn't see her frazzled expression right now. "I planned to be there but I got slammed with two new brides at the same time who drove over together from Boise. Apparently one of their friends wore one of my older designs so now they want me to customize their own dresses."

"That's fantastic! Your reputation is climbing, girl. Next thing you know, you'll be in all the bridal magazines and we can all say we knew you when."

Samantha's breath caught at the idea. Her designs in a bridal magazine. She couldn't even imagine it. "That's not going to happen any time soon."

"You don't know. Your designs are innovative and beautiful. I love the one you did for Dani's wedding to Ruben. It fit her personality so perfectly. Feminine and tough at the same time. That's your genius, Sam. You have the uncanny ability to see through what a woman thinks she wants in a dress to the style she really needs."

Sam appreciated the kind words but wasn't sure she agreed. That was her end goal but she acted more on instinct than any intentional effort.

That was also one of the reasons why she doubted she could ever take her wedding gown designing to another level. She created bespoke wedding dresses based on the wearer's personality, body type and design likes. She couldn't mass produce that with any degree of success.

"Are you sure you can't come?" McKenzie cajoled. "You're only a half hour late. If you can swing a break, even for a few moments, we'd still love you to drop by. Everyone missed you last week."

That had been another case where her best intentions had given way to expediency. She had been looking forward to the meeting after the fitting with Gemma the week before. Just as she had been about to walk across the street with Katrina, a bus full of tourists had pulled up and about a dozen of those tourists had headed into the store. She hadn't felt good about leaving her staff alone to handle the onslaught so had missed the meeting.

Right now, in contrast, the store was empty. Completely empty. Clarissa Wu, the salesclerk who had been scheduled to work that day, had called in sick that morning with a stomach bug she feared was food poisoning from a weekend picnic.

She didn't have any customers. The day had been a slow one so far. Could Sam afford to close the shop for an hour so she could spend time with her friends?

Her mother would have had plenty to say if she knew Sam was even considering closing the store. Though they both tried to attend the Helping Hands meetings when they could, Linda always refused to close the store for something she considered frivolous, even when business was painfully slow. If one of their employees couldn't cover the lunch break, Linda would stay herself.

Samantha rolled her eyes a little now, remembering the very well-honed martyr act her mother could pull. "You go on and have fun," Linda would say with a long-suffering look. "I'll be fine here by myself."

Those had been other instances where Sam had felt like a terrible daughter. While she may have felt a pang of guilt, quickly squelched, she would invariably attend anyway instead of offering to stay behind so her mother could go in her place.

She justified it at the time by reminding herself that she needed those breaks away from Linda. Anyway, every woman needed time with her friends to recharge her soul.

Now, when she didn't have anyone else to consider but herself and any potential customers who might be inconvenienced, she wavered for a few more moments, then hurriedly grabbed a piece of paper and scribbled a note saying she would be back in an hour.

She owned the store alone now. If she wanted to go see her friends, who was stopping her? She might miss a sale or two, but if someone wanted an item badly enough, they could come back after lunch.

She flipped the sign on the door to Closed, stuck the note below it with tape, then locked the door behind her and hurried down the street to McKenzie's store, Point Made Flowers and Gifts.

The moment she opened the door, the familiar sounds of women laughing and the warm, welcoming scent of cinnamon and cloves filled her with comforting peace.

Right decision, she assured herself as she made her way to the workroom in the back. She needed this, especially after missing the last one.

Kenzie opened this room for craft classes and for regular meetings of the Haven Point Helping Hands, a loosely organized group whose goal was to help and lift others in the community. Usually that involved working on craft projects together and selling them at local events, then using the proceeds from those sales to benefit various causes.

When she walked in, conversation around the table stopped as everyone greeted her enthusiastically. She saw a few faces were missing. Devin Barrett, McKenzie's sister, wasn't there and neither was Dani Morales. The two of them had demanding careers, one as a physician and the other as a veterinarian, which meant they often couldn't come to the midday meetings of the group.

"You made it!" McKenzie beamed at her. "I'm so glad."

"I don't have long but it feels like it's been forever since I've been able to come to a meeting, and I needed lunch, anyway, so I decided to close the store."

"Good for you." Julia Caine, who ran the town library, smiled.

"Grab some salad," Kenzie ordered. "There's plenty left."

She knew better than to argue with the woman so she filled a plate with a large green salad and some of Barbara Serrano's famous Italian pasta salad, then added a bowl of fresh strawberries.

She sat down at a long rectangular table surrounded by her friends.

"How's the wedding planning?" Charlene Bailey was asking Gemma Summerhill.

Gemma lit up at the question. "Everything is coming together perfectly."

"Three weeks now, isn't that right?" Eppie Becker asked kindly.

"That's right."

"It will be here before you know it," Eppie's sister, Hazel, said. The two sisters were in their eighties and had spent their entire lives living no farther than a few houses away from each other. They had even married brothers. Though Hazel's husband had died several years ago, Eppie's husband squired them both around town to various functions.

"I know," Gemma said. "I can't believe the wedding is

less than a month away. I'm utterly thrilled that Eliza and Aidan are allowing us to marry at Snow Angel Cove."

"Oh, it's our pleasure," Eliza assured her. "Aidan is hoping that you'll stick around at Caine Tech for a long time, now that you're marrying someone local."

Eliza's husband, Aidan, was CEO of the largest employer in town, which had mainly been responsible for the rejuvenation of Haven Point. Samantha didn't want to think about where the town might be if Aidan and Ben Kilpatrick hadn't decided to open their research and development campus onto the site of the old boatworks that used to be owned by Ben's family.

The town had been dying before that, sustained only by fleeting tourism during the summer months.

Those tourism dollars had been appreciated but weren't enough to spur growth and keep the younger population from fleeing for other job opportunities elsewhere after high school.

Even Linda had agreed Caine Tech had been good for Haven Point, though she still complained about the new housing developments and increased traffic in town.

Fremont Fashions had benefited tremendously from the new growth. Samantha only had good feelings toward the tech company, especially because of the friends like Gemma it had brought into her life.

Right now, her friend seemed to glow with happiness and Sam sighed inside. All this talk of weddings made her feel like the only single person left in town. Except Hazel, anyway.

"How nice that your family is able to come," Eppie went on. "By the way, we met your brother and niece and nephew the other day at the supermarket."

"How did you know he was my brother?" Gemma looked surprised.

"We don't have that many people in town with posh British accents who sound like they could be on *Downton Abbey*. Plus, the two of you look like you could be twins."

Gemma gave a faint smile. "We're not. He's the older by two years. But when we were younger, people often used to mistake us for twins."

"We saw the similarity between you two, and Hazel stopped him and asked straight out if he was related to you," Eppie went on. "The children both were polite and well-mannered and your brother was ever so helpful. We couldn't reach a can of tomatoes on the top shelf and he kindly agreed to get it for us and then we enlisted his help in the cereal aisle with that granola Ronald likes. He seemed like a lovely man," Eppie said.

"Inside and out," Hazel piped up with a wink to the table in general.

Everyone giggled except Sam.

"I haven't met this paragon of a brother yet," Roxy Nash, the only other unattached female in the group, said in a voice that sounded like a purr. "Maybe I need to time my grocery visits better."

Sam chewed salad greens that suddenly tasted bitter. She usually liked Roxy but she didn't care for that predatory tone. Anyway, Ian Summerhill wasn't a topic she wanted to discuss. It was bad enough that she couldn't seem to stop thinking about the man, especially after their encounter with him in the moonlight the night before. She didn't need to talk about him on her lunch break.

She tried to come up with another topic but Charlene Bailey spoke before she could.

"How nice that he can come in early. Is he helping you with all your wedding preparations?"

That seemed to amuse Gemma. "I would like to say yes, but I'm afraid that's not really the case. He would be hopeless at it. Ian is a biologist and he's writing a paper on a species of salmon native only to Lake Haven."

"Oh, yes. The Lake Haven kokanee," McKenzie said knowledgeably.

"How on earth do you know that?" Charlene stared at her.

Wynona, Charlene's oldest daughter, laughed. "Surely you know that Mayor Kilpatrick knows everything that goes on within a hundred-mile radius of Lake Haven. She can tell you every rare bird that ever made a visit, even if it only stopped in a treetop for a few moments to eat a worm during its migration."

"I can't help that I like to stay informed," McKenzie said haughtily, though she looked amused at Wynona's teasing. "There's an entire book at the city offices on the flora and fauna in and around Lake Haven. Though it was written in the 1930s, it still contains valuable information about some of the unique species of the area."

"I'll have to mention it to Ian," Gemma said with interest. "I'm sure he'll want to take a look at it. He's trying to narrow down historical populations of the salmon as part of his research."

"I would be happy to show it to him. We only have the one copy, though, so I'm afraid we can't loan it out."

"How wonderful that your brother could coordinate his research with your wedding and a vacation for his children," Eppie said.

"Did his wife come on the trip with him?" Hazel asked.

"I didn't see the children's mother at the grocery store with him."

Gemma's mouth tightened. "I'm afraid not," she said. "Susan died last year."

"Oh, no." Andie Bailey, married to Katrina's brother, Marshall, looked sorrowful. "Those poor children. She must have been young. What happened?"

Andie was one of the most compassionate people Samantha knew, maybe because she had walked a hard road herself. She had been a young widow when she arrived in Haven Point with her two children. Now she had a busy, joy-filled life and a houseful of children, including Marshall's teenage son, a toddler and a new baby.

"Cancer," Gemma said, still with that odd, closed look on her face. Her expression wasn't sorrow exactly. It was closer to anger, for reasons Samantha didn't understand. "She was diagnosed with breast cancer a few years ago. By the time they found out, it had metastasized throughout her body."

What a horrible way to die, she thought again. Samantha didn't want to think about it. Her mother's death had been shocking, yes, completely unexpected. But at least Linda had died in her sleep of what doctors suspected was a massive heart attack and probably hadn't even known what was happening. She hadn't had to deal with a long, lingering, painful death, knowing she would be leaving behind those she loved.

Those poor children.

Her heart ached again for all of them.

"It's been a hard year for them all," Gemma went on.

"How nice that your wedding gave them a reason to take a vacation together," Charlene Bailey said. "I've always found travel to be a great comfort."

"Yes. This is the first vacation Ian and the children have taken since she died."

"Well, they couldn't have chosen a more beautiful time of year to visit our lake," Barbara Serrano said loyally. "I was thinking this morning what a perfect June we're having. I don't think my flower garden has ever been this lush so early."

To Samantha's relief, the conversation shifted to gardening and the next cruise vacation Charlene and her husband, Mike, were taking later that summer.

Sam finished her lunch, her thoughts still centered on Ian and the children while she listened to the flow of conversation around her, which now focused on the Lake Haven Days celebration in a few more weeks and the group's effort to raise funds to build a playground for children of all abilities at one of the city parks.

Ian's children needed to grieve for their mother and they couldn't do that by ignoring her life or her death. She knew firsthand how that only led to more pain.

She really didn't want to talk to Ian about what Amelia had told her, that he was discouraging the children from talking about their pain. It was none of her business. She barely knew the man and was only connected to him at all because he was renting a temporary home near hers.

She couldn't forget how much it had wounded her when her mother tried to erase the memory of Samantha's father.

She wished her mother had given her an age-appropriate explanation about how mental illness and depression could sometimes lead unhappy people to take desperate action.

If she could have talked about Lyle more, remembered good times, received counseling when she was a vulnerable teenager struggling with the loss and pain and missing her father, perhaps she wouldn't have this gaping hole in her heart.

How could she bring it up to Ian? And how would he respond to having a woman who was virtually a stranger question his parenting skills?

She knew one thing at least. Once she told him she thought he was wrong to discourage his children from dealing with their grief, he would probably no longer look at her with that glimmer of awareness in his eyes.

CHAPTER SIX

HE WAS BECOMING addicted to these mountain evenings.

After the children were in bed, Ian walked outside the house toward the allure of the lake, with the gently lapping water and the glitter of stars overhead.

The grass was wet and rustled under his feet, the air sweet with the scent of pine and water and night.

He drew it deeply into his lungs, wishing he could bottle that scent and take it back with him for those times when the demands of the life he was stepping into became too much.

In England, he didn't take nearly enough time to simply *be*. He was always too busy caring for the children, working with students, handling the day-to-day details that filled a life.

He was not sure the last time he had a moment simply to think.

The owners of the house he was renting had thoughtfully placed a bench just on the lakeshore. He sat down and looked out at the moon reflecting on the water, its glow shimmering on the surface of the lake.

A fish jumped in the water and he smiled a little, wondering whether it was one of the salmon he was studying.

He felt tension trickle out of him with every passing moment. Ian released a breath, closing his eyes and listening to the water and the breeze.

The children seemed to have had a good day. The best in a long time. They had returned home from caring for the puppies with a new energy, bubbling over with stories about what the little dogs had done and how cute they were.

"They're the most precious puppies in all the world," Amelia had said firmly.

"I wish we could take one home," Thomas said, his tone wistful.

"I would choose Coco," Amelia had declared.

"No, Oscar. He's the littlest and the cutest."

He had loved seeing their animation as they debated the merits of each puppy. It made him realize how subdued they had all become, as if afraid to let too much light and joy into their lives.

He would have to seriously consider getting them a dog, as he had promised, when they moved into the small cottage at Summerhill. His parents had their four dogs at the main house that would fill some need in the children to have an animal to love and care for, but his parents' dogs were older, set in their ways. Perhaps the children needed a dog of their own to train, to feed, to walk.

What sort of dog? A retriever was a good family pet, hardy and calm. He'd had one himself when he was young and had adored it.

Would it be better to find a dog shortly after they moved or wait until the children had a chance to acclimatize to their new schools, new home, new surroundings?

He sighed, looking out at the water and considering his options.

Trying to, anyway. There was a small chance he may have become *too* comfortable out there on the bench. One moment he was thinking about the lake and about the children and retrievers and fitting the demands of a puppy into their life when they would already be dealing with so much upheaval; the next he gradually became aware he wasn't alone.

He opened his eyes to find a little brown-and-black dog watching him, as if his canine musings had conjured her.

Samantha's dog, Betsey, he realized.

"Hi there." He scratched her ear and was touched when she immediately jumped up to settle beside him on the bench.

Where was her owner? He looked about for Samantha Fremont and couldn't see her. Not quite sure what to do with the dog, he continued to pet her and she rested her chin on his thigh, seeming perfectly content to snuggle next to him.

It wasn't a bad thing at all to sit out on a cool evening next to a vast lake, petting a little lapdog. Perhaps this was the sort of dog they needed, something small and cute and cuddly.

"I think you're supposed to be somewhere," he said to Betsey. In answer, she edged closer to him.

A moment later, he heard Samantha calling her. Betsey lifted her head but didn't move from his side.

"Over here," Ian called softly. He should probably send the little dog on her way but he was enjoying himself too much for that. If he were honest with himself, he could admit he didn't mind the idea of her owner coming out, as well, to share his bench and the beautiful night.

Samantha approached him, carrying a leash. "Betsey. What are you doing, bothering our neighbor? I opened the door for only a second and she raced out here as if she were late for an appointment. I'm sorry."

"She's no bother. I've been enjoying her company."

I would enjoy yours more, Ian wanted to say but the words caught in his throat.

"She is very calming, isn't she? I thought so from the moment I brought her home. Until I found out she was expecting puppies, anyway, and would deliver them in less than a month. Since then, I've been the opposite of calm."

"Seems like a fairly important detail her previous humans should have shared."

"One would think, right?"

"You didn't know about the puppies when you got her?"

She sighed. "No idea. I didn't have a clue. If I had known, I would have been a nervous wreck and probably wouldn't have taken her."

He couldn't hide his smile as he imagined what a shock that must have been. "How did she come to live with you? Is she a shelter rescue?"

He was further delighted when Samantha Fremont settled on the bench beside him, much as her dog had.

"That's a very long story." She gazed out at the water. "I suppose you could say it started when my mother died unexpectedly in January."

She probably wasn't even aware of the thread of sadness twisting through her voice. He heard it, though, and fought the urge to hug her as compassion seeped through him like water through limestone.

"I'm sorry. That must have been difficult." He adored his parents and couldn't imagine his world without their supportive presence.

She accepted his sympathy with a nod. "Thank you. She died in her sleep. For her, I suppose it wasn't a bad way to go, but I'll admit, I haven't been handling it well. My father died when I was young and for most of my life it's just been me and my mother. Living without her has been an adjustment."

"I can only imagine."

She sent him a swift look. "I'm sorry. That probably sounds pathetic to you. I'm a grown woman. I understand that losing my mother, while difficult, is not the same as you losing a wife and Amelia and Thomas losing *their* mother."

Guilt pinched at him, as it always did when someone showed him sympathy. "I've learned on this journey that you can't compare your pain to someone else's. We all have hard things."

"But I didn't lose the love of my life."

Neither did I, he wanted to say, but swallowed the words. "I would never tell you that I had more right to grief than you do," he said instead.

"My mother made a sampler when she was a girl that said, *If all our troubles were hung on a line, you'd take home yours and I'd take home mine.* It's still hanging in her bedroom."

What if they all simply left their troubles hanging on that line and let the wind eventually carry them away? He was tired of wearing his, like a too-tight hat always pressing against his skull.

"It sounds as if you were very close to your mother."

She released a sigh, pulling her dog onto her lap, and said nothing for a long time while small waves licked against the dock.

"I wanted to be close to her. I suppose we were in a way since we only had each other to lean on after my father died. But my mother was a...difficult woman."

"She and my ex-wife had that much in common, then." The words slipped out before he could stop them.

She stared at him. "Ex-wife? The children's mother was your ex-wife?"

Instinctively, he wanted to jump up and hurry back to his house, feeling horribly exposed.

Why had he told her that? Ian never talked about his marriage with anyone. It was the reason he went along with the fiction the world had created about him, a man who had lost the love of his life.

Now that he had brought it up, he found he wanted to tell Samantha the truth.

"Her name was Susan and she left me for another man months before she was diagnosed with cancer. We had just signed the papers when she found out she was ill."

"I thought you were a grieving widower."

This time it was his turn to sigh. "It's easier than trying to explain the whole story."

"She left you."

He found her shock rather gratifying, he had to admit. He was certain it was his imagination but he thought Samantha sounded as if she couldn't quite understand why any woman would do such a thing.

"We were never a good fit," he admitted, something he had come to see early in their marriage. "She taught at Oxford, as well. Psychology. We met when we were both graduate students."

They had dated only a few times but had slept together one night when they'd both had too much to drink after a party with friends.

She'd become pregnant with Amelia. While he had used protection and she had told him she was on birth control, he suspected she had lied.

He wasn't necessarily much of a catch, a too-serious biology student obsessed with his research. But his family was wealthy and not without influence and she had adored that part of their life far more than the quiet world of an Oxford professor.

She had never said so outright but he suspected that wealth and influence was the main reason she had dated him in the first place.

"We tried to make it work for the children's sake," he said now to Samantha. "Whatever else I could say about her, she was a good mother who loved her children. We might have stayed together and figured out a way to cobble together a happy life but three years ago she fell passionately in love with a visiting guitar instructor from Spain."

"Oh, no."

Samantha sounded so distressed he had to sigh. "My heart wasn't broken, I promise. At least not for myself. Divorce is always hardest on the children. Thomas was young enough he didn't really know what was happening but Amelia was struggling to process all the changes. We were figuring things out together and then Susan was diagnosed with cancer after a routine mammogram."

"What happened to her guitar instructor?"

"He decided radiation and chemotherapy weren't what he signed up for and went back to Barcelona."

"I would say that's just what she deserves but that seems a little cold since she was dealing with such a hard diagnosis."

He had thought much worse than that, he had to admit. "Susan was devastated, of course. On both counts. By then I was mostly numb. My brother had died a few months earlier and Gemma was seriously injured in the same accident. Our family was still reeling from that."

Again, he couldn't believe he was telling this woman he scarcely knew all his deep, dark secrets. If they had been sitting beside the lake in the warm light of a sunny summer afternoon, he probably couldn't have been able to be so honest, but there was a quiet intimacy here in the dark.

He didn't tell her the rest of it, how he felt as if his entire life had completely spun out of his control.

In a handful of months, his world had turned upside down—one minute he was a relatively happy if boring fisheries biologist, coming home each day to his wife and children and secure about his place in the world; the next he was the custodial parent of two young children and trying to adjust to the idea he would have to give up everything he loved.

And then his children's mother had been diagnosed with a terminal illness.

"You took her back."

"Technically, yes, but not really. We were still divorced. But yes. She lived with me and the children as she went through cancer treatment. We were able to let go of some of the bitterness and anger between us and become...friends, of a sort, I suppose you could say. I am sorry she lost her battle with the illness, but for the children's sake much more than my own."

"You cared for her at the end?"

The shock in her voice made him wince. "You sound like Gemma. She thinks I was crazy to let Susan come back to live with us during her treatments after she walked away from our marriage."

"I don't think you were crazy." Sam's voice was soft.

"I don't, either, for what it's worth. Susan had nowhere else to go and was frightened and terribly ill. Whatever else she might have done, she was still the children's mother. Caring for her was the right thing to do."

"Of course it was. You gave her the chance to be close

to her children toward the end of her life. She was lucky to have you," she murmured.

He wanted to close his eyes and let her words heal the raw places in his heart.

"Thank you for saying so. It was an easy decision but not an effortless one, if that makes sense."

"It makes perfect sense to me."

"I couldn't have lived with myself if I had known I allowed the mother of my children to die alone."

"Of course you couldn't. You did exactly the right thing."

He didn't know precisely why but her firm approval warmed a cold and hollow corner inside him. So many of his friends and associates had believed him crazy to allow Susan back. Even his own parents questioned the wisdom of opening that door to her again after all the harm she had caused.

He had weighed his options and had ultimately gone with the one that felt right to him. The children had grown much closer to Susan in her remaining months than he would have imagined possible. While that may have magnified their grief at her loss, he wouldn't have deprived her or the children of the opportunity to share those last weeks.

Beside him, Samantha shifted on the bench. The scent he was coming to associate with her floated on the breeze toward him, strawberries and clotted cream with lemon biscuits.

His mouth watered.

"It sounds to me as if you did everything right."

"I don't know about that. I just did my best. There's no right or wrong in a complicated situation like ours."

"Other than leaving your husband and children for a

Spanish flamenco musician. I would say that definitely falls under the *wrong* column."

He had to smile at her tart tone. "I can agree with you on that point. But forgiveness can be powerful, too. I'm not sure we could ever heal all those wounds, even if she hadn't become so ill, but at least I no longer hated Susan for walking out. I accepted my part in not being the husband she needed. In the end, I mostly felt…sorry for her."

"I owe you an apology," she said after a long moment.

"Why is that?" he asked, startled.

"I've been gearing up to lecture you on your parenting skills. But I have a feeling perhaps I don't know the full story."

"Oh, trust me. You could probably lecture me night and day about my parenting skills. What did I do this time?"

"Probably nothing. The other day, Amelia told me you didn't want them to talk about their mother, that you told them it was time to move on. I was prepared to think you were an unfeeling jerk, if you want the truth. Children need time and space to grieve. They might seem as if they're handling things fine, but often there can be far more going on inside than they will ever share."

He didn't want her to think poorly of him. He wanted her to keep looking at him with that admiration in her eyes that seemed as genuine as the moonlight.

He also wanted to know why she spoke with such firm knowledge. She said her father had died young. Had she been discouraged from talking about him?

"I make plenty of mistakes where the children are concerned, but I promise, I've never told them not to discuss their mother. They went to grief counseling from the time she was put on hospice until only a few months ago. I try to talk to them about their memories of her as often as possible without making the topic oppressive for them."

"Why would she say they weren't supposed to talk about her?"

He frowned. "I have no idea. Maybe she misunderstood something I said. Thank you for telling me. I'll try to make it clear to both of them that it's healthy to talk about her, that it's okay to feel sad and miss her."

She shifted on the bench beside him. "You're welcome. I was all ready to yell at you the next time I saw you. I feel a little let down now."

He laughed, which seemed to surprise both of them. "Go ahead. I probably deserve it for something else I've done wrong."

"I would guess you're an excellent father," she said after a moment. "Only a loving parent and an honorable man would be concerned enough about his children's mother that he would be willing to care for her as she was dying, even after they were divorced. It couldn't have been easy."

He didn't know quite how to respond to that. He was only aware of a soft, seductive warmth flickering to life inside him. "Thank you," he said gruffly. "You're right. It wasn't easy. But I don't regret it, despite what my family and friends might have thought."

They lapsed into silence again, but it was far more comfortable this time. He could feel some of the tension ease from his shoulders.

How did he find her presence so relaxing, especially with this attraction he couldn't seem to fight?

"Tell me more about your research project. What led you to salmon, of all things?"

He seized on the topic, grateful to have another reason to stay with her for a few more moments. "I've always found them fascinating. The word *salmon* is believed to derive from the Latin word *salmo* or *to leap*. They fight against rapids and strong currents, work their way past snags in the water, all so they can return to the place of their birth. It's unbelievable, really. The salmon in Lake Haven fight their way two miles up the fast-moving Chalk Creek waters, with six separate small waterfalls and a hundred obstacles, until they reach the place where the females create their nests, called redds. Each female will lay around a thousand eggs. Many of them die in the effort but enough survive to spawn so that a new generation can repeat the process."

He caught himself again. "I'm sorry. I've been told I tend toward pedagogy when I talk about my favorite subject."

"I don't know what that word means," she admitted without a trace of embarrassment. "But it sounds terrible, whatever it is."

He laughed, finding her honesty refreshing. Okay, the truth was, he found *her* refreshing. Full stop.

"When I talk about my research, I tend to come off like a lecturer reading from a textbook."

"I disagree. If you're a lecturer, you're a very good one. You make even salmon sound interesting."

"They are interesting."

She smiled. "No doubt. Of course, it might be your accent. You could be talking about plumbing fixtures and I would still find it fascinating. You know how we American girls are about you sexy Brits."

He blinked. No one in her right mind would ever call him sexy. Good grief. He was staid and boring, focusing only on his work and his children.

"You don't have to mock me," he said stiffly.

She shifted to stare at him. "I wasn't mocking you, Ian. I assure you, I was wholly sincere."

This bright, vibrant, beautiful woman couldn't possibly find him sexy. The idea was laughable.

"At heart, I'll always be a boring biologist who knows more about the mating habits of salmon than I do about what makes a woman tick."

She cuddled her dog closer. "Oh, somehow I think you do all right in that department."

He almost laughed. What would she say if he told her he hadn't been with a woman in longer than he cared to remember?

He wasn't a saint by any means. He had dated here and there after the separation and had been in the early stages of a relationship with a very nice woman when Susan had been diagnosed with cancer.

Joann had been the one to gently break things off between them, telling him it was clear he wasn't in a good space for a relationship with his attention fragmented between his children, his students and Susan's worsening condition.

Dating had, of course, been impossible after Susan came back to live with them. Even if he had the energy or desire, which he hadn't, how did he explain to a woman that he wanted to take her to dinner—oh, and by the way, she needn't worry because he had caregivers at home with his dying ex-wife?

The past year had been a blur of helping the children grieve, wrapping things up at his college and frequent trips back to Summerhill to begin assuming some of his new responsibilities.

"I appreciate the confidence," he said, his voice gruff. "Misplaced as it might be."

"I don't think it is. And believe me, I should know."

"Why is that?"

She was quiet for a long moment, gazing out at the water. Finally she faced him with a determined set to her jaw. "I'm surprised you haven't heard the rumors, considering you live next door to me."

"Rumors?"

"I have something of a reputation around town as a man-hungry flirt."

She said the words in a lighthearted tone as if she were making a joke, but somehow he sensed she was serious.

"Is that supposed to be some kind of a warning?"

She gave a little laugh that almost sounded sincere. "You're perfectly safe with me. You could say I'm a reformed flirt. I used to be one, a lifetime ago. But then my mother died and I ended up with a pregnant dog, a lemon of a car and more wedding dress orders than I have hours in the day to finish. I'm not the same person I was six months ago."

He had the feeling they were both at a crossroads in their lives, both trying to find their way amid earthshaking changes.

He shouldn't be so drawn to her but he couldn't seem to help it. He wanted to set her dog gently on the ground and pull Samantha into his arms, both to take that bleak tone out of her voice and to ease the aching hunger he realized had been curling through him since she walked out through the darkness to join him.

"Give it time," he said. "I'm sure you'll rediscover your inner flirt."

"Maybe I don't want to. If you want the truth, the woman I used to be was silly and shallow and focused on all the completely wrong things."

He again had that sense of unexpected intimacy in sitting here in the darkness beside the lake with her, sharing truths neither might not feel comfortable revealing in bright sunlight.

He wanted to know more about her. He wanted to know everything.

"What used to be important to that old Samantha?"

"I cared about the kind of clothes a man wore or the type of car he drove or how much was in his bank account."

He understood that mind-set. How could he not when Susan had only dated him in the first place because of his family's prominence and because of the Honorable that had preceded his name in those days as a younger son, before David died and Ian became the viscount?

He wasn't the kind of man likely to interest a woman like Samantha. He dressed comfortably but didn't follow trends and in England he drove an eight-year-old car he had picked more because of its safety record than style.

"What matters to you now?" He found he desperately wanted to know the answer.

She gazed out at the lake. "I'm not looking for a relationship. If I were, I hope I would choose a man who is kind to his family, who respects and supports me and who makes choices based not on what the world might think but about what his conscience tells him is right."

"Sounds like a boring prat."

She laughed. "Apparently that's what I need these days."

He liked her, more than he'd liked another woman in a long, long time. Maybe ever. "Well, when you're ready, I hope you find him," he said, and was astonished that his voice came out gruff.

"Thank you."

Her gaze met his and he was fiercely drawn to the

laughter in her eyes, the smile that tipped the corners of her mouth. The intimacy of the night seemed to swirl around them, soft and sweet.

She swallowed, her smile trickling away, and he saw something flicker in her eyes, something that sent a hot ache coursing through him.

She folded her hands tightly on her lap but he thought he saw her fingers tremble.

He should get up from this bench, right now. A smart man would simply say good night, walk away and return to his house, where he was safe.

He couldn't seem to make himself move, either unable or unwilling to do that. He wasn't sure which.

Her gaze flickered to his mouth and then back to his eyes and that was it. He knew he had to kiss her.

He tried to talk himself out of it, even as he angled his body toward hers and set her dog down onto the ground. Nothing good could possibly come from kissing his next-door neighbor when he would be leaving in only a few weeks.

He couldn't offer her anything but this, ever. When this summer idyll ended, he had to return to Summerhill and immerse himself in family concerns that seemed far removed from this little Idaho lake town.

Beyond that, she was his sister's good friend. Gemma would kill him if he indulged in a summer fling that could end up hurting this sweet, perfectly nice woman.

This wasn't a fling, he argued. It was only a kiss.

He knew it was a justification, but in that moment he didn't care. As he lowered his mouth, all the reasons why this was a bad idea flashed through his head in rapid succession, but none compared to the urgent hunger inside him to kiss this soft, enticing woman.

When his mouth brushed against hers once, then twice, Samantha gave a sexy little intake of breath. He started to ease away but didn't make it far before she wrapped her arms around him, returning the embrace with a heat and passion that sent all thoughts of salmon and Susan and the children completely out of his head.

The kiss was every bit as delicious as he might have expected. Her mouth was sweet, warm, and tasted like fresh-picked berries. He wanted to explore every inch of it.

She gave that delicious sigh again, her hands tight around his neck.

Bad idea, that warning voice said as he tightened his embrace. This was more than a simple kiss.

He ignored it. Right now, with a soft, enticing woman kissing him back like she couldn't get enough, this felt like the absolutely best idea he had ever had.

THIS HAD TO STOP.

Right now.

The thought pushed through her consciousness but Samantha shoved it right back out. She couldn't seem to think straight, lost in the magic of kissing a fascinating man in the pale moonlight.

He was warm, strong, his hair silky under her fingers, and he smelled so good, like some kind of masculine soap and a laundry detergent that smelled like a mountain meadow.

His mouth tasted like chocolate cake and she couldn't seem to get enough. She wanted to close her eyes and pretend the rest of the world didn't exist, that only this moment mattered.

She gave in for several moments, telling herself it was only a casual kiss and didn't mean anything. The man was only here for a few weeks. She could indulge in a few kisses in the moonlight with him, couldn't she?

No.

This was a mistake. She was not the kind of woman who kissed a man she barely knew. Or at least she wasn't that kind of woman anymore.

She had to be stronger than this. As tempting as Ian Summerhill might be with those stunning blue eyes and that accent and the casually messed hair she wanted to smooth down, she could no longer afford to make decisions she knew deep in her heart were bound to turn out disastrously for her in the end.

Only a moment more, she told herself as he deepened the kiss, his tongue licking at the seam of her mouth, his body strong and hard against her. What was the harm in two unattached adults sharing a kiss on a cool summer's night?

It's not like she was going to fall in love with the man. She knew he was leaving in a few weeks. She might have been stupid about men once upon a time but surely she had a little more common sense now.

She wrapped her arms more tightly around him, feeling hard muscles against her that told her he might be a scientist but he was also athletic. He made a low sound in his throat that seemed to slide down her spine, making her shiver.

Oh my.

They kissed for a long time, tasting, discovering, savoring. She didn't want it to ever end. How had she forgotten how intimate a kiss could feel, as if he could learn everything about her by a simple brush of his mouth against hers?

This felt anything but casual. It felt...profoundly moving somehow, as if something significant had just shifted in her world, something she didn't quite understand.

The night murmured around them. The water, the chirp of crickets, an owl in the treetops. She vaguely registered all of those sounds on some level but they couldn't pierce the soft, dreamy haze surrounding her and Ian until Betsey suddenly gave a sharp bark.

The sound dragged her back to hard reality, to the knowledge that she was kissing a man she barely knew with an eager hunger that belied everything she had told him about looking for something deeper in a man than physical attraction.

What was she doing? She knew better. This had been a grave mistake, one she feared she would pay for eventually.

She slid her mouth from his and edged away on the bench, her heart pounding.

"I need to, um, go."

He gazed at her, those blue eyes glittering in the moonlight. Why did he have to be all kinds of gorgeous?

"Do you?"

That voice. That accent, the low timbre. He hit every single one of her buttons, including several she hadn't known existed until this moment.

She inhaled sharply, ignoring every instinct that urged her to simply slide back into his arms.

"Yes. Betsey and I have been gone too long. The puppies will be anxious."

"Right." He stood up abruptly and she shivered as cool air blew off the lake.

She couldn't read his features clearly in the darkness. Was that regret she saw in his eyes? Was it because they had kissed? Or because they had to stop?

"Good night."

She scooped up her dog, grateful for the buffer Betsey provided, and headed for the house. She had only made it a few steps before she realized Ian was following closely behind. They were in her own backyard. Did he really think he had to escort her to the door?

She wanted to tell him he didn't need to bother, but by then they had reached her back step and she couldn't see the point.

"Good night," he said, some of his earlier stiffness returning to his voice.

She wanted to kiss him again, to wrap her arms around his neck and return to that magical place they had found by the water's edge. Instead, she nodded, then let herself into the house, feeling as if something fundamental had changed inside her, something she didn't want to examine too closely.

As soon as she closed the door, Betsey rushed to her water bowl and took a healthy drink. Sam followed her example, turning on the tap and filling a large glass with cold water.

Instead of drinking it, she pressed it to first one flaming cheek and then the other.

Holy moly. The man could kiss.

She didn't know when she had ever completely lost her head over a kiss.

Starry-eyed Sam. That's what her mother used to call her, in a mocking voice Samantha had hated, because of what Linda perceived as her daughter's tendency to fall in love at the drop of a hat.

That was her past, one she wasn't particularly proud of.

This wasn't her first time letting her emotions get carried away.

Even with the other men she had kissed, she didn't remember an embrace ever leaving her so breathless.

Contrary to popular belief, she was not really an expert when it came to men. At least when it came to sex. She had gone all the way with only two guys. One was her high school boyfriend, who was married now and living in Shelter Springs with his wife and their three kids. He worked at a home improvement store in the larger town. Yeah, that had led to a few uncomfortable conversations when she had to go in asking about garden hoses and pipe fittings.

Another had been a guy she dated while finishing her degree in business in Boise.

She had lived at home to help her mother with the store after class and on the weekends so she hadn't had much of a social life. She did manage to date occasionally and had gone out for about six months with an economics major who was a few years ahead of her in school, Craig Bothwell.

She told herself she was in love and thought he felt the same. She spent those six months dreaming about the adventures they would have and how she was going to tell her mother she was leaving the boutique to go with him when he graduated.

He had taken a job in Dallas a month before graduation. As he prepared to pack up his belongings and move, she waited for him to talk to her about going with him. He didn't. Finally, a week before graduation, she had gathered her courage and brought it up.

She could still remember the devastation scorching through her when he had told her that while he'd had fun these past few months with her, he didn't see a future for them and he certainly didn't want her to go to Dallas with him.

Brokenhearted, she hadn't dated anyone else seriously in college, too busy licking her wounds. Only after graduation, when she turned her full attention to the boutique, did she begin to realize how limited the dating options were here in Haven Point. She lived at home with her mother in a town where everybody always seemed to be watching her. She couldn't just sleep with any random tourist without word trickling back to her mother.

She went on dates here and there and seemed to convince herself this was it...she was in love. This one would last forever.

They never did, though, and finally she'd gotten tired of trying.

She closed her eyes, reliving the kiss with Ian. Nothing in her past had prepared her for that kind of fast and furious response to a man. She still couldn't quite catch her breath.

How ridiculous. She didn't even know him. Not really. Yes, he seemed to be a good father. Yes, she was attracted to him. But the only thing she really knew for certain was that he would be leaving in a few weeks' time. Even if he were interested in a fling, which he clearly wasn't, she couldn't do it. She wanted more. She wanted the kind of life Katrina had with Bowie, and Wyn had with Cade Emmett.

They each had found deep and lasting love. Bowie and Cade would both give everything they had for their wives. Being around the couples was both inspiring and depressing, reinforcing just how shallow her previous relationships with men had been.

No one she had ever dated had once looked at her with even a small portion of the tenderness she saw her friends receive from their husbands.

She wanted that. Not right now, maybe, but someday.

If she gave in to her attraction, something told her Ian Summerhill would leave her far more devastated than Craig ever had.

With a sigh, she returned Betsey to her puppies, then headed to her own bedroom, the one she had slept in since birth, feeling more alone than ever.

CHAPTER SEVEN

APPARENTLY SHE WAS a genius all these years and had no idea.

Genius might be too strong of a word. She couldn't use it toward herself without feeling uncomfortable. Then again, maybe she had spent too much time listening to certain negative voices and struggled to give herself enough credit.

There was no maybe about it, she acknowledged. Samantha didn't trust her own instincts, always questioning and second-guessing every decision, from the kind of toothpaste to buy to the best way to pick out ripe watermelons at the grocery store.

In the months since her mother died, she had tried to break herself of the habit but it was proving harder than she expected. She wanted to think she was getting better at figuring things out on her own.

In this case, she had made an impulsive decision and it had paid off better than she could have dreamed. The plan to have Ian's children watch the dogs seemed to be working like a charm. This week had been a dream. Since the previous Monday when Amelia and Thomas had started checking on them and playing with them a little during the day, Betsey and the puppies seemed so tired by the time Samantha returned home from work that they only needed a little love and cuddles and then they were asleep for the night.

She was utterly thrilled with the results. Not having to entertain a dog and three pups left her with more time to work on dress designs and at her sewing machine.

She was so thrilled, in fact, that on Friday she made a stop at her favorite bakery in town after a long day at the shop to pick up some of their huge fresh chocolate chip cookies for the children to thank them.

Bag in hand, she rang the bell at the house next door. Perhaps her luck would hold and Ian wouldn't be there. She could hand the cookies to Mrs. Gilbert or the children and be on her merry way without having to face that particular temptation.

Alas, when the door swung open a moment later, Ian Summerhill stood on the other side, his collar askew and his hair messed in that gorgeous way, as if he had just raked a hand through it. She fought the urge to straighten the collar and smooth down his hair.

She thought she saw something hot leap into his expression for an instant before he blinked it away. "Oh. Hi."

Nerves jittered through her. She hadn't seen him since the night they had kissed beside the lake earlier that week. That didn't mean she hadn't done her share of obsessing about the heat of his mouth on hers, the delicious taste of him, the hard muscles beneath her hands.

She drew in a shaky breath and held up the bag full of cookies. "Hi. I'm sorry to bother you. Don't mind me, I'm only the neighbor who shows up with sugary treats for your children."

"Is that right?"

She found some small satisfaction that he looked as uncomfortable to see her as she felt to face him again.

"There's this fabulous bakery in town that makes gigantic cookies as big as your hand. I hope you don't mind but I picked up a couple each for your amazing children, along with their paycheck."

"They are quite amazing. I must say, it's nice to see someone else recognize it."

She smiled. "I included a few for you and Mrs. Gilbert, with my grateful thanks."

"I'm afraid she and the children are not here right now. She took them to the cinema in Shelter Springs so I could catch up on some work and make some uninterrupted phone calls."

"And then your neighbor stopped by to interrupt you with sugary treats. Sorry."

"No bother. I finished earlier than I expected and was only reading on the back deck."

Her friends at her book group might have said there was no such thing as *only reading* but she didn't want to correct him. "Well, I'm sorry to interrupt that."

"You didn't. Really. Come in, won't you?"

She hesitated, remembering what had happened the previous time they had been alone together. She had lost sleep she could ill afford, haunted by memories of their kiss. She ought to just toss the bag of cookies at him, trot back down the steps and return to her own house, where she was safe.

She was being ridiculous. He wouldn't kiss her again. Even if he did, surely she could summon the fortitude to withstand this attraction. She was a grown woman and could have an adult conversation with a man without wanting to fall into his arms.

She stepped inside, noting as she did that the house seemed to feel more as if a family lived in it than it had the last time she had been inside, when the previous owner still lived there.

Ian and the children had left an indelible mark—a red ball in one corner, a pair of children's rain boots by the door, a stack of what looked like scholarly manuals on the end table.

It was a warm, comfortable house. She had always thought so. Somehow having Ian and his children here made the house feel perfect.

"I'm sorry I missed Amelia and Thomas," she said, handing the cookie bag to him along with an envelope that contained cash for their labors.

He set them on a table piled with books inside the entryway. "They'll be happy for the biscuits, trust me. And for the spending money."

"It's the least I can do for all their work with the puppies this week. I meant what I said earlier. Your children have been absolutely terrific. I don't know exactly what they're doing, but this has been the best week since the puppies were born. Seriously. All three puppies and Betsey seemed happier and more tired than I've ever seen them at the end of each day."

He gave a soft laugh that sent sparks shivering through her. "The experience has been mutual, then. Amelia and Thomas have been utterly thrilled at the chance. I feel like I'm the one who should be delivering treats to you. Babysitting for those puppies has been a wonderful distraction for them. They look forward to it all morning and talk about it all afternoon. They've loved it. I'm not sure they would have enjoyed their time here in Haven Point half as much without having cute puppies to entertain."

"Kids and puppies just go together, don't they?"

"Yes. Like bangers and mash."

"Or spaghetti and meatballs."

"Or salmon and bears."

They shared a smile and Samantha was suddenly breathless again. Oh, for heaven's sake. She had to cut this out.

"How's the research coming?" It was a logical question, especially since he had been the one to bring up salmon.

"Good. I've managed to hike to the redd—that's the breeding spot—nearly every day this week. It's been fascinating to watch them."

"I will have to take your word for it."

"You've never hiked up the Chalk Creek?"

"I'm afraid not."

"It's beautiful, though fairly rugged. The children are asking me to take them but it's not a maintained trail, more like a deer path, and there are several rock screes you have to cross." He suddenly gave her a considering look. "I'm glad you stopped by actually. I could use some advice from a local."

"What sort of advice?" she asked warily.

"I don't want to take the children to Chalk Creek as I am afraid that's a bit too intense for them. They have been after me to take them hiking, however. When I had breakfast at the café in town today, the server mentioned Bridal Veil Falls as a good hike for children. Do you know it?"

"Sure. The falls are beautiful and the trail isn't difficult. It's fairly level for most of it, only a few small hills."

"Would you happen to know where we can find the trailhead for that? The server tried to explain it but I'm afraid the directions weren't terribly clear."

"You can reach it from a couple of different spots around town. That might be why you were confused. The best access is not far from here actually. In fact, you can even walk there from your house. It's about three blocks down the road. You turn left past Sugar Pine Trail and walk along the creek there about a mile or so. It's a beautiful trail, especially this time of year. I haven't done it since high school but I remember it being very family-friendly. I'm sure the children will have fun."

"Amelia enjoys hiking but Thomas isn't much for it, though I hope that will change as he gets older. He comes along with us simply because he hates to be left out."

She smiled, wondering if she should tell him that both of his children had captured her heart. She had talked to them a few times about the puppies since they started coming over. Amelia was solemn, mature for her age, taking her responsibility to care for the animals so seriously. She had even done research about puppies apparently, because she had talked to Sam about some of the ways to wean puppies from their mothers.

"One name for a mother dog is a *dam*," she had informed her the other day. "Did you know that?"

"I did not," Sam had answered, grateful Amelia hadn't called Betsey a bitch.

Thomas did his part to care for the puppies, as well, though she could tell he mostly just loved dogs. Something told her the boy had a mischievous streak just waiting to come out.

She wanted children of her own.

The desire wasn't new, but as she headed toward thirty, the yearning seemed to have increased. It would hit her when she saw one of her friends holding their new babies or when she would spot a toddler at the park while she was walking Betsey. She would even feel it when mothers would come with their teenage daughters to the store, whether the girls were sweetly enthusiastic and happy to be there or sullen and reluctant to be seen shopping with their mothers.

What sort of mother would Samantha be? It was a question that sometimes kept her up at night. Had her own mother's negative influence scarred her forever?

She would hate, more than anything, if she turned into Linda, letting her unhappiness with life's inevitable disappointments sour everything around her.

She didn't have to become her mother. She was a seamstress who knew that simply because you might have been given a pattern, you didn't have to follow it.

People broke free of the bad examples from their childhood all the time. If others could do it, she could, too.

She could be a good and loving parent, like Ian appeared to be toward Amelia and Thomas. She turned her attention back to him, embarrassed that she had let her thoughts wander.

"If you have trouble finding the trailhead, just ask anyone. Someone nearby can show you. I'm sure you will have a wonderful time. They'll both enjoy it. You have a very pretty view over the lake from there. Waterfall on one side, a spectacular view on the other. It makes for a great combination."

"Like bangers and mash," he said with a smile.

"And salmon and bears."

His smile deepened and she couldn't help returning it. For an instant, his gaze flickered to her mouth ever so briefly and then quickly away.

She felt her cheeks heat. Was he remembering that kiss as she was?

"I've just had a brilliant idea," he said suddenly. "Would you like to go with us?"

She stared, taken completely by surprise at the idea. "You…want me to go hiking with you?"

"And the children," he hurried to answer. "It wouldn't be a date or anything, I assure you."

As he said the words, she thought she saw color rise on his rugged features.

"I never thought otherwise," she said just as quickly. They were quite the pair, the two of them, both dancing around this attraction neither seemed willing to acknowledge.

"I simply thought it would be nice to have someone local along, someone knowledgeable about the trail system, so we don't wander off into the wilderness somewhere."

She had to laugh at that. "I'm afraid if you're looking for an expert, you will have to find someone else. I've lived here my entire life, just a few blocks from the trailhead, yet I've only been to Bridal Veil Falls a handful of times."

When she *had* hiked that trail, it had usually been with friends. Certainly not her mother. Despite living in one of the most beautiful places on earth, Linda wasn't big on outdoor activities. She gardened a little but mostly had preferred to be sitting at home with a book or watching television.

Maybe if her father had lived longer, he might have taken her on more of the trails around the lake. He had been a deep lover of nature, both the pristine mountain setting around Lake Haven and the Redemption Mountains and the wildlife who lived all around them.

"No matter," Ian said now. "We don't really need an expert. We can always use a trail map to guide our way. I'm sure the children would still enjoy having you. Maybe we could take a picnic lunch on Sunday."

Oh, that sounded lovely. She could imagine sitting beside the falls, enjoying a summer day with them.

Before she could answer, Ian winced a little, as if only now remembering to whom he was speaking. "You will probably be working in your store, though, won't you? Forget I said anything."

It was a logical assumption. Between all the custom dress orders she was sewing mostly at home in between overseeing daily operations at Fremont Fashions, she was working every single day without a vacation. She had been since her mother died.

Suddenly the idea of spending a few hours with Ian and his children was undeniably appealing.

Not the smartest idea, her mother's voice seemed to whisper in her ear. She had to admit, this time that voice was probably right.

She was already concerned about growing too close to Ian and his children. After all, they would be leaving in only a few more weeks. Spending the afternoon with them hiking through the backcountry was not a good way to maintain boundaries around her heart.

She was about to tell him no when she caught herself. Was she really still letting the thought of what her mother might say in a given situation dictate her actions and tell her who she should associate with and when?

Linda was gone now. If Sam wanted to hang out with Ian and his children for a few hours in the mountains on her day off, what was the harm? She had been working endless days, harder than she had ever worked in her life. She deserved a few hours for herself.

"I hope to be finished with Gemma's dress and another one I'm working on by Sunday. A hike in the mountains to celebrate finishing the work sounds lovely actually."

He looked delighted and a little surprised that she had agreed. "Great. Let's plan on it. How long do you figure it will take us to reach the waterfall?"

Katrina would die laughing if she knew Ian Summerhill was looking at Samantha, of all people, for backcountry guidance.

"Again, I'm not the expert on local hikes. I hope you don't expect that from me."

"Not at all," he assured her.

"I can ask around to be certain. I have friends who have done it many times. As I recall, it's a little bit uphill at the beginning and then the trail levels. I believe it usually takes the average hiker about an hour. With the children, you might want to give it an hour and a half, since there are interesting things to see along the way."

"Not to mention that Thomas can literally drag his heels if he gets the slightest bit tired."

She smiled at the visual imagery. Again, he gave her that intense look that made her skin feel hot and itchy.

"Let's plan to leave around ten thirty in the morning. Does that work with your schedule?"

She could fill her day with a thousand things to do. None of them appealed to her as much as taking a short hike into the mountains with Ian and his children.

"Sounds perfect. It's still cool enough on our June mornings that we should be comfortable. Can I pack a lunch?"

"I'll have Mrs. Gilbert fix some for us, as it was my invitation."

"All right. I'll look forward to it. Meanwhile, please convey my thanks to your children for their loving care of my puppies, won't you?"

"I'll do that."

They gazed at each other and she could see the memory of their kiss flicker in his eyes. The butterflies in her stomach seemed to flutter out of control.

"Ms. Fremont," he began, but she cut him off.

"Samantha. Or Sam, even. I don't think we need to be so formal with each other, do you? I mean, we've kissed. Remember?"

A little frown formed between his eyebrows. "Remembering isn't a problem. It's forgetting that seems to be the struggle."

The air between them seemed to crackle with awareness and she didn't know what to say.

"I'm glad you brought up our, er, kiss actually. I feel as if I should apologize for my inappropriateness that night."

She had to laugh at his formal tone. Conversely, it made her suddenly feel far more at ease. "You make it seem like we're stuck in Victorian times and you're some stuffy lord horrified to find himself messing about with a downstairs scullery maid. This isn't Queen Victoria's time, Ian."

He blushed more, which she had to admit she found quite adorable.

The truth was, she found *him* adorable. She wasn't sure she had ever made a man blush before.

"I'm aware," he said stiffly. "It was still inappropriate on my part. I want to assure you that my invitation to go hiking with me and the children shouldn't lead you to surmise that I expect…more kissing."

Would that be so terrible?

The thought slithered through her consciousness. With no small degree of shock, she realized she wanted more kissing between them. Quite desperately actually. Right now, she wanted nothing more than to wrap her arms around his waist, stand on tiptoe, bury her hands in that slightly disordered hair and kiss him until she couldn't breathe.

She straightened her spine, vertebra by vertebra. *No. Stop that*, she told herself, clenching her fingers into fists before they could reach for him. She didn't need more heartbreak right now, when she was in the middle of trying to rebuild her life.

She would go on this hike with Ian and his children. They would have a lovely time appreciating the gorgeous scenery around Haven Point and perhaps enjoy a nice picnic lunch together, packed by his children's nanny.

He and his children were her neighbors and she owed them much more than a little guide service for helping her with the puppies. Showing him a few of the local sights was the least she could do for them.

She was strong enough to spend a few hours with him, especially if she continued to remind herself that he and Thomas and Amelia would be leaving in a few weeks.

She couldn't allow herself to care about them more than she already did. It would be a disaster and would prove once and for all that her mother was right about her— Starry-eyed Sam still led with her heart and not her common sense.

Not this time.

"I'll see you on Sunday," she said, trying not to wonder how she would make it through the next few days until then.

An hour into the hike with Samantha on Sunday morning, Ian knew inviting her along for this outing had been a grave mistake.

Oh, she was wonderful company. He couldn't complain about that part. The children both seemed to adore her and vied for her attention, taking turns telling her in quite astonishing detail about other hikes they'd gone on together at home or when Ian or their mother or both had taken them on holiday.

Samantha, in turn, was warm and friendly to them as they walked, pointing out landmarks along the way, like a spot local Native Americans tribes still considered sacred and an almost-buried foundation of one of the early European settlers' cabins.

The children were captivated by her stories. Thomas had warmed to her more than any other woman Ian could remember and Amelia was obviously impressed by her fashion sense and style. Both children loved her puppies, of course, which went without saying.

No, the problem had nothing to do with how she was interacting with the children and everything to do with the trouble he was having controlling his growing attraction to her.

He was well on his way to becoming besotted. Every moment he spent with Samantha Fremont only increased his desire to continue spending time with her. She fascinated him on so many different levels. He liked everything about her, from the way the sunlight caught in her hair to the patience she showed with Thomas's endless questions to her rather chagrined acknowledgment that she wasn't much of a nature enthusiast.

If he wasn't extraordinarily careful, he was in danger of making a complete fool of himself.

When the children hurried ahead on the trail a short way, leaving him and Samantha walking alone together, Ian had to fight the urge to tug her into the trees and kiss her senseless.

What was happening to him?

"Gorgeous day, isn't it?" she asked after a rather awkward moment.

"Lovely," he answered, which was nothing less than the truth. He couldn't remember a prettier June day. The morning was cool at the higher elevation and birds seemed to follow them in the treetops.

The sky was so open here in this part of Idaho, a vast blue peppered with only a few clouds, and the air had a sweet, citrusy scent as they walked through groves of pines and ancient aspens he knew were probably hundreds of years old.

"Do you have many trails like this near where you live?" she tried again.

"England has an extensive walking trail system but nothing quite like this. If you want this sort of wild and untamed mountain terrain, you have to typically go north to the Lake District or into Scotland."

"Those of us who live in the Rocky Mountains sometimes take the wilderness outside our door for granted. At least, I do. When all I see is my house and my shop and the road between them, I often forget I live in such a spectacular place. It's good to have this reminder. I should make more of an effort to get out into the backcountry."

She drew in a deep breath of mountain air, while he only wanted to breathe in the essence of Samantha.

He was being utterly ridiculous.

"I'm sorry you couldn't bring your dog along. The children would have enjoyed having her here."

"I know, but for now she still needs to stick close to the puppies. They'll be gone before we know it, then she and I can start walking together. She can be my hiking buddy after you leave."

She gave a smile that looked slightly forced and he had the oddest feeling she wasn't looking forward to their departure any more than Ian was.

"Do you have new homes picked out for all three of them, then?"

"They're going to friends of mine, which makes me happy. I have this idealized image—probably silly—but I imagine them having regular playdates with each other. It's hard to think of giving them away to new homes, though it's inevitable. I can't keep them all. That would be completely impractical. Still, I can't help thinking about how sad Betsey will be once they're gone."

"I have great sympathy for her. I can't imagine being particularly thrilled when the children are old enough to go off to university."

"Maybe they won't. Maybe they'll stick around and go to Oxford, then you won't have to let them go."

Except he would no longer be there after the end of the summer and certainly not by the time Amelia and Thomas left for university. He would be at Summerhill House, wrapped up in the mundane business of the estate.

He didn't want to think about that. He was still on vacation and didn't have to immerse himself yet in his responsibilities. Ian quickly changed the topic. "Did you go away to university?"

She shook her head. "I went to college in Boise and commuted to class or did online coursework. I lived on campus for one semester but my mother needed help at the store so I moved back home and did the long-distance thing."

He frowned, wondering about the sort of mother who would deprive her daughter of the necessary experience she would gain living away from home.

"What did you study? Fashion design?"

She looked down at the trail in front of them with a distant sort of look. "I wanted to major in fashion but it didn't make a great deal of sense, considering I knew I would be coming home to run the boutique. Fashion design would have been fun and exciting but a degree in business administration made much more sense."

Something told him her mother, the one she had previously told him had been difficult, may also have had a strong influence in that decision.

"Do you enjoy what you do?" he asked after they walked a few hundred more feet beside a softly singing creek, the children just ahead of them now.

She looked startled at the question. "Of course. Would I keep doing something I didn't enjoy?"

He thought of the years stretching out ahead of him, taking over the family concerns from his father. "People stick with all manner of jobs they don't enjoy, for a whole host of reasons."

"I guess that's true." She gazed out at the landscape in front of them. His children were having a wonderful time, he could see. They had picked up walking sticks somewhere along the trail and were comparing them to see whose was tallest.

"I have always thought I would run the boutique forever," Samantha said after a moment. "Lately, though, I've started to wonder if that's really what I'm meant to do, you know?"

He understood completely. "A few years ago, I switched from full-time research to teaching a few upper level classes. I discovered that while I love the research, I have something to give to students, as well."

Or at least he did, Ian thought with a familiar pang.

"Yes. That's it exactly. I love elements of running the boutique. Ordering in precisely the items I think my clients will like, helping to find the perfect outfit for someone who considers herself hopelessly unfashionable, seeing a client leave the store feeling better about herself than she did when she walked in."

"That does sound rewarding."

"It can be. But other parts make me cringe. I hate dealing with personnel issues. I had to fire someone a few months ago and it was one of the worst experiences of my life."

"What happened?"

"She was someone my mother hired without talking to me first and Gwen's personality was difficult. No one else seemed to get along with her. Not the customers, not the other employees. If that had been the only issue, I would have tried to work with her about her people skills. But when inventory started disappearing, always coinciding with her shifts, I studied our security cameras and found proof she was slipping items into her bag and carrying them out. Only one or two a shift, but that could add up. I know of other small boutiques that have gone completely under because of one employee's dishonesty."

"I'm shocked that someone would do that so blatantly here in Haven Point, where everyone seems to know everyone. Didn't she know you had CCTV?"

"I think she didn't think I would ever catch her. She wasn't a local," Samantha said. "Her husband transferred from out of state to Caine Tech and she applied after they moved to Shelter Springs."

"Well, that explains everything, then."

She made a face at his dry tone. "I don't mean to imply that every local is necessarily perfect. We have our problems, too. I only meant that I didn't know her from a mannequin when my mother hired her. She didn't really have references, either. At least none that I ever saw. My mother was impressed because she drove a nice car and had trendy clothes."

That only reinforced his negative impression of her mother, which he knew was probably not fair. Still, he had the distinct impression from a few things Samantha had said that her mother had spent a lifetime undermining her confidence in herself.

She had much to offer the world but he was beginning to suspect she wasn't able to see that clearly herself.

"I've never had to fire anyone and can only imagine how difficult it must be. Do you still encounter this woman around town?"

"No. Fortunately, her husband took another job shortly after that in California so they moved away. I can't tell you how relieved I was when I heard she was leaving, especially because she had begun spreading rumors around the community that she had been fired unfairly and had even told people she was considering suing."

"You didn't press charges?"

"No. Her husband paid me back the cost of the merchandise she had taken. They could well afford it, which was another thing I didn't understand. Why not just pay for it with her employee discount, which is substantial? He was embarrassed about the whole thing, and to be honest, I just wanted to forget it."

"That must have been difficult, coming only a few months after your mother's death. Especially when your mother had been the one to hire her."

"Yes. I think she was dishonest from the day my mother hired her but I didn't realize it for several weeks. I might have acted sooner if I hadn't still been feeling a little lost, trying to run things on my own. It was a tough time."

"I'm sorry."

"Thanks. If you want the truth, the whole incident left me a bit scarred."

"In what way?"

"I need to hire a few more people to pick up the slack at the shop since I've become so busy on the wedding gown side of things, but I'm afraid of making the wrong personnel decision. What if I end up having to fire someone again? I'm not sure I have the fortitude to do that."

"You do," he said confidently. "You've done it once. It will probably be easier the second time around."

She laughed a little. "I would much prefer if the first time was the only time."

"Look at it this way. You'll be the one doing the hiring this time. You can vet candidates as carefully as you need to so you can be absolutely sure of a person's character before you take on a new salesclerk."

"You're right," she said with a surprised kind of look. "Thank you."

"You're welcome."

He was finding so much more to admire about Samantha Fremont than he'd ever imagined when he first met her.

"If you weren't running a boutique, what would you do?" he asked after a few more moments.

"Design dresses." She answered with such alacrity, he almost laughed.

"You could give it a moment's thought," he suggested.

"I don't need to. That's my favorite part of the job. I love creating the ideal wedding dress for someone to wear on her perfect day."

"Ah. You're a romantic." He didn't need confirmation. He had figured that out about her already. He supposed any woman who designed wedding dresses would have to be something of a romantic.

"In some ways, I guess."

"If you love it so much, why don't you design dresses full-time, then?"

She appeared to give his question serious thought, her cheeks slightly pink from the exertion as they walked up-hill.

The children didn't seem to be bothered by the climb. They appeared to be having a wonderful time, scampering ahead like mountain goats. Mountain goats with walking sticks, anyway.

"It's not that simple, I'm afraid," Samantha finally said. "If I wanted to focus solely on making dresses, I would have to close the boutique and I have no idea if I could make a living designing wedding dresses alone. If you do the math, there can't be that many brides in the Lake Haven area to keep a business going indefinitely."

Pursuing her passion seemed an easy enough decision to him, especially in his own circumstances. He didn't have a choice about how he would be spending the rest of his life.

"If designing wedding gowns is what you love, why not take the chance?"

"I can't throw away a thriving business with a long history in Haven Point to pursue a fly-by-night dream. It's just not practical. I have employees. Payroll. People who depend on me."

He wanted to argue that dreams were important, too, but knew that would be hypocritical, given his current situation, so he said nothing.

They walked without speaking for a few more moments, accompanied by the murmur of the creek next to the trail and the twittering of birds in the trees. It was a singularly peaceful endeavor, walking in nature, surrounded by wild beauty. He had always loved it but there was something about this place that called to his soul.

She stopped at the top of a rise to take a drink from the water bottle in her daypack and he called ahead for the children to do the same.

Amelia trotted back and grabbed her and Thomas's water bottles that Ian was carrying in his pack, then returned to her brother, carrying them.

"May I ask you a question, if it's not too presumptuous?" Ian asked after his daughter was out of earshot.

"Until you ask it, how can I know if your question is too presumptuous?" Her eyebrows raised with both curiosity and humor. That was one of the things he was discovering he liked best about Samantha. She never seemed to take herself too seriously.

"How about this? I'll ask the question, then you can decide whether it's too presumptuous to answer."

"Fair enough."

He didn't quite know how to ask the question now that he'd started this.

Finally, he just blurted it out. "Speaking of wedding gowns, why haven't you had your own, er, perfect day? Why aren't you married with a bunch of little ones of your own?"

He winced. "And now that I hear that out loud, never mind. It *is* too presumptuous and none of my business. Not everyone wants that traditional life. More and more these days, it seems to be the exception and not the rule. I'm also perfectly aware a woman does not need a man to be happy."

He was rambling, mostly because he couldn't believe he'd brought up such a stupid question. To his relief, Samantha didn't seem offended.

"Did you want to leave space in there for me to answer?" she asked with that same amused look.

"Yes. Sorry. Go ahead."

Her brow furrowed as she appeared to consider his question. "I'm not married, I suppose, because I haven't found someone I wanted to marry. Or, if I'm honest, anyone who wanted to marry *me*."

"That can't possibly be true," he said.

She laughed, though he thought there was a hollow sound to it.

"You might be surprised. Don't you remember I told you about my reputation as a man-hungry flirt? My mother used to call me Starry-eyed Sam because I have a terrible tendency to fall in love with regularity."

His heart ached at the thread of loneliness he thought he heard in her voice and Ian decided he was beginning to heartily dislike her mother.

"There's nothing wrong with falling in love."

"I agree. When it's real, love can be a beautiful thing. You said it yourself, I'm a romantic. I have enough friends who have found their perfect person for me to know the real deal when I see it. Josh and Gemma, for example, or my best friend, Katrina, and her husband, Bowie. I haven't found that yet…and that's okay with me right now."

THIS LINE OF questioning left Samantha feeling exposed, vulnerable.

Not very long ago, finding her soul mate seemed like the ultimate aim of her life. As each of her friends seemed to be finding her happy-ever-after, Sam had been ridiculously eager for her own.

When she should have been trying to figure out who she was and what she wanted out of life, she had been worried if she was wearing the right kind of eye makeup, if her hair was perfect, if she was on the right dating sites or dressing the right way or asking the right questions.

Her mother's death had changed her somehow, given her an entirely new perspective on herself and on the life she wanted to create.

Instead of trying to find the perfect man who would make her life complete, she should have been trying to make out of her life what she wanted and needed so that she could look for a good man who might add to it.

She knew why the men she had dated hadn't stuck around. She had been obsessed with perfection, with becoming exactly who they wanted her to be instead of being herself and finding out if they were willing to take a chance on Samantha Fremont, warts and all.

"What about you?" she asked. "It's been a year since Susan died. Will you start dating again?"

"I made a mess of things the first time around, didn't I?" He gestured ahead to the children. "Anyway, they're my priority now. They have to be, as I'm all they have. The children are still dealing with their mother's death and...other changes in our life. I can't complicate things by starting a new relationship."

"There you go. We're both in the same boat. Good thing you're leaving in a few weeks." She smiled, trying for a lighthearted tone.

"Isn't it?" he murmured, though she thought his tone said something entirely different.

She was relieved when the children paused on the trail, waiting for them to catch up.

"Dad, I'm hungry," Thomas called before they could reach them. "Did you bring any snacks?"

"I've got some granola bars in my pack," Samantha offered quickly. "Will that do?"

"That sounds delicious," Thomas said.

She dug in her bag until she found what she was after, then handed one to him and to Amelia. "There's one left," she said to Ian. "Would you like it?"

"I can split it in half."

He did so, offering Samantha the larger half, she couldn't help but notice. They both chewed as they continued walking the trail. Ian seemed to be lost in thought. She had to hope he wasn't wondering about the revelations she had spilled out, like water gushing from the Hell's Fury Dam.

"I'm sorry about earlier," Ian said a moment later. "I shouldn't have asked such an intrusive question and started us on that topic. It really was unconscionably rude of me to pry."

She swallowed the last bite of her granola bar, already feeling a little less hangry. "I didn't consider it rude. I'm just embarrassed when I look back at my journey and the person I used to be. I want to think I've gained a new perspective over the past few months. I hope so, anyway. I'm only sorry it took me so long."

"You said the other day that your mother was difficult. In what way?"

She gazed out at the landscape, wondering if it was disloyal to tell him the hard, uncomfortable truths she had finally acknowledged to herself since Linda died. No. She couldn't believe it was. Ian didn't know her mother and he never would.

"You have to understand that I loved my mother very much. She was a tremendously hard worker and also fiercely loyal to Haven Point and the people who live here."

She paused, trying to find the right words. "But she could also be critical and overbearing. I'm only now beginning to realize how I let her strong personality dominate mine. For the first time in my life, I'm making my own decisions based on my needs and desires. I'm not only acting in ways that are expected of me. It's empowering and terrifying at the same time."

"Why terrifying?"

"When things go wrong, I have no one else but myself to blame. That can be hard. Look at Betsey. My mother would never allow a dog in our home, even after I was an adult. She said they were too much bother, messy to clean up after and a nuisance to have around. The first chance I got, I pick up a random dog a couple of strangers were selling outside the supermarket. Who does that without checking first to make sure the dog is not expecting puppies?"

He smiled. "It hasn't been all bad."

She couldn't lie. "It hasn't been. You're right. But instead of a sweet, gentle companion who would sit at my feet while I sewed and keep me company in that empty house, I also ended up with three noisy, troublesome puppies."

"Three noisy, troublesome, *adorable* puppies. You mustn't forget that part."

"They are pretty adorable," she admitted. "But I was barely keeping my life together as it was. Four dogs is a lot to handle. It doesn't help that I keep hearing my mother say *I told you so* in my ear."

"You need to give yourself a break. You're doing the best you can. You're finally on your own and that can be scary for all of us, no matter what age. After I moved away from home, I found myself calling my parents at least three or four times a day—until my mother gently told me I needed to stop, that it was time I started making my own decisions. That was quite a shock, I'll tell you that. Especially when I only wanted to know which sort of washing-up liquid she favored."

She smiled, charmed at his confession. "It can be empowering to feel responsible for your own mistakes. I'm trying to focus on that instead of the fear."

"Good for you," he said, and she wanted to turn toward the approval in his voice like a sunflower reaching for the sun.

Oh, this was bad. She liked this man so very much. She had to continually remind herself that falling for him would be a terrible mistake—far worse than taking home a pregnant dog.

"Are we almost there?" Thomas asked.

Sam released a breath, grateful for the distraction. "Nearly," she replied. "If I remember correctly, it should be just around that curve in the trail."

She really hoped she was remembering things correctly. The last time she had been here had been on a hike with Katrina several years ago and they had been in the middle of a deep conversation about the guys they had met the night before at a bar in Shelter Springs. She barely remembered the hike, though she oddly had a vivid memory of the conversation and of the guys.

"I think I hear it," Amelia said.

Samantha listened closely. "I hear it, too," she said at the low rushing sound that seemed to grow louder as they neared the bend in the trail ahead.

They walked on a little farther and then suddenly the falls dominated the landscape ahead of them, much more beautiful than she remembered from previous trips. Bridal Veil Falls did indeed look like a veil, plunging through a narrow break in the rock and rippling down at least thirty-five feet, glinting in the sunlight like it was sewn with diamonds. Around it, pine and fir trees seemed to have sprung out of bare rock, clinging precariously.

She caught her breath at the majesty of it. She lived an hour away. Why on earth didn't she make more of an effort to come up here?

She would from here out, she promised herself. She would come hiking with Betsey again this summer and into the fall, when the sugar maples would be on fire with color. When she did, she knew she would always remember the day she came here with Ian and the children.

"Wow. That's really pretty," Amelia said. She stopped in her tracks, her expression captivated.

"It's bigger than I thought it would be," Thomas said, eyes wide. "Can we swim in it?"

"Brrr. That water would be terribly cold," Samantha told him. "It's basically melted snow coming down from the tops of the mountains."

"I believe I would still like to go swimming."

"Not here," Ian said firmly. "Why don't we take some photos in front of it, though, to send to Nana and Grandfather?"

"I'll take your picture," Sam offered.

For the next few moments, she tried to pose them in a way that allowed her to catch them and the falls in one frame, which turned out to be a difficult shot. Either they were tiny in the frame or she cut off the top of the water, which was the most dramatic part of the waterfall.

After a few different angles, she managed it.

"That's a good one," she finally said, handing Ian's phone back to him so he could see it.

"We should take a photograph with all of us," Amelia

said. "That way we can always remember today and how much fun we had on our hike together."

"Great idea," Ian said. "I can set my phone up and hit the camera shutter with my watch."

As she had done, he experimented with angles for a few moments and she and the children made funny faces that made them all laugh until he set it just right.

She felt a little odd being photographed with them in what was really a family picture but decided to just go with it.

"That should do it," Ian said after several frames. "Wait right here while I make sure the pictures worked."

He crossed to where his phone was propped on a rock facing them and looked at the images with a curiously intent look on his face. "Wonderful," he finally said. "They're perfect."

"I want to see, Dad." Amelia hopped down from their spot to where her father held his phone and took it from him. "Oh, it *is* wonderful!" she exclaimed. She held it out for Sam to see.

She looked at the image and felt a funny little catch in her throat. They all looked so *right* together. The children smiled brightly, as did Ian. She hadn't seen him smile very often. It made him look young and handsome, even with his perennially messed hair.

"Can you text me these?" she asked. "It will make a wonderful memento of today."

"Certainly. I'll do it as soon as we get back to a signal."

She handed the phone back to Ian. As he took it from her, their hands brushed and Sam hoped he didn't notice her shiver.

"Who's ready for lunch?" Ian asked.

Sam and both of the children raised their hands at the same time, then smiled at each other, in full accord.

SAMANTHA COULDN'T WAIT for Ian to send her those pictures, but she knew she wouldn't need that tangible evidence to recall what had turned out to be one of most delightful days she had enjoyed in a long time.

The picnic was simple roast beef sandwiches Mrs. Gilbert had prepared, but they were made on fresh-baked bread with a creamy mustard and horseradish sauce and tasted better than anything from the best restaurants around the lake.

Sam had a vague memory of going on a camping trip with her father once when she must have been six or seven. She could remember him saying something about how food eaten outside always tasted better. Was it a true memory or something she had imagined? It didn't really matter, she supposed. Either way, it was definitely true.

They ate under a tree with the waterfall in the background, serenaded by birds as a light breeze made the wildflowers dance around them.

Samantha wanted the moment to go on forever.

When Amelia finished her dessert of shortbread cookies, she gave a happy sigh. "This has been the *best* day. Thank you for showing us such a beautiful place," she said. "I shall remember this always."

"As will I," Samantha said softly.

"I still wish we could go for a swim," Thomas said mournfully.

"You wouldn't enjoy it, trust me," his father said.

After lunch, they walked around trying to identify wildflowers. Sam shared as many as she knew, mostly Queen Anne's Lace, wild iris, columbine.

"June is still a little early at these higher elevations for flowers. That's what my friends who are experts say, anyway. In another month, there will be many more wildflowers up here, of all colors. It's quite a spectacular display."

"We'll be back home by then," Amelia said with a little pout. "Maybe you could send us a photograph."

"I'll do that," Sam said, trying to ignore the pinch in her heart to think about them leaving. How had they all wormed their way into her life so quickly? She adored the children and was well on her way to developing a terrible crush on Ian.

So much for her intentions to remain distant but friendly. She had crossed that line a long time ago.

It didn't feel like any crush she'd had before, though. She didn't remember oversharing so much with another man. He knew things about her she had never shared with anyone besides Katrina.

Funny thing, though. He hadn't seemed disgusted by her honesty. There was a lesson in that for her, she supposed. Maybe she needed to stop being so ashamed and focus on moving forward instead of looking back.

They were all more quiet on the way down the mountain than they had been heading up. Some of the fun seemed to have gone out of the day. Maybe they were all tired or maybe Ian and his children were thinking about the end of their holiday. They had a few weeks in Haven Point still, though, until after his sister's wedding.

They had almost reached the trailhead, the children just ahead of them again, when Ian spoke.

"Would you, um, have any interest in going as my plus-one to Gemma's wedding?"

To her dismay, she chose that inopportune moment to

stumble on a rock and he reached out to help her catch her balance, his hand warm and strong on her arm.

"Sorry. I didn't mean to startle you. That may seem like it's coming out of nowhere but it's not. I've been thinking about it for a few days."

"You have?"

"Gemma suggested I take someone." He made a face. "All right, that's not exactly true. She suggested the two of us go together."

Sam didn't know how to respond to that. She already had her own plus-one invitation to the wedding and had informed Gemma she wasn't planning to take a date.

Why would Gemma encourage the two of them to go together when the bride knew perfectly well Samantha would be there, anyway, to help with her dress and any last-minute alterations? She frowned. Was her friend match-making?

Ian quickly disabused her of that idea. "She said something about the seating being easier if we attended together. But if you already had plans or prefer to go alone, please forget I said anything. Gemma can figure out the seating without having to match everyone up for her own convenience."

"I wasn't planning on taking a date," she said. "I already told Gemma that."

Finding someone she wanted to spend an entire evening with had seemed like too much bother. She had anticipated that she would sit with other Helping Hands at the ceremony only so she could see Gemma in her spectacular dress as she married the love of her life and then Samantha intended to slip away before the reception and inevitable dancing and socializing began.

"All right, then. Totally understandable. Again, don't worry. Forget I said anything."

His smile looked slightly off. Was he genuinely disappointed at her answer? She couldn't quite tell. She did know the wedding would be far more fun if she attended with Ian and his children rather than going on her own, at least judging by how much she had enjoyed today's outing with them.

"I would be delighted to go with you," she finally answered.

She would simply have to remember the only reason he asked her was to appease his sister. It certainly wasn't because of that earthshaking kiss they had shared.

CHAPTER EIGHT

"Super. That would be terrific."

There. That wasn't so hard. He had a date for Gemma's wedding and he would have at least one more excuse to spend time with Samantha Fremont before he and the children left Haven Point.

He hadn't been looking forward to the wedding festivities. He couldn't say he had been dreading them exactly. He was thrilled for Gemma. She deserved happiness and a good man who cherished her, as she had found in Josh Bailey.

Gemma's wedding, while joyous for her sake, represented a turning point for Ian. The time when he had to put away his passion and focus on the necessary work of helping his father and taking over as the heir to the earldom.

For the first time, though, he was aware of a real sense of anticipation for the wedding, something he suspected had nothing to do with Gemma's happiness and everything to do with his own at being able to spend an evening entirely with Samantha.

Letty would be there to take care of the children. She certainly would never miss Gemma's wedding. That would leave him free, perhaps, to have a dance or two with Samantha under the moonlight.

Nothing would come of it. She had just told him she wasn't looking for a relationship. Neither was he, even if such a thing between them was possible. But he was a man and she was a beautiful woman to whom he was fiercely attracted. He wanted to dance with her. Wanted it quite urgently in that moment.

He had a strange, bubbly feeling in his chest. Under other circumstances, he might have even called it...giddy.

They walked down the street toward home, the children obviously tired out from the hike.

"Can we play with the puppies for a moment?" Amelia asked as they approached the house. "We only saw them for a short time when we left to go hiking and I've missed playing with them."

"I think we've taken up enough of Samantha's day, don't you?" Ian said.

"Not at all. I'm sure the puppies would love to see you, too." Samantha smiled at his daughter with an honest affection that sent soft warmth seeping through him.

She led the way into her tidy house, where they were greeted by a chorus of yips and yaps. As soon as she opened the gate into the room, three little pups emerged, wriggling with delight at seeing the children.

"Let's take them outside quickly," Samantha said, handing him one of the puppies before Ian could respond.

The children picked up a puppy each and the mother dog followed them all out to her garden.

Outside, they set them in the grass and the children giggled as the puppies urinated immediately, then waddled about, sniffing at each blade of grass.

They were quite adorable, he had to admit, with their tricolored ears and curly hair.

Samantha smiled as she watched the scene and he couldn't tell if she was amused by the children or the puppies or both. Either way, looking at her in the soft afternoon sunlight left a strange ache in his chest, one he couldn't quite identify.

They had only been outside for a few moments when he saw a vehicle pull into his driveway next door. Samantha noticed it, as well.

"Looks like you have company."

He frowned, not recognizing the vehicle. The only other person he knew in Haven Point was his sister and she drove a little electric hybrid she had purchased after moving here.

Who would visit him driving a sleek, luxurious town car? Curious, he headed in that direction just as the door opened and his father climbed out, tall and commanding.

The heavy weight of expectation seemed to settle on Ian's shoulders as if someone had draped a blanket lined with lead over him.

His mother alighted the vehicle from the other side, graceful as always.

The children didn't notice them at first, too busy playing with the puppies. Thomas was the first one to spy his grandparents.

"Nana! Grandfather!" he exclaimed, forgetting the puppies completely and heading toward his grandparents at a steady run.

"Hello, darling." Margaret Summerhill beamed at her grandson, holding her arms out wide to catch him in a tight hug. She must have been traveling all day but she showed no sign of it, looking as lovely and elegant as always.

Margaret had modeled in her earlier years, until she grew too bored in front of the camera and decided she wanted to be the one holding it instead. She was a gifted photographer who had lined the walls of Summerhill House, his parents' London townhome and his own flat in Oxford with her landscapes.

When Amelia finally noticed the commotion, she gave a little shriek and rushed toward her grandparents. "You're here! I thought you weren't coming until next week!"

Wishing he could put off the inevitable but left with no choice, Ian followed his children to greet his parents. Samantha, he noticed, hung back, as if she didn't want to intrude on the family reunion.

He kissed his mother's cheek and shook his father's hand, as was their strange, formal way. He loved his father and respected him more than any man he knew but Henry Summerhill was not particularly comfortable with excessive affection or emotion.

"Gemma will be thrilled you've come early," he said.

Margaret smiled. "Your father decided at the last minute to attend meetings in New York for a few days. Since we were already halfway here, we decided to bump up our plans a bit to see if there is anything we can do to help Gemma with the wedding."

"That's wonderful," he said, which was mostly the truth.

He loved his parents and was deeply grateful for all the help they had always given, first during his separation and divorce then Susan's diagnosis.

Despite that debt he knew he could never repay, he still wasn't completely thrilled to have them here. It felt too much like real life intruding on a delicious dream he didn't want to end. His time in Haven Point would be over soon enough, wouldn't it? He thought he had one more precious week of freedom before he had to put away what he loved to focus on the inevitable changes to his life when this summer idyll was over, and he found himself suddenly resentful at the glaring reminder.

"Look, Nana." Amelia thrust out one of the multicolored puppies. "Isn't it adorable?"

Margaret smiled and reached for Coco. Or was it Oscar? He couldn't seem to keep them apart.

"Hello there. You are a cutie. What's your name?"

"That one is Calvin," Samantha said. "The others are Coco and Oscar."

"All designers?" Margaret asked, clearly delighted.

Samantha gave an embarrassed sort of smile and Ian wanted to give himself a head slap. He hadn't even realized that. Trust his mother to make the connection.

"Yes. Oscar de la Renta, Calvin Klein, Coco Chanel. Their mother was already named Betsey when I got her, which I decided was short for Betsey Johnson, who is one of my favorite designers. It seemed right that her progeny should have designer names, as well."

"I wholeheartedly agree. I suppose Saint Laurent or Givenchy would have sounded too pretentious."

She smiled. "Those are names better suited for purebreds."

Margaret laughed with delight, leaving Ian to remember his manners.

"Mother, Father, this is my neighbor and friend, Samantha Fremont. She's the one sewing Gemma's wedding gown."

"Hello," Henry said politely.

"Oh," his mother exclaimed. Before Samantha could respond, Margaret reached out and wrapped her arms around her, pulling her in for a tight hug.

"Thank you, darling. The dress is spectacular. Gem sent me a selfie from your last fitting and I was overwhelmed with gratitude. It's utterly perfect for her."

Samantha looked touched and overwhelmed at the praise. "I… Thank you."

"You are truly gifted, my dear. I say that with the deepest sincerity."

As he watched, a rosy glow stole over Samantha's delicate features, as if someone had switched on a light inside her. "Thank you," she said again, clearly thrilled at the praise.

He couldn't help smiling at her astonished delight, then regretted it when his mother's gaze sharpened. She sent a swift look between him and Samantha and he saw the questions in her eyes. Mercifully, for once, Margaret kept her mouth shut and her opinions to herself.

"I wish I had your talent," his mother said after a moment. "I always wanted to be a designer but I'm horrible at it. I decided a long time ago that I'm much better at taking pictures of other people's designs."

She cuddled the dog, then handed him back to Amelia. "And you raise puppies, too?"

"Not on purpose," Samantha assured her. "It's a long story. I adopted a dog but didn't realize at the time she was expecting puppies."

"We're puppy-sitting while we're here," Thomas informed his grandparents.

"Are you?" Henry said.

"It's been such fun," Amelia said. "They're darling little things who just want some company while Miss Fremont is working."

"I live next door," Samantha explained, pointing to her house. "The children have been wonderfully kind to help me out with the puppies."

"And it's given them something fun to do while I'm busy with my salmon research," Ian said.

He didn't miss the way Henry gave a pained sort of look at the reminder. His father just as quickly hid his reaction.

He knew his father hated asking him to give up what he loved, just as Ian knew neither of them had a choice.

"Are you staying with Gemma?" Ian asked his parents.

"No. She's booked the sweetest cottage for us near her house," Margaret said. "We dropped our bags there a short time ago before following her directions to this place in search of you and the children."

"Oh, that's a nice part of the lake," Samantha said.

"It's a fine view," Henry said. "But I'm not sure one could find a poor one around here. This lake is quite spectacular."

"I completely agree," Samantha said with a smile for his father. "Lucky for you, you've picked one of the best times of the year to visit, when everything is green and gorgeous."

"I don't know. I would think fall would be stunning, as well," Henry said thoughtfully. "How's the fishing around here?"

"You're asking the wrong person, I'm afraid, though I've heard it's wonderful. Ian likely knows more about that than I do, at least when it comes to the kokanee salmon in Lake Haven."

Again, his mother looked interested to discover Samantha knew about his research.

Drat. He didn't need Margaret to discover his fierce attraction to Samantha or the unlikely friendship that had begun to develop between them.

"We should go," Ian said pointedly to his children and to his parents. "We've taken up quite enough of Samantha's day. Where would you like the puppies? Back inside or in their enclosure?"

"The pen is fine," Samantha said. She seemed a little

taken aback by his clumsy efforts to escape from her before his entirely too-perceptive mother saw through him.

The children carefully lowered the puppies into the fenced area where they immediately began toddling around in the grass.

To Ian's astonishment, Amelia hugged Samantha. "Thank you for going with us on our hike today," his daughter said.

"You've been hiking?" his mother said, raising her eyebrows.

"We saw a giant waterfall," Thomas said. "It was as high as the Eiffel Tower."

The waterfall, in fact, didn't come close to being as high as the tower, which they had seen a few years earlier on a weekend trip to Paris. At nearly a thousand feet, the tower would dwarf the hundred-foot waterfall, obviously. Through a child's eye, everything was relative and Ian didn't want to correct his son.

"How nice to see you're getting around and exploring the backcountry around here," his father said.

"And how nice of your neighbor to show you around." By now, his mother looked positively giddy. How would she react when she found out he had invited Samantha to be his date to the wedding?

Oh, lord. Why had he invited Samantha to be his date for the wedding?

Should he back out? Tell Samantha he had reconsidered? That might be the safer route, all the way around. He hadn't thought things through and now realized that his mother was bound to sit up and pay attention when she found out he had asked her to the wedding. If he didn't do something, he was very much afraid he and Samantha would both find themselves on the receiving end of his mother's determined matchmaking efforts.

"Wait. I've just had an idea," Margaret said suddenly.

Ian swallowed a groan, afraid it was too late to stop her now.

"I still don't have anything to wear for the wedding. Nothing decent, anyway. I brought along a couple of options I picked up here or there but I'm not particularly fond of either. I don't suppose there's any chance you might have time to help me with something new, would you?"

Samantha's eyes widened in surprise. As he swallowed his own relief that Margaret had something else to focus on besides her son's love life, or lack thereof, he could almost see Samantha performing a complicated mental inventory of her workload.

He knew she was overwhelmed right now but he guessed she also didn't want to disappoint a potential customer. Especially one who happened to be the mother of her good friend.

"I... Perhaps," she said tentatively.

"It wouldn't have to be anything elaborate," his mother assured her. "I tend toward simple styles, anyway. Just something flattering for the mother of the bride."

"Still, that's a high order," he protested when he saw Samantha waver. "The wedding is only two weeks away, Mother."

Margaret looked abashed. "You're right. There wouldn't be enough time, would there? Especially as you're working on Gemma's gown. Forget I said anything."

"Gemma's dress is nearly finished," Samantha said. "You're right, we don't have much time but I can look through a few pattern books tonight and perhaps come up with a few ideas that might work. If I hurry, I might be able to finish something in time. Why don't you come into the boutique tomorrow and we'll do some measurements, then you can look through some of my designs to see if anything pops for you?"

"Are you sure? I don't want to burden you."

"Positive," Samantha said firmly.

"That would be perfect. Thank you." Margaret beamed and Ian tried to put away his unease. His mother couldn't have an ulterior motive for going to Samantha's boutique, could she?

"Great. I'll see you tomorrow," Samantha said with a general smile for all of them. "If you'll excuse me, I have errands to run this afternoon. Thank you for a lovely day."

"Our pleasure," Ian said, meaning every word.

She looked at the children, still watching the puppies as they talked to their grandfather. "Please don't worry if your children are too busy visiting your grandparents to check in on the puppies for me this week. I easily can make other arrangements."

"They'll do it," Ian said firmly. "They made a commitment to you and will be happy to fill it."

"If that changes, please let me know. They're on holiday and should feel free to visit with their grandparents all they would like without having to worry about my puppies."

A few raindrops suddenly splattered on the grass from one of those quicksilver showers he was discovering hit the lake on many summer afternoons.

"Everyone inside," Ian said to his parents and children, ushering them toward his door.

"What about the puppies?" Thomas asked. "They'll be soaked."

"I can take care of them," Samantha assured his son with a warm smile.

"I'll help her," Ian said as more drops began to pour. "You all go into our house where it's dry."

His mother gave one more pleased look at him and Samantha before she grabbed a child with each hand and hurried toward the house.

SHE HAD TO ADMIT, the man looked utterly adorable carrying Oscar and Calvin as they hurried into the house with Betsey trotting after just as a rumble of thunder shook the trees.

"That came up out of nowhere," Ian exclaimed.

"That seems to be how our summer storms go around here. You've probably noticed that already. One moment it's lovely and feels like the perfect summer day, the next everyone is ducking for cover. It's worse in August but we have a few in June and July, too."

She was able to keep Coco dry by tucking the puppy under her shirt. Inside her house, she set the puppy back down on the pad inside her mother's sewing room, then stepped away so Ian could do the same with Oscar and Calvin.

"Thank you," she said, suddenly nervous to find herself alone with him again, which she told herself was ridiculous.

"Glad to help."

"I like your parents very much. They seem to adore the children. Do you live close to each other in England?"

"Not really. The children and I live in Oxford, which is northwest of London while Summerhill House, the family home, is in Dorset, closer to the south coast. It takes about two hours to travel between our homes. We do meet up in London where possible as they live there part of the year, and usually we spend a week or two at Summerhill House. We talk often on the phone and video chat where we can."

He gestured to the puppies. "You've made a cozy little room for them here."

"My mother is probably rolling in her grave to know I've transformed her sewing room to a puppy playroom. I didn't know what else to do with them."

They were side by side, both looking in on the puppies as Coco and Oscar wrestled and Calvin chased after a ball.

He smelled delicious, rugged and masculine with that undertone of some kind of expensive soap. Exactly as she might expect of someone who spoke casually of his family home with a grand-sounding name like Summerhill House. She again couldn't help picturing something out of *Pride and Prejudice*, the Keira Knightley movie version, something with statues and Doric columns and vast, ornate gardens.

His home in reality was probably nothing like that, but that didn't keep her from imagining it that way.

"You called this your mother's sewing room, not yours," Ian said. "Do you have a sewing room of your own?"

"I've always kept my sewing machine in my bedroom. Since my mother died, I've moved the machine into the sunroom, where I have a view of the lake and can watch television."

She gestured behind them to the comfortable space she had carved out by taking several ugly pieces of furniture to a charity thrift store in Shelter Springs. Rain still pattered against the glass, creating a warm, intimate bubble.

He took in the fabric swatches, the table covered with scissors and thread, the sewing machine set up in front of the windows.

"It seems like a good workspace. Very calming."

"I like it."

She thought he would leave then but he seemed reluctant to rejoin his parents. Was he drawn to *her* or was he simply trying to avoid his family?

"What programs do you like to watch?" Ian asked, gesturing to the television.

When was the last time any man had seemed genuinely interested in what she liked? She couldn't remember, which probably said a great deal about her choices in men.

"A little of everything. From Hallmark movies to true crime to travel shows and everything in between. I'm an equal-opportunity viewer and change channels a lot. What kind of shows do you watch?"

He shrugged. "I don't watch much telly, if you want the truth. Give me a good book and maybe a little Glenlivet and I'm sorted for the night."

He winced a little. "That makes me sound like my father, doesn't it? Sorry. At least I didn't say a cup of tea instead of the Scotch, which is probably closer to the truth most of the time."

She smiled at his honesty. "Either way, it sounds nice. You don't need to apologize for what makes you happy, Ian. Some people like haute couture while others are most comfortable in jeans and a T-shirt. I learned early on working at Fremont Fashions that neither choice is bad, simply individual preference."

"I'm obviously the jeans and T-shirt type. For now, anyway," he added under his breath.

She wanted to ask what he meant but he didn't give her the chance.

"We really did have a lovely day on our adventure. The children will remember it always. Thank you for showing us the falls."

"I'm the one who should be thanking you for inviting me and pulling me away from my sewing machine. I loved it. Your children are a delight."

"Most of the time. They do have their moments. But on the whole, yes. I would have to say I've been extraordinarily lucky in the offspring department."

Oh, she liked him. Entirely too much. With a sigh, she decided she might as well confess all.

"I enjoyed their company and yours," she admitted softly. "And that's not flirting, I promise. It's truth."

"I enjoyed yours, as well." His voice was so low it seemed to whisper through the room, giving her goose bumps she hoped he didn't see.

Her gaze met his as the moment seemed to swirl around them. She saw that hunger in his eyes again and knew he wanted to kiss her.

She should walk away now. She only had to shift slightly and put a little more space between them. She knew it would be the smartest thing to do, the best choice for self-preservation, but she couldn't seem to get her muscles to cooperate. Instead, she leaned forward slightly, her mouth slightly parted, unable to help herself.

That hunger flared brighter and then he kissed her, as she wanted him to with a fierce ache that astonished her.

At first, the kiss was soft, gentle, his mouth barely touching hers. She caught her breath, swept away by sensation. If his mouth had been hard, aggressive, she might have been able to resist him, but this gentleness completely enchanted her and left her wanting more.

She twisted her hands around his neck and returned the kiss, her fingers playing in his thick, dark hair as she had longed to do all day.

She could fall in love with Ian Summerhill so easily,

she thought as his mouth demolished all her good intentions. It would only take the merest push.

Oh. She was such an idiot. She couldn't do this again, set herself up for heartbreak with a man who couldn't be hers. She had to break the pattern.

Ian Summerhill wasn't the man for her. He had a life away from here, a family, a complicated past.

Even as the thoughts passed through her mind, Ian deepened the kiss and she shivered, letting him push her against the wall, his body hard and muscled against hers.

She gave in for a few more moments, caught up in the magic and the wonder and the sheer delight of the kiss.

Why did it have to be so blasted hard to make the smart decision here? She didn't want to. She wanted to keep kissing him for the rest of the afternoon while the rain clicked against the windows.

Each moment she spent in his arms made it harder and harder to do the right thing. Finally, though everything inside her urged her to stay right here, she managed to find the strength necessary to slide her mouth away from his. They stared at each other, both breathing hard, for a long moment as a suddenly awkward silence spread between them.

He sighed finally, a wistful, hungry sound that left her restless, needy.

"I did it again, didn't I? I completely lost my head."

"We both did," she murmured.

"And after we talked about why we're both not looking for a relationship right now. I'm sorry, Samantha. I should never have kissed you. I don't know what came over me."

"Maybe the rainstorm," she suggested, though she knew that wasn't the reason. This particular storm between them had been building all day. Every moment she had spent with him that day had left her wanting to kiss him again.

"That might be. Whatever the reason, I promise it won't happen again."

She knew she shouldn't feel this twinge of sorrow. She didn't want to think about never kissing him again. "It's fine. It happened. Let's move on."

He opened his mouth, then closed it again. "I'm not that sort of man, in case you were wondering. The kind who looks for dalliances everywhere he goes."

She was quite sure she had never heard anyone outside of an actor on a film or television show use the word *dalliance*.

"I never thought you were," she assured him.

He made a rueful sort of sound. "You seem to bring out a side of me I don't quite recognize."

"I'm sorry," she said, not sure what else she could say. He made her sound like some femme fatale with unlimited power.

"I certainly don't blame you. It's not your fault, it's entirely my own."

He was silent, his features tense. "You must know I'm becoming quite ridiculously infatuated with you."

She had to catch her breath. In all her life, no man had ever told her such a thing.

"Are...are you?"

His cheeks turned slightly pink. "I know. It's quite juvenile. You don't have to say anything. I'm embarrassed enough as it is."

"You shouldn't be embarrassed," she assured him. "If you want the truth, I'm touched that you trusted me enough to tell me. I find it rather sweet."

She didn't want to tell him that she had plowed past infatuation the first or second time she met him.

"I suppose *sweet* is better than *pitiable*."

She frowned at his word choice. "I would certainly never pity you. Why would I?"

"Lonely widower goes on vacation with his children where he meets a beautiful woman next door who compels him to promptly make a fool of himself."

"Are you lonely?" She focused on that word rather than the heat glowing inside her that he would call her beautiful.

"I probably wouldn't use that word to describe my day-to-day life. I'm too busy to register that I might be lonely. I focus on the children, my family, my work. But yes. At the heart of it, I suppose I am."

Something inside him called to her, an echo of her own loneliness.

She had been lonely for a long time, long before her mother died and left her alone. She had tried to mask it, to be the life of the party everyone seemed to expect while inside she had yearned most of all for someone to cherish her, to treat her as if what she wanted mattered more than anything else in the world.

Starry-eyed Samantha.

She could almost hear her mother's strident voice ringing through the house with the familiar words.

"I like you very much, Ian," she said. "You and your children. I wish I were the sort of woman who wouldn't mind a bit of, er, dalliance."

"I understand. Good to know where we both stand."

"There's no reason we can't remain friends. You live next door and we are bound to run into each other here and there."

She would do her best to make sure she avoided her

dock at night. Or finding herself alone with him in a quiet hallway during a thunderstorm.

"I won't hold you to your invitation from earlier, to be your plus-one at Gemma's wedding. I would never want to make things awkward for you."

"You wouldn't," he protested.

"You don't have to worry about me, truly. I'll be there anyway, fussing over Gemma's dress. And I suppose your mother's now, if we can find her a dress design she likes that I can pull off in less than two weeks."

She tried not to panic at the reminder.

"I would still like to go with you and I know that would make the children happy, too."

She should tell him no. Spending more time with him was a *terrible* idea. She had no willpower around him, as the past few moments had amply demonstrated. Despite their conversation, she still wanted to fall right back into his arms.

Didn't he understand how weak she was, how she should be spending all her time shoring up her defenses around him so she didn't wind up with a broken heart when he took his adorable children and returned to England?

Maybe it was that weakness that made her unable to back out of going with him to the wedding. "All right," she said.

His serious expression lifted and she saw relief in his gaze. "So that's that. It's a date."

"Yes."

She would have to be so careful to keep things in perspective for the next couple of weeks before Gemma's wedding, she thought after he left her house to return next door to his children and his parents.

She was making a new start here, figuring out life on

her own. That life didn't include a long-distance relationship with a man whose world was thousands of miles away.

She and Ian couldn't be together, no matter how she might feel herself falling for him.

She remembered his words with a little thrill.

You must know I'm becoming quite ridiculously infatuated with you.

Wouldn't it be wonderful if circumstances were different and they could both act on these feelings growing between them? But they weren't and they couldn't. They might share a mutual infatuation but it could never move beyond that.

Something told her that if she gave her heart to Ian Summerhill, it would be damaged forever.

IAN WALKED BACK to his rented house, his thoughts whirling and his face hot with mortification.

Good Lord. He really *was* an idiot. Had he really blurted out that he was infatuated with her?

What had he been thinking?

The answer to that was quite simple. He hadn't been thinking at all. The words had slipped out without a moment's thought behind them.

He was hopeless. Utterly hopeless. Put a beautiful woman in his arms and he completely lost his head.

He should never have kissed her. He still didn't know what had come over him. That was twice now that he had acted without thinking and had simply taken what he wanted like some kind of Neanderthal. And that was probably being unfair to Neanderthals.

He had to be far more careful around her. He meant what he had told her earlier. He wasn't looking for a relationship, even if one between him and a woman who lived five thousand miles away was even possible. The children needed him right now. It would be hard enough for them to pack up their lives and move at the end of the summer. They had already endured far too many life changes for children so young. He had vowed he wouldn't date anyone until Thomas was at least through grade school, which right now seemed eons away.

The thunderstorm had blown over as quickly as it had arisen, leaving the air cool and the lake churning and restless—much as he felt inside.

He hurried through the wet grass, managing to wrestle most of his emotions under control by the time he entered the house. Inside, he found his father reading the newspaper. Amelia and Thomas were showing Margaret their assortment of stones collected in the short time they had been in Idaho.

"Puppies all managed?" Henry asked.

Ian could feel his cheeks heat and hoped like Hades that his father wouldn't notice his reaction.

"Yes," he answered. "All tucked in, safe and dry."

"Nice of you to help out your neighbor," Margaret said, looking up from a heart-shaped stone Thomas had found along the lakeshore.

"More like she's helping me. Samantha has been very kind to us."

"She's letting Dad park his boat at her house," Amelia informed her grandparents.

"Is that right?" Henry asked.

"When we rented this house, I thought the dock out there belonged to our rental," he explained. "I must have misunderstood something the estate agent said. It turned out the dock belongs to Samantha's property. She's been kind enough to let me moor my research boat there and use it whenever I need it."

"She's very pretty," Margaret observed.

"Isn't she?" he replied as blandly as he could.

"Gemma says she's nice, too. I just spoke with your sister to tell her Samantha had agreed to help me find a new dress for the wedding."

He could only imagine how that conversation had gone. He had a feeling the topic of mother-of-the-bride dresses had only filled a portion of it. The idea of his mother and sister in cahoots, working together to push him and Samantha Fremont together, filled him with apprehension.

It didn't matter how hard they pushed, Ian thought. Nothing would come of their efforts. How could it? He might be infatuated with her but anything beyond a few kisses was completely impossible.

"I UNDERSTAND YOU went hiking this morning with Ian Summerhill and his children."

Samantha gaped at Katrina later that evening as they sat together on the terrace of Serenity Harbor, the luxurious house where her friend lived with her family.

"How on earth could you know that?"

"Jennifer Hyer said she saw you going up the trail to Bridal Veil Falls when she was coming down."

She barely remembered bumping into Jen on the trail among all the other hikers they had passed on their way up, maybe because she'd been so busy trying not to wheeze her way up the trail and to keep her attraction to Ian under wraps.

Now that she thought of it, she remembered seeing Jen running down the trail with another of her fit friends and having a completely petty urge to trip her skinny butt. One she would never act on, of course.

"And she had to phone you the moment she had cell service again so she could gossip about it?"

"Are you kidding? When Samantha Fremont is caught out and about with the most exciting new arrival to hit Haven Point in a long time, tongues are going to wag, my dear."

Well, she had to agree on one point at least. Ian Summerhill was exciting. She wasn't sure her heart rate had settled down yet, hours after that seductive kiss. Even now, sitting with Kat after her friend had spontaneously invited her over for dinner, Sam was having a hard time focusing on anything but the memories she couldn't seem to shake.

Those were *her* memories, though, and she didn't want anybody else in town ruining them with prurient gossip.

"The busy tongues in Haven Point can mind their own business. There's nothing going on between me and Ian Summerhill."

It wasn't precisely true but she wasn't prepared to divulge anything more to Katrina.

Her best friend had enough on her plate right now and far more important things to worry about than Sam's pathetic love life problems.

"Nothing? Are you sure? Apparently you're getting along well enough with him that you were even willing to go out into nature to enjoy our gorgeous surroundings," Katrina teased.

Though they had been BFFs since they were in grade school, she and Katrina had always had different tastes. Katrina was far more outdoorsy than Sam, frequently taking advantage of the lake and the mountains to kayak, ski, hike. Her friend's latest craze was stand-up paddle board-ing, which Sam had tried with minimal success.

"You know I'm happiest with my sketchbook and a good TV show," Sam said.

She had a sudden mental picture of Ian sitting by the fire somewhere in England, maybe wearing a nubby Irish fisherman's sweater—jumper, he would call it—his hair a little messy and a distracted look in his eyes. She would be sitting beside him, sketching a new design while she alternated between watching him and watching the chil-dren playing a game on the floor at their feet.

Yearning swelled through her at the imaginary scene until she caught herself and pushed the picture away.

She had to cut this out. She was *not* destined for a fu-ture with Ian and his children. There was no possible way anything would work out between them and she had to get that straight in her head now before she started weaving all kinds of dangerous fantasies.

Starry-eyed Samantha. She couldn't seem to stop spin-ning impossible dreams.

"I'm glad you tore yourself away from your sewing machine long enough to go with them. Summer feels so fleeting this year, for some reason."

Their winters could be harsh here on the lake, which was one reason locals tended to cram as much outdoor recreation as possible into every available moment until the snow began to fly again.

By the time frosty mornings returned to the lake, Ian and his children would be gone. She tried to ignore the sharp pang in her heart.

With the uncanny perception that came from years of close friendship, Katrina gave her a careful look. "You like this guy, don't you?" she asked, her voice soft.

To her horror, Sam's throat felt tight, achy. She ruthlessly swallowed down the emotion. "I barely know Ian. But yes. He seems very nice and his children are so sweet." She did her best to sound brisk, businesslike. "Unlike Gemma, however, he won't be uprooting his life to take a job in a new country. And since I have a life here and am not a fan of long-distance relationships, pursuing anything more than a friendship between us is kind of pointless, isn't it?"

Katrina gave her careful look. Her friend knew her better than anyone else on earth. Even better than Linda had. Katrina knew how much Sam longed for a family of her own. She yearned for a man who would love her without restraint and would never leave her, children she would treat with kindness and respect, cherishing every moment she had with them instead of constantly finding fault and criticizing.

She wouldn't be able to bear it if Katrina said anything about that right now so she quickly changed the subject. "Did the gossips also tell you Gemma's parents are in town? They showed up a week before they were expected."

Kat shook her head. "Interesting. I hadn't heard that news. Apparently it hasn't made the rounds yet."

"They've only been in town a few hours. Give it time."

Kat smiled. "Are they staying with Ian and his children?"

"No. They're staying at a cottage near Gemma's house. Their names are Margaret and Henry and they seem charming, just as you would expect Gemma's parents to be. Their father seems a little formal but Margaret was very kind."

"I wouldn't expect anything else, knowing Gemma."

They lapsed into a comfortable silence, broken only

by the water lapping at the shore and the laughter of Gabi and Milo.

Bowie and Katrina had created a warm and loving family here. Sam always had the best feeling when she came to Serenity Harbor. The place was aptly named, offering a calm and contentment rarely found anywhere else.

"I have news," Katrina announced after a moment with a funny, half-wary and half-excited expression that told Sam she'd only been waiting for the right moment to spring it on her.

"What news?"

"I haven't even told my family yet. Only Bowie knows."

"You're pregnant," Sam guessed instantly without a bit of surprise in her voice.

Katrina's mouth opened with shock. "How did you know?"

Sam made a face. "How long have we known each other? It's a little obvious. You always glow when Bowie's around but I've noticed something more the last few times I've seen you. I could tell the moment I arrived that there was something different. That's why you invited me over tonight, to spring the news on me, right?"

Katrina looked over at Bowie, who was monitoring the steaks on the grill and keeping a careful eye on the kids. The joy in her eyes made Sam's heart squeeze again.

"We had decided that Milo and Gabi were enough for us but apparently Mother Nature had other ideas," Katrina confided. "It wasn't planned. For the record, even the best birth control methods aren't a hundred percent effective."

"Are you okay with it?"

"More than okay." Kat looked luminous with happiness. "Some of life's best gifts come in unexpected packages."

"Then I think it's wonderful," Sam said promptly. "Congratulations. You're a fabulous mother already and will only have more love to give this little one. And Milo and Gabi will be wonderful older siblings. When are you due?"

"Not until the new year."

"I'd better get busy sewing, then. You'll have the best-dressed baby in Haven Point, whether it's a boy or a girl."

Katrina laughed, then abruptly grew teary. "I love you, you know. You were the first one I wanted to tell as soon as the plus sign showed up on the test. I haven't even told my family yet. I'm springing the news on them tomorrow."

Sam reached out and squeezed her hand. When Katrina married Bowie, she had worried their friendship would end now that their lives were going in different directions. It was wonderful to know the bond between them was as strong as ever.

"I love you right back. You are the sister of my heart, you know."

"I hope that never changes," Katrina said. "Even if you end up with a handsome Englishman who steals you away across the ocean from me."

"You don't have to worry about that," Sam said with that little pang in her heart again. "I'm not going anywhere. I'll be the doting maiden aunt to this baby and any others who come along, spoiling them with toys and clothes and candy their parents don't let them have."

Katrina snorted a little, but before she could argue the unlikelihood of that, Bowie called to them.

"Steaks are ready," he said.

Katrina sighed. "I don't want to move. I don't remember when I've been this comfortable."

Sam smiled. She had to agree. It was a perfect Sunday evening, here by the lake.

"Mama! Get up!" Gabi ordered in her bossy voice. "I am hungry."

Samantha laughed and scooped up the little girl, twirling her around. "It's all right. I'll eat her share," she said.

Gabi giggled as Samantha carried her over to the table with Katrina close behind.

It was a perfect Sunday evening, she thought as she sat down on the terrace overlooking the water. Good food, dear friends, joyful news to savor.

Too bad she eventually would have to go back home to her empty house and her empty bed and her empty life.

CHAPTER NINE

WHAT IN BLAZES was he doing heading into a dress shop for a wedding fitting?

Ian grabbed his mother's arm and helped her up the curb to the pavement along the road in the charming business district of Haven Point.

This area of town had a cozy feel to it, Ian had to admit. It reminded him a great deal of the village near Summerhill House. He admired the historic-looking lampposts and their hanging flowerpots overflowing with blossoms that sent a sweet smell to stir the morning air.

They headed in the direction of Samantha's shop, clearly marked by a light blue awning out front emblazoned with the words Fremont Fashions in fancy script. He could see several dresses in the display window and he noticed with approval that the store had a park bench out front, presumably so dutiful husbands—or sons, in this case—could stay safely out of the way during the serious business of shopping.

"Thank you again for giving me a ride, darling," his mother said, squeezing his arm. "The idea of tackling the roads here where everyone drives on the wrong side fills me with utter dread."

"Once you get the hang of it, driving here isn't bad. I find it simply takes a little practice."

"Well, you rescued me. I didn't know what I would do

after your father ended up having to schedule a conference call this morning. The difference in time zones gives him a very narrow window for taking care of things at home."

"I'm sure."

"Your sister is coming straight from her office, as well, and I didn't want her to have to pop out of her way to pick me up, especially when you were just a few streets over."

No two addresses in Haven Point were particularly far from each other. Gemma no doubt could have picked up their mother without any bother. He had been available, though, and hadn't seen any good reason to refuse her request.

"I don't mind," Ian told her again. "While you're busy trying things on, I'll just head over to the bookshop down the street and catch up on some reading."

"You should at least come in and say hello to Samantha. It's the neighborly thing to do, right?"

He narrowed his gaze at his mother, certain again that she had more than dress shopping on her mind. Despite her best efforts at subterfuge, Margaret was wholly transparent. He suspected the entire reason she had asked him for a ride had more to do with her ill-fated matchmaking efforts on his behalf than any real need.

In this case, though, she was probably correct. Since he had agreed to bring his mother to her shop, Samantha would find it odd if he didn't at least say hello.

"Yes. All right," he finally said. "I'll pop in, but only for a moment. I am quite sure I'll only be in the way."

"You could never be in the way, darling," his mother said, which both of them knew was a complete falsehood. He didn't see the point in arguing with her and decided to keep his mouth shut.

By then, they had reached the front entrance to the shop.

He was aware of a little burst of anticipation as Margaret pushed open the door, which gave a cheerful little chime.

When he walked inside, he immediately felt out of place. The store was decorated in pink and gilt with Tiffany-blue accents. Something told him this decor hadn't been Samantha's choice, though he couldn't have said exactly how he knew that with such surety.

A young woman with choppy dark hair who seemed to be around the age of his students was rearranging the display in one of the windows. She gave them a friendly smile. "Hello. May I help you find something?"

"Yes," his mother said, smiling in return. "I'm looking for my daughter. Gemma Summerhill."

"Oh, of course. She's just arrived. She and Samantha are in the largest fitting room. It's just through that door there."

As Margaret turned to go in that direction, the store clerk gave Ian an appraising look. "I know you're not the groom. I've met Josh Bailey. I have to ask, are you part of the wedding party?"

"I'm Gemma's brother."

And I absolutely don't belong in this soft, sweet-smelling, feminine space, he wanted to add.

"Oh, how fun that you came for the dress fitting!" she said. "It's a true family affair."

"I'm only the chauffeur," he quickly explained. "I'm not here for the fitting."

His mother headed toward the back of Samantha's shop where the clerk had indicated. She slipped through the door, leaving Ian uncertain about what to do. Should he accompany her, wait here or head over to the bookshop?

He hesitated, feeling big and male and out of place amid all the flowers and gilt and fabrics.

He was about to turn and escape when the door through

which his mother had slipped opened again and Samantha bustled through, making notes on a clipboard. She was dressed in a plain white blouse, navy slacks and matching sandals. He caught a fleeting glimpse of pink-painted toes that for some ridiculous reason made his heartbeat kick up.

She almost ran into him before she realized he was there. "Oh," she exclaimed, looking up from her clipboard. "Hello."

He couldn't seem to stop staring, wishing more than anything that he had the right to pull her hair out of that loose bun and run his fingers through it.

Oh, lord. Had he really told her he was infatuated with her? He was such an idiot.

"Hi," he managed.

A little hint of pink appeared on each cheekbone and he immediately wanted to touch his mouth to both spots.

He closed his eyes, mortified at himself. "My, uh, mother rang me for a ride. I've just dropped her off."

Of course he had. She must have seen his mother only seconds earlier. What other possible reason would he have for being there?

"That's nice of you. Thank you. I only needed to find a particular pattern book I think your mother might like."

"She's very much looking forward to working with you," he said.

For some reason, his words seemed to spark panic in her eyes.

"How am I going to find the perfect dress for your mother and finish it in less than two weeks?"

He didn't want her upset. He wanted to tuck her against him and make everything all right for her, no matter what it might take. "Easy enough," he said. "You only have to tell her you don't have time. She brought two dresses along that she picked up at home. One of them will be perfectly fine."

"Not if she doesn't like them."

"She liked them well enough when she bought them," he pointed out in what he thought was a perfectly reasonable argument. "If it will help, I suggested she bring them both along so that you might have a better idea of her tastes. They're both in the car. Would you like me to fetch them?"

She stared at him, eyes wide and a dawning relief on her lovely features. "Ian. You're brilliant!"

"Am I?"

"Yes. I can't believe I didn't think of that. Maybe instead of starting from zero, I can simply alter one of the dresses your mother brought along to make it more to her liking."

"From what I've seen, I'm sure you have the necessary skill to work magic with the dresses she has. If I were a woman, I would definitely want to shop here."

It was a stupid thing to say but somehow seemed to hit the right note, anyway. She gazed at him, eyes wide again but this time with a stunned, luminous happiness. "Thank you for saying that."

"You're welcome," he said gruffly.

They stared at each other long enough that it began to feel awkward. He cleared his throat. "Right, then. Shall I fetch the dresses?"

"Yes. Please. And thank you. A thousand times, thank you."

It was a small thing to feel heroic about but he decided to take his small victories where he could find them. He unlocked the vehicle where the dresses were hanging. As he reached in to grab them, a man approached him.

"Need a hand with anything?"

He frowned at Gemma's fiancé. "What are you doing

here? You're not supposed to be anywhere in the vicinity. Gemma is inside trying on her wedding dress and you know she'll have a fit if you see it before the wedding."

Josh Bailey made a face. "Where am I supposed to go exactly? Haven Point isn't that big and my store is just across the street. I spotted you from inside a few moments ago when you showed up with your mother."

"Anywhere but inside Samantha's shop is fine."

"Have you had breakfast? I was just about to head over to the café to grab something and would love to have you join me."

Ian considered his options. He wouldn't mind sitting on that conveniently placed bench outside the store with his book. On the other hand, he had been hoping for an opportunity to become better acquainted with his sister's fiancé. Every other time they'd been together had been with Gemma as a buffer.

"I already had breakfast with the children this morning but I wouldn't mind a cup of coffee." He was going to say tea but decided coffee made him sound a little less British. "I only have to deliver these dresses to Samantha inside the boutique."

Josh looked confused. "Don't people usually take dresses *away* from the boutique, not the other way around?"

"It's a long story. I'll tell you about it over coffee. You had better wait out here. I'm afraid if you walked into that shop right now, there might not be a wedding and all this fuss over dresses would be for nothing."

"Probably wise advice. I'll wait right here and keep my gaze carefully averted."

Ian had to admit, he liked the man. Joshua Bailey seemed smart, centered and chill, exactly what Gemma needed.

When he pushed open the door to the shop, he saw his mother and Gemma had come out from the back room but he only had eyes for one woman.

Samantha's features seemed to light up when she saw him, her hazel eyes looking more green against the colors of the store. Wouldn't it be wonderful if he could put that look on her face all the time?

"Thank you again. This is perfect. Brilliant," she said.

"I don't know if having these dresses will help," Margaret said.

"Well, if nothing else, it will give me some insight into your tastes. Something must have appealed to you when you bought them."

"Right now as I look at them in your shop surrounded by all these lovely clothes, I have no idea."

Sam smiled as she took the dresses from Ian. He tried not to notice the scent of strawberries and clotted cream that swirled around him.

"These aren't bad," Sam said, studying them carefully. "Not bad at all. Margaret, why don't you try them on while I finish Gemma's fitting and then we'll see what we can do."

His mother took the dresses with a sigh and turned to head into a dressing room he could see at the rear of the store.

"I bumped into the groom-to-be outside," Ian told Samantha. "He and I are grabbing coffee at the café down the street. He's waiting outside, as I knew none of you would like it if he followed me inside."

"Good thinking," Samantha said.

"Have Mother call me when she's ready to go," he said to his sister.

"I can drop her off, if you have other things to do," Gemma said, just as he suspected would be the case.

It would be easy enough to say yes, go outside and tell Josh never mind on the coffee. He could head back out to the lake and perhaps log more salmon heading up to the Chalk Creek redds. But he was here and had already blocked off the morning to play chauffeur.

Besides, when he returned to pick up his mother, he would at least have another chance of seeing Samantha again.

"I don't mind," he said quickly before he could change his mind. "Besides, why would I pass up an opportunity to interrogate your intended?"

"Behave yourself," Gemma said, her voice stern.

He always did, unfortunately.

Maybe it was time he tried misbehaving once in a while.

"Oh, my darling. You look exquisite."

Margaret's reaction to seeing Gemma in her wedding dress was everything Sam would have hoped for. The older woman's features were soft, almost tearful, as she looked at her daughter.

"I do, don't I?" Gemma gazed into the mirror with a shocked expression, almost as if she didn't recognize herself.

Sam smiled as she adjusted the neckline a little more solidly on Gemma's elegant shoulders and smoothed the small train that rippled out behind her.

"It's so much better than the pictures, which I thought were amazing enough. Oh, Samantha," Margaret breathed. "It's a masterpiece. An absolute masterpiece. What a marvelous dress."

She had to admit, she had outdone herself on this one. It

looked like something out of a medieval fairy tale, with a scooping neckline, snug bodice and flaring skirt, all made of hand-embroidered fabric.

No one else would be able to wear this dress so well. It highlighted Gemma's ethereal features perfectly.

"When he sees you in this, Josh is going to think he's the luckiest man in the world," Margaret said.

"As he should." Gemma spoke with a confidence Sam hadn't seen in her before.

"Oh, quite," Margaret said tartly. "And you never want to let him forget that."

She had to smile at the woman's tone. She genuinely liked Ian and Gemma's mother. The past hour of working with her had been sheer delight. She was funny, kind and had a keen eye for fashion.

"What about you?" she asked the older woman. "Are you happy with our plan to alter the peach dress instead of starting from scratch? I think those few changes we talked about to the neckline and the sleeves are all you really need to make it work for you."

"After seeing what you've done with that wedding dress, I have complete faith that you know exactly what you're talking about. Gem has sent me pictures of her gown all along the way, from the time you showed her the first sketches, but I'll admit, I didn't envision the full glory of it until I had the chance to see it in person. Honestly, I couldn't be more thrilled."

Sam glowed under the other woman's approval. She wanted to lap it up like the puppies at their feeding bowl.

The past hour truly had been a delight. She didn't need therapy to understand why she was so drawn to Margaret, considering supportive older women in her life were fairly thin on the ground.

That wasn't precisely true, she corrected herself. She had dear friends in the Haven Point Helping Hands always ready to provide a positive influence. Eppie and Hazel. Charlene Bailey. Barbara Serrano.

Still, Linda's dominance and Sam's own weakness and inability to stand up for herself cast a wide shadow over her life.

"Thank you," she said now to Margaret. "I'm so thrilled with the way it turned out. I'm never quite sure if everything will come together until the final fitting."

"Well, I can't imagine a more perfect gown for my daughter to wear for her wedding," Margaret said. "Well done."

After Gemma had changed back into her regular clothing, Samantha carefully tucked the gown into the long white custom garment bag emblazoned with the store's swirly logo she had designed herself.

Margaret watched the whole process with interest.

"What a marvelous shop you have here," she said. "I'm astounded. I'll be perfectly honest, when Gem told me she was having someone local make her dress instead of choosing a more well-known designer, I was a bit concerned. She's never cared much about what she wore and I worried about the quality she would be able to find in a little town in Idaho. I'm not ashamed to admit I was far off the mark."

"I'm so happy you like it," Samantha said.

"She's going to be a gorgeous bride," Margaret said as Gemma came back to join them. "You'll be there, won't you?"

"Or course. I wouldn't miss it."

"I know you told me you weren't taking a date but have you changed your mind yet?" Gemma asked on a teasing note.

She made a noncommittal sound, not sure how to respond. She found herself suddenly reluctant to tell Margaret and Gemma that Ian had asked her to go with him, especially if he hadn't told them himself.

"What does that mean?" Gemma looked suddenly interested. "*Have* you changed your mind? Are you taking someone?"

She could see no reason to lie. "Ian and I have decided to, um, go together."

"Is that right?"

Margaret and Gemma exchanged a look that immediately put Samantha on edge.

"Yes. He asked me yesterday on our hike. He said you were hounding him about taking someone. Something about seating arrangements and so forth. As he knows no one else in Lake Haven County, he asked me to go as his plus-one."

"My son, the romantic," Margaret muttered.

"It's not a date," Samantha assured them quickly. "He and I are merely friends."

"Too bad," Margaret said.

"Mother," Gemma chided. "Stop."

"Why? I love my son and want him to be happy. Ian deserves to date a beautiful, smart, talented woman, after what he's been through. You probably didn't notice but he lit up around you yesterday in a way I hadn't seen him do in years. You can't blame a mother for wishing there could be something more between you."

Sam shifted, deeply uncomfortable. Margaret surely understood why anything between Sam and her son was impossible. Anyway, the other woman had to be mistaken about Ian's reaction to her. Samantha hadn't seen anything like that.

"I'm afraid there's nothing more than friendship," she finally said. Her chest burned a little at the awkward lie but she certainly couldn't tell Ian's mother about the two delicious kisses they had shared...or how she ached for more.

"I'm sorry. I didn't mean to make you blush," Margaret said.

"Drop it, Mother," Gemma said.

"You're right." She hugged Samantha. "In whatever capacity, I'm glad you will be going with Ian to the wedding. Now, I believe finishing a gown of this caliber calls for a celebration, don't you think? Let's all three of us go to lunch or something."

Sam's extensive workload flashed through her head. It sounded lovely but she had *so* much work. Before she could make her excuses, Gemma stepped in.

"I wholeheartedly agree with you about the celebration," Gemma said. "Unfortunately, I have a meeting in an hour I can't miss so I have to go back to work."

"That Aidan Caine is a slave driver."

Gemma looked regretful. "He's really not, we're just in the middle of a big project right now and I'm trying to finish as much as possible before Josh and I leave for our honeymoon."

"If you can't do lunch, what about dinner later?" Margaret asked. "Would that work for both of you?"

Gemma appeared to consider. "Yes. I believe that would fit our schedule. We didn't have plans tonight and were planning a quiet night."

"Perfect. Do you want to pick a restaurant? You know more about the best places to eat than I do, though I did enjoy the place we ate last night."

"Instead of going out again, why don't we throw something on the grill?" Gemma suggested. "That's what Josh and I had planned. I've got a couple of chicken breasts marinating. It would be no problem to stop at home before I head back to the office and toss a few more in."

Her mother beamed. "That sounds perfect. Samantha, what about you?"

She had so much to do, including finishing the alterations for Margaret's dress. A responsible business owner would refuse, citing her heavy workload.

On the other hand, she had to eat. How much extra time would she pick up, eating by herself in front of the TV? She could work after dinner. Altering a dress wasn't nearly the job she thought she would be facing, starting from nothing.

Anyway, she had worked terribly hard on the gown for Gemma and wanted to celebrate a job well done. She deserved at least that, didn't she?

"I think I can make dinner work tonight," she said.

"Perfect." Margaret beamed. "Shall we do it at our cottage? Last night we had a lovely view of the sunset over the mountains and I expect tonight will be the same."

"We can do it at my place," Gemma said. "Same view, with a little more space. Plus Josh knows how to work my barbecue grill and I doubt Father can say the same."

"That works. But I'll take care of dessert and all the sides," Margaret insisted. "Should we say seven?"

"Yes. That should be great," Sam said. It would give her just enough time to go home and check on the puppies before she left again for dinner with them.

Before Margaret could respond, the bell on her front door chimed and a moment later Ian walked inside, his hair messed a little by the breeze.

She wanted to smooth it down, straighten his collar, then mess it all up again with a kiss.

"Ian, darling. Tell me you don't have dinner plans,"

Margaret ordered. "We're planning a dinner party to celebrate the fabulous dress Samantha has created for your sister. You and the children must be there."

"Must we?" he said faintly.

"What Mother means is you're invited to dinner," Gemma said with a grin. "I'll have Josh grill chicken and would love to have you and the children and Mrs. Gilbert join us."

"Well, in that case, of course."

He didn't look at Samantha but she somehow sensed his attention, anyway.

Margaret looked pleased. "Do you know Gemma's address?" she asked her. "I can write it for you."

"I know where it is," she said, declining to point out that Haven Point was small enough that she knew where nearly everybody lived.

"Great. We'll see you there, then. Or better still, you should ride with Ian and the children, since you live just next door. I don't see the point in taking two cars."

"Think of the environment," Gemma said, a teasing look in her eye as she looked at her brother.

He frowned at her. "Right. The environment. I guess that seals it. What time is dinner?"

"Seven."

"Shall I pick you up at 6:45?" he asked Sam.

"That would be good. Thank you."

"My pleasure," he said solemnly.

She was becoming more enmeshed in his life with every passing day, Sam thought after they left and her store was quiet again. First with the children and Ian, now with his mother.

She liked them all so much. She liked being part of

something, even though she had to remind herself it wouldn't last.

Except for Gemma, the Summerhills would only be here a few more weeks. She had to keep that in mind. Her relationship with all of them was temporary, as fleeting as the Haven Point summers. Ian and his family would return to England when the wedding was over, leaving her alone with only her memories.

How on earth would she go back to her solitary life when they left?

CHAPTER TEN

As Ian waited on Samantha's doorstep for her to answer Thomas's vigorous ringing of the bell, he felt ridiculously tongue-tied.

"Do you think she forgot we were coming?" Thomas asked anxiously.

"You only rang the bell fifteen seconds ago, son. You have to give her time to answer."

"I hope she didn't forget. I like Miss Fremont."

So did Ian. Entirely too much. That must be why he had butterflies jumping inside him as he waited for her to open the door. He couldn't say that, of course. He didn't even want to admit it to himself.

A moment later, the door opened and Sam stood there.

"Hello." She smiled, looking as fresh and lovely as a summer day. He wasn't the kind of guy who usually paid attention to things like clothing but he couldn't help noticing she had changed her clothes from work and now wore a turquoise sundress and carried a navy jumper over her arm. Her messy bun of earlier in the day looked softer somehow, more enticing. He again wanted to pull the whole thing free.

More than that, he wanted fiercely to step forward and kiss her. The urge was an actual ache in his chest. Only his children's presence stopped him. What a relief that they were there to keep him from making that mistake again, he told himself, but wasn't quite sure he believed it.

"Hello," he answered, feeling as if his thoughts and words were as slippery as fish out of water.

"It's very kind of you all to give me a ride."

"It's no trouble," Amelia assured her, as if the eight-year-old would be doing the driving.

"It's really not," Ian had to agree. "It's not as if we had to go far out of our way."

"We didn't have to go out of our way at all," Thomas said. "You're just next door. How are the puppies? Are they in their room?"

She gave him a soft, warm smile that didn't help Ian's turmoil. "Yes. Safe and sound for the evening."

"They were silly this morning when we played with them," Amelia told her. "You should have seen them. Coco was running around in circles and Oscar kept jumping on everything."

"We played fetch with them and Calvin always caught the stick first but wouldn't bring it back." Thomas giggled at the memory.

"You've both helped me so much. I can't tell you how much I appreciate you watching over the puppies for me. You've done me such a huge favor."

She was the one doing the favor for them. She had to know it. The puppies would be the highlight of this particular trip for the children, besides Gemma's wedding, of course. Without the distraction of three cute balls of fluff, Amelia and Thomas would have been bored and troublesome.

"I wish we could take one home with us," Amelia said, her voice subdued.

"So do I, sweetheart. But I'm afraid all three have been

promised already to other homes. Plus, that would be a very long airplane ride for a little puppy."

She sighed. "I know. It's a long airplane ride for me, as well. I'll be so sad to say goodbye to them."

Samantha's expression softened as she ran a gentle hand over Amelia's hair in a gesture that made a lump rise in Ian's throat. "Saying goodbye can be hard, can't it?"

"Yes. I wish we didn't have to."

"The puppies already have homes they'll be going to in a few weeks. If you took one, that would leave someone here very sad."

"Dad says maybe we can get a puppy of our own when we go back home," Thomas announced.

Samantha smiled at him, as well. "Oh, that will be fun. You've had good practice taking care of mine, then, haven't you?"

His children both seemed to drink in her attention. They both wanted to hold her hands as they walked the short distance from her house to his vehicle. Samantha had a way of drawing people to her, something he suspected she didn't consciously realize.

At the vehicle, she looked surprised. "No Mrs. Gilbert?"

"She begged off," Ian said.

"She said she wanted a quiet night at home with her book and the telly," Amelia said with shock in her voice that clearly conveyed what she thought of that idea.

Ian thought that sounded perfectly lovely, though he couldn't deny he was looking forward to the evening ahead in Samantha's company.

"You have made quite an impression on my mother," he said. "When I took her home, she couldn't stop talking about how well the fitting went. What did you think?"

"I think your sister's dress just might be my favorite of all the wedding gowns I've created."

"My mother's exact word was *exquisite*."

"I believe I quite love that word," Samantha said with a smile. "I'm planning to incorporate it into my daily vocabulary."

He was finding Samantha such a funny mix of contradictions. She seemed full of life and light and energy at some moments, then seemed almost paralyzed by doubts in others. Was that because of her own mother's influence?

She seemed to have so much love to give but was almost afraid to offer it.

"How was your afternoon?" she asked. "I don't imagine you could give the salmon much of your attention while you were busy running your mother to dress fittings and having coffee with your new brother-in-law."

He had thoroughly enjoyed his time with Joshua Bailey. His first impression of him had been spot-on. He was a good man with a kind heart and a deep love for Gemma. Ian expected that even despite the distance, the two of them would form a strong and lasting friendship as the years went on.

"The salmon will be there tomorrow, I imagine. They're very patient."

She settled into her seat as Ian drove the short distance to his sister's house. After a few weeks in America, he was almost used to driving on the opposite side of the road. He only hoped he didn't have a big adjustment back to the other way once they were home.

"I'm still fascinated by the fact that you've chosen to study salmon," Samantha said after a moment. "Of all the things in the world a person could choose to research—

elephants, aardvarks, honey badgers. There's no limit. So why salmon?"

"Salmon are vitally important to the world. They are considered a keystone species for the environment, particularly in the Pacific Northwest. That means a great deal of other life depends on them. When ocean-dwelling salmon swim upstream to spawn, they bring their nutrient-rich bodies and end up feeding wildlife, microorganisms, even trees, if you can believe that. When eagles and bears and other predators take a fish out of the water to eat it, they distribute what's left on the forest floor and that feeds the trees. It's estimated that fully one-third of the nitrogen in old-growth forests comes from salmon runs, which I find fascinating. In England and across Europe, we no longer have the historic numbers of salmon and we'll likely never get that back, but there's still hope for the Pacific Northwest salmon to recover."

He caught himself before he could start lecturing on. "I'm doing it again, aren't I? I'm sorry. I didn't mean to bore you."

"You didn't bore me," she said, a curious light in her eyes. "I like seeing you so animated and excited."

She met his gaze, then quickly looked away, her cheeks suddenly turning pink for reasons he couldn't have explained.

She turned back to the children. "Amelia, Thomas, I understand from your grandmother that you took a field trip with Mrs. Gilbert to the children's museum today," she said quickly, as if in a hurry to change the subject. "What did you like about it?"

"That it had a great display about the weather."

"I liked floating things down a little creek inside," Thomas said.

While Samantha engaged the children in a discussion about the museum, Ian kicked himself for going on and on about his work. Susan often would tell him how pedantic he could be on the subject.

He could almost hear her voice echoing in his head. "Of all the people on the planet, maybe four of them care about this as much as you do. Sadly, none of them is here right now."

In retrospect, she had been nothing short of dismissive of his work. Really, of everything about him. They never should have married. In trying to do the right thing, he had made everything worse.

He had admitted to himself some time ago that he would have sought a divorce eventually, even if she hadn't walked out on the marriage. He had been bitterly unhappy, though he hadn't wanted to admit it.

He sighed, earning a curious look from Samantha that made him annoyed with himself for dwelling on the past. He was heading out for an evening with a beautiful woman who made him smile and whom his children adored.

He refused to let memories of his marriage ruin his enjoyment of this perfectly lovely evening, Ian decided.

When he pulled up in front of Gemma's house, the sun had begun to slip behind the Redemption Mountains. Full sunset was still at least another hour or more away but the sun started to go down early on this side of the lake in the shadow of the mountains.

It was a beautiful summer evening, cool and soft and smelling of cut grass and the lake.

He loved it here, he thought as he went around the vehicle to open Samantha's door. The lake, the people, the jagged mountains that stood as sentinels around the community.

These few weeks had given him an appreciation for the choice his sister had made to start a new life here with Josh. He easily could see himself living here with the children, starting over, as she had done. He could study Pacific Northwest salmon, both anadromous and nonanadromous, to his heart's content.

If only that were possible. If only he didn't have the inescapable demands of the earldom weighing on him.

He suddenly missed his brother with a fierce ache. David's death had changed everything.

As he opened the door for Samantha, the fading sunlight gleamed on her features. She was smiling at something one of the children must have said and he suddenly felt breathless.

Oh, he was in trouble. He was growing to care for her entirely too much. She was open and honest, like that sunshine.

If he wasn't careful, he was going to make an even bigger fool of himself over her than he already had.

CHAPTER ELEVEN

IF SAMANTHA WERE ever asked to describe her perfect evening, it would be very much like this one.

When they arrived at Gemma's cottage, a small but tidy clapboard house with a shake roof near downtown, the air smelled delicious, of barbecue chicken and roasting vegetables.

Sam's stomach growled, reminding her that the quick salad she'd taken from home to work for lunch had been a long time ago.

Few places on earth could be as gorgeous as Haven Point on a summer evening.

The setting sun sent long shadows across the lake, which gleamed silver in the light. A flock of ducks or geese—she couldn't tell which—flew overhead while a few boats darted across the water.

Ian's mother stood on the porch of Gemma's house. She waved a hand in greeting as they approached, her features bright with affection for her son and grandchildren. "There you are. I was afraid we would have to eat all this food among the four of us."

"Hi, Nana." Amelia smiled and Margaret hugged her.

"Hello, Nana," Thomas echoed, hugging his grandmother in turn.

"And, Samantha, darling." Margaret turned to her, arms wide, and folded her into an embrace both welcoming and kind. "I'm so happy you're able to join us. Isn't this a beautiful evening?"

"I can't argue. I was thinking that very thing on the way over. Our summers are so short that each day feels like a precious gift."

"I understand your winters around here can be quite intense," Margaret said with interest. "That's hard for me to imagine, with these glorious temperatures right now."

"We can have up to three or four feet of snow at a time and spend weeks with the thermometer never hitting above freezing. You can see the mountains still have snow at the higher elevations. Some of that doesn't melt until late July."

"I believe I would like to see that much snow," Amelia exclaimed.

She smiled at the girl's astonished expression. "It's always beautiful at first. There is nothing prettier than the first snowfall clinging to the pine trees, but by the end of the winter, we're ready for it all to melt and our glorious summers to arrive again."

"Have you ever built a snowman?" Thomas asked.

"Oh, yes. Nearly every year. With as much snow as we can have, you could build an entire snow village if you wanted to. The people of our neighboring town, Shelter Springs, come together to build an elaborate ice castle every year, complete with turrets, slides, fountains, all lit by LED lights in various colors. It's quite spectacular."

"Can we come back to visit Aunt Gemma in the wintertime?" Amelia asked her father eagerly.

Ian looked taken aback. "We'll have to see about that. You'll have your school term."

Samantha had never considered that. She should have. All this time, she had been thinking she would never see them again once they returned to England, but she suddenly realized Ian would always have a link here. His sister and Josh were making their lives here, which meant Ian and the children would likely return at some point for visits in the future.

At that moment, the woman in question walked around the side of the house along with her fiancé.

Sam refused to allow herself to feel embarrassed, though she had once been quite enamored of Josh and had come close to making a fool of herself over him.

Water under the bridge, she told herself.

"You're here," Gemma exclaimed, leaning forward to kiss Sam on the cheek before hugging her brother. "We're setting up on the back terrace."

"Everything's ready," Josh said.

"Shall we?" Margaret gestured toward the gate.

Gemma led the way around the cottage she had rented when she came to town, where a picnic table had been set up in the shade of a weeping willow, branches rustling softly in the breeze. It was a charming scene, with tea lights in bottles hanging from the branches and fresh-cut flowers spilling over vases on the table.

Somehow she ended up seated between Gemma and Henry, Ian's father, who struck her as more formal than the rest of his family. He was the one she had spoken with least in the family.

He was friendly enough, though, and immediately asked her about her boutique.

"Margaret tells me you've done an excellent job making Gemma's wedding gown. They've both been talking about nothing else all evening."

"It's been my pleasure. Really. Gemma's been a delight to work with."

"I know nothing about fashion," Henry said. "If you

want the truth, without my wife I would be lucky to don socks that match in the mornings. But Margaret and Gemma say the dress is stunning and I trust them."

Stunning. What a marvelous endorsement, especially coming from someone as stylish as Margaret. She was deeply grateful her hard work had been so well-received. "I'm so glad they like it. It's one thing to have a bride love a dress. It's another thing entirely when her mother does."

Henry chuckled. "I imagine that's true. Mothers can be notoriously hard to please."

He looked across the table and down, where Ian was talking to Margaret.

"And you are neighbors with our Ian and the children, who have been helping you with your puppies."

Our Ian. She had to smile at the phrase. "Yes. Amelia and Thomas have been wonderful with them. You have dogs, I understand."

That was exactly the right topic to bring up. Henry's somewhat stern features warmed as he told her about his Jack Russell terriers.

By the time the delicious dinner of grilled chicken and salad was over, she and Henry were fast friends and he had given her several suggestions to help her begin initial training of the puppies to help transition to their new owners.

She pushed her plate away with a warm glow, having enjoyed herself immensely. Still, despite her pleasure in the evening, she felt a faint strain of sadness twisting through her like a stray thread that needed pulling.

As much as she had enjoyed the conversation with Henry, it somehow made her miss her own father, something she didn't do very often.

Losing her father to suicide at such a young age had left a deep wound inside her heart. She wanted to think that time had covered that wound in scar tissue, but sometimes out of nowhere she would remember something he had said or ache to share something with him and would realize the scar was paper-thin, the wound easily reopened.

What would it have been like if her father had been able to deal with his depression another way, if she'd had a father figure through her teens and young adulthood? Would she have been so prone to making stupid mistakes with men?

The sadness was edged with no small amount of anger that she'd had so little time with him.

"Nana, watch," Thomas called to his grandmother as he threw a stone into the water, skipping it two or three times.

"Nice work, Thomas," she called back with a fond smile.

"He's got a good arm, that boy," Henry said. "He ought to play cricket like his father."

"I played for two years, Father, and was never very good," Ian said.

"Watching you was still a joy," his father replied stoutly.

As she tried to picture a younger version of Ian playing cricket—which she knew absolutely nothing about—Samantha was envious suddenly of his life. His parents seemed so genuinely kind and he had two sweet-natured children.

His life hadn't been perfect, she reminded herself. His children had lost their mother, whom Ian had been in the midst of divorcing after she had left him for another man.

She also knew they had lost another brother, David. Gemma had mentioned him once when Samantha had asked about the accident that left her with a slightly uneven gait. Perhaps his death had brought the family closer together.

That's what families should do, she thought. Pull together to share each other's pain, not let their pain turn them bitter and hurtful.

"Tart?" Gemma asked, dragging Sam from her introspection.

"Thank you," she said, taking one of the berry-topped pastries from her friend and completely ignoring the strong possibility that she would perhaps have a hard time fitting into the dress she was to wear to the wedding.

"So, Ian, Samantha tells us she's going as your date to the wedding," Gemma said with a mischievous smile.

"Did you hear that, Henry?" Margaret said. "Ian is taking Samantha as his date to the wedding."

"I'm right here. Of course I heard," his father said gruffly, though he looked pleased at the news, as well.

Ian looked embarrassed, as if he didn't quite know how to respond, so Samantha did it for him.

"It should be a wonderful day," she answered with a smile for both Gemma and Josh. "You two are a great couple. I know the Helping Hands have been working hard on the decorations. I can't wait to see how everything turns out."

"Nor can I," Gemma said. "Everyone here has been so kind, from the moment I arrived in town."

"Because we love you," Samantha said. It was true. Gemma had endeared herself to all of them for her generous heart and her kind soul. Meeting her family gave Sam a very good idea where she had developed those traits.

"Guess what?" Thomas said, rejoining their table. "Aunt Gemma is teaching me how to dance. We've already learned the fox-trot and are working on the waltz."

"And you're a wonderful dancer," Gemma said.

"Excellent news," Henry said. "Dancing is a skill every young gentleman ought to have."

"May I have a dance with you at the wedding, Miss Fremont?" Thomas asked her formally.

She had to smile at the seriousness coming from a boy of six. "I would be honored to dance with you, kind sir. I'll definitely save you a dance."

As the sun finally dropped and the lights came on, they chatted about the wedding and about Lake Haven's history, with Josh filling in the many glaring gaps in Samantha's knowledge about her hometown. All in all, it was a delightful, relaxing evening, one of the most enjoyable she'd had in a long time.

She was so at peace she found herself yawning at one point and flushed when she saw Ian looking.

"Sorry," she mumbled.

"You put in long hours," he said with a smile. "We should get you home."

She didn't want the night to end but knew he was right.

"Do you mind if the children stay overnight at our cottage?" Margaret asked. "We would love to have them. You said you were going out on the lake early in the morning and this way Mrs. Gilbert can sleep in."

"Oh, may we, Dad?" Amelia asked, looking as if she would be crushed if he refused.

Ian looked trapped for a moment but ultimately shrugged. "If you're sure it's no trouble, I'm sure Mrs. Gilbert will be happy if she doesn't have to wake early. Someone here likes to be up at first light."

Thomas raised his hand with an unashamed grin, making all the adults smile.

"I don't mind if you're up early, either of you," Henry assured his grandchildren. "I wanted to take a hike to that waterfall you were telling me about in the morning. As you've already been there with your father and Samantha, you can point me in the right direction."

She hoped Henry knew what he was doing, relying on the children as his wayfinders. As she remembered, Amelia and Thomas hadn't paid much attention to where they were going and had constantly wanted to explore some of the side trails during that trip. She had to hope they all didn't end up hopelessly lost.

"We've things they can sleep in," Margaret said. "Don't worry about that. And we can run them back around lunchtime tomorrow."

"All right," Ian said. "Good night, darling children. Don't keep your grandparents up all night."

Amelia and Thomas both giggled as they hugged their father.

Only as she and Ian headed out to his SUV did Samantha realize the children's sleepover with their grandparents would mean Thomas and Amelia wouldn't be available to provide a buffer between the two of them on the drive home. It was only a short distance, she told herself. She could handle being alone with Ian for the time it would take them to make the trip.

His entire family walked them to his vehicle, as if the two of them were heading out on a grand trek instead of merely driving across town.

He hugged his children again, admonishing them once more to behave for their grandparents, and shook his father's hand.

Samantha was astonished when Margaret hugged her as if they were old and dear friends.

"I'm so happy you could come to dinner," Margaret said. "It's been a delight getting to know you better. What a stroke of luck that Ian ended up renting a house next door to yours."

Good luck or bad? She wasn't sure about that yet. "Thank you for including me in your family dinner," she said.

"Nonsense. It was all in honor of you, for that beautiful dress."

After another round of goodbyes, Ian opened the vehicle door for her and she slipped past him to climb inside, chiding herself for the sudden acceleration of her heartbeat as the scent of him tantalized her senses.

When he climbed into the vehicle, she was again reminded that they were alone, truly alone, for the first time since that devastating kiss the day before.

"Thank you for making time to have dinner with my family," he said as he backed out of the driveway and began driving around the lake. "I know how busy you are. I think it meant a great deal to my mother to be able to raise a glass to you in thanks for your work on Gemma's gown."

"I'm the grateful one," she assured him. "If not for your mother's dinner invitation, I would have been stuck with a frozen dinner and then likely would have spent the evening at my sewing machine and cleaning up after puppies otherwise. This was a vast improvement."

"You work extraordinarily hard."

Was that a criticism or merely an observation? She couldn't quite tell. She decided to take it as the latter. "I feel incredibly lucky to have clients who need wedding dresses and who have asked me to design and sew them."

"Can't you hire someone to help you? Don't you worry about burning out from the sixteen-hour days?"

"Right now, I'm happy to have the business. I have to

hustle while I can. It's probably the same reason you're working on research while you're here with your family."

He looked as if he wanted to say something but they reached her driveway before he could, making her wish she lived a little farther away from Gemma.

He started to turn into her driveway but she held out a hand to stop him. "No need to drop me off here. Park where you usually do and I can walk next door to my house. It makes more sense than you having to move your car again in five minutes."

He appeared reluctant but did as she suggested, parking in his driveway, then walking around to let her out. The night was soft, sweet. Intimate. She found she didn't want to go inside just yet to deal with puppies and work and reality.

He seemed to feel the same reluctance for the night to end. Instead of walking directly next door to her house, they both seemed to move as one toward the dock between their houses.

"Forgive me if this question is out of bounds," he said after a moment. "You can tell me it's none of my business. But do you and Josh have some kind of past?"

"Did he say something to you?" she asked, suddenly mortified.

"No. Nothing," he assured her. "I just thought I picked up some kind of vibe. You were almost overly polite when you talked to him, if that makes sense. You seemed comfortable talking to everyone else but him. But that might have been my imagination. I could be completely misinterpreting the situation. I'm not always the best at picking up social cues."

She shoved her hands in the pockets of her sweater. "You didn't misinterpret anything. I suppose you could call it a history. Josh and I have friends in common, sort of. In a small place like Lake Haven, people around the same age tend to socialize in the same circles. His cousins Katrina and Wynona are my best friends."

"Ah."

She might as well tell him the rest of it. "Yes. Josh and I dated a few times. It was never anything serious."

"Things didn't work out between you? Since the man is about to marry my sister, I would like to ask why. You don't have to tell me, if you feel like it's none of my business."

Her first impulse was to make some kind of excuse about how people didn't always click romantically, even after two or three dates. It was true, as she certainly knew.

That wasn't the whole truth, though, and Samantha found she was reluctant to lie to Ian.

Having grown up with a mother who always spoke her mind, no matter how harmful her thoughts, Samantha had been the recipient of enough slings and digs to know that honesty wasn't always the best policy. Still, she didn't want to hide things from him, especially when he would likely find out the truth, anyway.

She curled her fingers together inside the pockets, choosing her words as carefully as she would thread. "I've already told you that I've made some poor choices when it comes to relationships. I'm not proud of my history. In the past, I've had a terrible habit of jumping from Nice to Meet You to Let's Get Married in about five minutes. That's what happened with Josh, much to my chagrin. We dated a few times after his cousin Wynona's wedding a few years ago and I...wanted things to go faster than he did."

Her face felt hot, her skin stretched tight over her cheekbones. She wanted to disappear into the darkness. Why had she answered him with such blunt honesty? She should have kept her mouth shut and simply answered that after a few dates she and Josh realized they didn't suit.

"You must have cared for him a great deal," Ian said gently.

She couldn't back out of the conversation now. "I thought I did. I imagined I was in love with him, which seems so ridiculous now when I think of it. But unfortunately that wasn't the first or last time. I think I've always been more in love with the idea of being in love, if you know what I mean. It's always provided a kind of escape."

He gave her a sharp look and she again wished she had kept her mouth shut. She didn't need to reveal that to him.

"An escape from what?" he asked, his voice curious.

She sighed. "It doesn't matter."

"I think it matters very much," he said quietly. "I would like to know, if you would like to tell me."

The darkness provided a certain freedom. If not for the night, she wasn't sure she would have been able to tell him the truth.

"I told you that my relationship with my mother wasn't an easy one. Since college, I've dreamed about leaving and going to work somewhere else."

"But you stayed. You didn't even go away for university."

"I did for one semester but it didn't work out. I've always felt a great sense of family obligation since it was only the two of us. She was a single mother for most of my life after my father died and worked very hard to take care of me, and I suppose I felt as if I owed her somehow."

"You have that backward. Children don't owe their parents. It's the other way around."

She could see that now but her mother wouldn't have agreed.

"How old were you when your father died?" he asked after a moment.

"Eight."

"That's a tough age to lose a parent."

"Yes. I don't think I was nearly resilient as Amelia and Thomas seem to be. I'm not sure I've ever really gotten over it."

"How did he die? Do you mind me asking?"

She debated how to answer him. Usually she gave the same sort of answer her mother had given her, that he had been ill. It was easier than explaining what had really happened.

"He killed himself," she said quietly. "My father suffered from clinical depression. One summer night he came out here to this very dock with a handful of painkillers from a surgery he'd had a few years earlier. He swallowed the pills with an entire bottle of gin, passed out and never woke up."

"Oh, Samantha. I'm so sorry." The compassion in his voice made her want to cry suddenly, to howl out her sorrow and loss as she hadn't done for her father in a long time.

He looked as if he wanted to embrace her and she suddenly wanted to sink into his arms, lean her head on his chest and give in to the jagged pain.

Instead, she swallowed hard and took a few steps away from him, sliding down onto the bench where she often came to remember her father.

"As you can imagine, losing her husband like that was hard on my mother. Her personality changed. She changed. It must have been so difficult for her, losing the love of her life that way. I can only imagine how betrayed she must have felt."

"You stayed because you didn't want to abandon her, as well."

She stared at him, struck by the truth of his words. "I... I suppose you're right. I've never really looked at it that way. I stayed. And, quite frankly, I opted for the path of least resistance when it came to dealing with her. It was easier to do what she wanted than deal with the guilt of disappointing her. I suppose that makes me sound horribly weak."

"Not weak," he corrected gently. "You sound like a loving daughter who simply failed to see that the number one job of parents is to prepare their children to go out and conquer the world without them."

"Whether they want to or not."

"*Especially* if they don't want to," he answered.

That was the sort of parent she wanted to be, if the time ever came when she had children. Loving and supportive, yes, but wise, as well.

"That might be a parent's job but it can't be an easy one. How did Henry and Margaret cope when Gemma said she was moving to take a job in another country, especially now that she's making it permanent by marrying Josh?"

He was quiet. "They miss her, especially after losing David. But it's obvious that being here, working at Caine Tech, has been the best thing possible for her."

"It's good that you're only a few hours away from your parents."

"For now," he said.

"What do you mean?"

"We're moving closer to them as soon as we return to England."

"You are? But what about Oxford and your salmon research?"

Ian looked out at the water. "I'm leaving my work behind. My father needs me to help him with the, er, family business."

She stared, sensing there was something he wasn't telling her. "But you love what you do. You can't just walk away from your research, simply to make your father happy."

He gave a stiff-looking smile. "It might seem that way from the outside but the reality is not nearly as clear-cut. My father needs my help."

They were in very similar situations. She could so relate to what he was saying. No one else could understand unless they had experienced it.

Kat, for instance, had been telling her for years to move out and leave her mother behind in Haven Point, but even her best friend hadn't understood all the complicated reasons she had stayed, the murky reality she had been wading through for years.

That fear of abandoning her mother as Lyle had done, which she was only now beginning to realize.

"That's what I always told myself. My mother was older and had health problems. I told myself I was only being a dutiful daughter. If I left, she would have no one. So I stayed, unhappy and dreaming of a different life than the one I had. I suppose dreaming a handsome prince would come and take me away from it so I wouldn't have to make any hard choices on my own."

The stark self-scrutiny made her want to cry again. She blinked the tears away.

"And then she died and I realized I was almost thirty years old and my life has been wasted, waiting for something else."

"Not wasted," he corrected softly. "You have created

a good life here. Friends you care about. A thriving business. Puppies."

"You're right. It is a good life, even though it was designed for me from the time I was a girl. I didn't buy my own clothes until I was in college, if you can believe that. My mother had a very strong personality and I let the force of her consume me. It just seemed easier to go along with what she wanted, all these years."

If her father hadn't killed himself, maybe that overbearing aspect of her mother's personality wouldn't have come out so strongly. Or maybe she and her father together might have been able to keep it in check.

She couldn't believe she had blurted all this out to Ian. She wasn't sure she had ever really been so transparent with anyone, even Kat.

What must he think of her?

"I'm sorry. I didn't mean to dump all of this on you."

"I asked. And I'm glad you told me, that you feel as if you can talk to me."

He reached out and grabbed her hand, his fingers warm against her. She found deep comfort in the contact of skin against skin and wanted to lean her head on his shoulder.

She was doing it again. Falling in love at the drop of a hat.

This time felt different somehow. Ian was different.

He was a good man. A kind one. She had loved seeing him surrounded by his family. His teasing of Gemma, the deep affection for his mother, the clear respect he had for his father.

She could love him very easily.

And end up with her heart broken, she reminded herself, when he walked away in a few weeks to return to his life overseas.

She stepped away from him, hoping a little physical distance would help her regain her equilibrium. His boat brushed against the dock and she seized on the distraction.

"What time do you usually leave in the morning? I often see the boat is gone before I leave for work."

She hoped he didn't guess that she always looked out the sunroom window first thing to see if she could see it moored here.

"Early," he answered. "I try to reach the Chalk Creek mouth before sunrise but don't always make it."

"You must be a very dedicated researcher for that kind of commitment. I hate thinking about you just...walking away from something you obviously care about a great deal."

He shifted in the moonlight and she saw reluctance and a hint of sadness in his eyes. "I don't have a choice, Samantha. I wish I did."

"There's always a choice."

"Not this time. As I said, as soon as we return to England from this trip, the children and I are moving to be closer to my parents. The wheels are already in motion."

He kept his voice carefully impassive but she thought she could hear a strain of sadness underneath.

"You don't want to leave your work, do you?"

"It's not about what I want." His mouth was firm, resolute.

"Ian. Please don't make the mistake I did, going along with what was expected of me simply because it was the easier route."

"It's not the same thing."

"If you don't want to work with your father, stand up for yourself. You love studying salmon and working with your students. Do you really want to throw that away to work in some stuffy office without a window?"

A little smile quirked at his mouth, though she saw it didn't quite reach his eyes. "Whoever said I was heading to a stuffy office without a window?"

"Wild guess. Am I right?"

"Not exactly. But close enough, metaphorically, I suppose."

"If that's not what you want, you need to tell Henry. You only have one chance at life. Why spend it living someone else's dream? Take what you want."

Before the words were out, before she realized what he intended, Ian was reaching for her, his mouth fierce and passionate on hers.

For an instant, she froze, not quite sure where the kiss had come from. This was a side to him she didn't recognize. Fierce, wild, passionate.

Wonderful.

His mouth was firm, determined, on hers, leaving no doubt as to what he wanted. Samantha kissed him back, her heartbeat racing and desire lapping at her like water against the dock.

So much for emotional equilibrium. All her emotions were raw and close to the surface.

She wanted him. Right here, right now. The attraction she had felt for him before had seemed powerful enough but this wild rush of her blood consumed her until she could think of nothing else but being with him.

She wrapped her arms around him, wanting to hold tightly to this man, this moment. The wedding was only a few weeks away and she knew he would be gone shortly after that, out of her life forever.

She couldn't let herself fall in love with him, as she had

done before with alarming regularity, but was it wrong to want to hold on to every moment she could while she had the chance?

SHE HAD TOLD him to take what he wanted and her words had triggered something deep within him.

She was what he wanted.

All evening, he had been fighting against the hunger prowling through him like a caged beast. Every time he looked at her while she laughed at something his father said or smiled at a joke Amelia made or listened, deep in conversation, to his mother and Gemma, he had wanted to grab her by the hand, tug her into the darkness and kiss her just like this.

He wanted to kiss her until she was making those soft, sexy sounds in her throat, until her heart beat as rapidly as his, until neither of them could remember all the reasons why they shouldn't be doing this.

What was it about her that turned him from a staid, rather boring professor to a man consumed by hunger?

The salmon he studied had a biological imperative to return to the waters of their birth to spawn. They could cross hundreds of miles to do it, swimming upstream against fierce currents, leaping up vast waterfalls.

For the first time in his life, after more than a decade of research, Ian began to understand the wild need that drove them.

When she pressed her soft curves against him, he lost all sense of reason. She kissed him with a hunger that seemed to match his own, her mouth tasting of strawberry tarts and the wine Gemma had served at dinner. It was an intoxicating combination that kept him returning to her mouth again and again.

Over her summer dress, she had put on the little jumper she'd brought along against the evening chill and he slid his hands beneath it to the warm, silky skin of her back. She shivered and made another of those sexy sounds that seemed to cut away all his restraints like a rigging knife on a bowline.

He wanted to make love to her. Right here on the dock, if he had to, or on his research boat, which bobbed softly on the waves. He wanted to be inside her, to feel that soft body arch against him, to lick and taste and savor all her hidden, delicious spots...

Some sort of lake creature splashed offshore, a small sound in the night but enough to jolt him back to his senses.

What was he doing?

Ian wrenched his mouth away from Samantha's, his breathing harsh.

He couldn't remember wanting anything as badly as he wanted Samantha Fremont in that moment.

She had shared with him deep pain from her childhood, and five minutes later he was kissing her like a prat who could only think about one thing.

Usually he prided himself on his control, his unfailing ability always to say and do the right thing in the right circumstances. Yet here he was, a heartbeat away from breaking all his rules and seducing this lovely, sweet, vulnerable American girl.

Good Lord. He had been willing to make love to her on a wooden dock, without any thought to privacy or dignity or, at the very least, comfort. Think of the splinters.

All right, yes, she had kissed him back. That didn't excuse his actions. He was mortified with himself at the lack of control, even while a large part of him was more than a little regretful that he had somehow found the strength of will to stop.

She gazed at him, eyes wide in the moonlight while she tried to catch her breath. He wanted to kiss her all over again, that charming cleft in her chin, the dimple that appeared only on the left side of her mouth when she smiled, those perfectly arched brows.

He wanted to kiss her everywhere.

He released a heavy sigh. "We are apparently a dangerous combination, Ms. Fremont."

"I fear you are correct, Mr. Summerhill."

He should probably correct her. Tell her the truth. Everything would be so much easier if he truly was still merely Mr. Summerhill.

He couldn't do it. Not yet. He had promised Gemma, for one thing. For another, he wanted to forget the rest of it for a few more weeks at least.

Instead, he rested his forehead on hers. "This is madness between us. I've never known anything like this heat we seem to generate."

"Neither have I," she said, her voice small.

"I'm leaving in only two weeks' time." Was he reminding her or himself? He wasn't sure.

Her smile seemed a little sad but it slid away as she reached on tiptoe to kiss him softy. He closed his eyes, pushing away the heat to focus only on the sweet, seductive whisper of her mouth on his.

"I know," she murmured. "And neither one of us is in the market for a summer fling. We've both made that clear."

He had moved far beyond the idea of a fling with Samantha. This seemed like so very much more. Somehow, when he wasn't paying attention, this woman had become vitally important to his world.

How on earth would he be able to say goodbye to her when this summer idyll ended?

"Neither of us needs a broken heart right now," she was saying.

"No. True enough."

"I've just told you that I have a very bad tendency to think I'm in love after just one or two dates. I can't lose my head over you, Ian."

"We wouldn't want that," he murmured, though he wanted that very much right now.

"So why don't we agree that we will just spend the rest of the time you're living next door as friends?" she suggested. "The children are still welcome to come over and help me with the puppies. We can still go together to Gemma's wedding. But it would be better for both of us if we refrain from any more of…this kind of thing."

This kind of thing was rapidly becoming an obsession for him. Only now in the intimacy of the night could he admit it to himself. This desire for her had been simmering inside him for a long time. He dreamed about holding her; he ached for it. He thought about it every time he looked out the window and saw her house next door.

Yes. She was absolutely correct. They had to refrain from these moonlight encounters beside the lake.

"I'm sorry," he murmured, not sure what else to say and wishing fiercely that things could be different.

"No. Don't apologize, Ian. We did nothing wrong. But you have to see that this is a mistake for both of us right now."

He might know that intellectually but the knowledge didn't make it any easier to drag himself away from her.

"I do see that. And you're absolutely right."

Her sigh echoed through the night, soft and filled with regret. The sound almost made him want to grab her, press her against a tree and kiss her until they both lost their senses and gave in to the heat between them.

Sometimes being a man of honor sincerely sucked. As much as he might want to take advantage of her regret, he couldn't do that, for her sake or for his own.

She turned toward her house, a clear signal he couldn't miss. He caught up with her after a few steps and walked her to the door, waiting as she unlocked it and slipped through the doorway.

"Good night," he said, mostly because he couldn't think of anything else to say.

She looked inside her house, then back at him. He could see she was going through the same internal struggle he was, torn between wisdom and desire.

"One more kiss probably wouldn't hurt," she said, not quite meeting his gaze.

She didn't need to say another word before he lowered his mouth, drinking her in. The door slammed shut behind her but neither of them noticed, lost in each other.

That single kiss turned into another and then another. Finally, more aroused than he remembered being in his life, he stepped away, knowing distance was his only saving grace.

"Walking away from you right now might be the hardest thing I've ever done," he admitted.

"I wish you didn't have to, but it's…it's probably for the best."

He wasn't entirely convinced of that.

"I need to say one more thing before you go. It…feels

important somehow. I don't know if that's only because I need to say it or because you need to hear it."

"Go ahead," he said warily.

She shocked him by returning to their conversation of earlier. "Your father isn't unreasonable, Ian. I only had one evening's worth of conversation with him, but on initial impression, I liked him very much. I'm sure he'll be disappointed if you don't follow in his footsteps but he loves you and I can't believe he wants you to work with him at the expense of your own dreams. He wouldn't want you to be unhappy."

If only the situation were that simple. Ian knew how deeply Henry still grieved for David, not only because he understood a father's love for his son but because Henry knew what his death meant for Ian. Neither of them had a choice and they both knew it.

Those out of the system didn't always understand primogeniture, the complicated, mostly archaic inheritance laws of the British nobility.

Henry couldn't live forever. He needed an heir and Thomas, next in line, was simply too young for the attendant responsibilities that went along with it.

Ian was prepared to do his duty. After a few years, he knew he would probably even begin to enjoy it. His father was a good, responsible land steward who treated everyone fairly and with kindness. Ian would try to follow in his footsteps.

He would do his best to learn all he needed to know before becoming the Earl of Amherst. The earldom and its attendant responsibilities might never be his passion as they had been David's, but Ian intended to fulfill his responsibilities to the best of his ability.

He loved his family far more than he loved a few salmon.

"Talk to your father," she urged. "Tell him what's in your heart."

The things in his heart right now concerned Samantha and his growing feelings for her, things his father didn't need to know anything about.

"Thank you for the advice," he said. Despite the impossibility of it, he was touched she was concerned about his future. "Good night, Samantha. Sweet dreams."

She gave a raw-sounding laugh that somehow matched everything he was feeling inside, then slipped into her house.

He watched her go, knowing his own dreams that night would be filled with the scent and taste and wonder of Samantha Fremont.

CHAPTER TWELVE

SHE DIDN'T SEE Ian for several days after the dinner with his family and the revelations and heated kisses that followed.

It was for the best, she told herself. She was too busy right now to worry about her growing feelings for him.

The puppies had unfortunately discovered they could chew things other than their toys and each other's tails. The wooden knobs on her mother's dresser had been catastrophes, as had the edging of one of the old blankets she had put into their playroom.

She was trying to finish Margaret's dress. In addition, two more brides—one from Shelter Springs and one from clear over in Meridian—had come to the shop requesting custom wedding dresses. This brought her current orders for the next six months to eleven, a number that filled her with panic whenever she thought of it.

By Thursday, she wanted to climb into her bed, pull the covers over her head and block out the world. Instead, she came home from work and hurried to finish the vegetable tray she was taking to Eliza Caine's house.

Eliza was hosting a party at Snow Angel Cove that night, a shower for Gemma Summerhill.

She considered two social events in one week about two too many with her plate so overflowing, but since she loved Gemma, she would make it work.

As she walked to the back terrace of Snow Angel Cove

a short time later with her gift in one hand and the vegetable tray in the other, she looked around at all the friends gathered and decided the effort in this case was more than worth it.

A chorus of hellos greeted her arrival, each one buoying her more. Katrina immediately came over to take the vegetable tray from her and hand her a glass of wine.

"I need you to drink this," she said under her breath. "I'm not ready to tell everyone about the baby yet, but I couldn't figure out how to refuse when McKenzie handed it to me."

"Sure. I'll take one for Team Callahan."

"You're definitely the godmother," Katrina said, grinning as Sam took the wineglass from her.

The Helping Hands had outdone themselves on the decorations. A huge balloon arch greeted those coming to the shower and six round tables all held more balloons and luxurious-looking flowers.

"I can take your present to the pile," Katrina offered, and Sam handed over the machine-embroidered pillowcases she had made for Gemma and Josh, then made her way to the circle of women who were chatting about their summer plans.

She found an empty chair next to Charlene Bailey, who beamed with pleasure when she spotted her.

"Oh, Samantha. I've been thinking of you this week. How are you doing, honey?"

It took her a moment to register why Charlene would be looking at her with concern. Her mother's birthday would have been the week before. Of course Charlene would remember that. She was always the first to keep birthdays and anniversaries in mind.

"Better," she said, which was mostly the truth, even as she suddenly had to blink away tears.

Katrina's mother had always been the warm and loving mom Sam had dreamed of when she was a girl. Charlene was kind, supportive, fun. Sam had been drawn to the Bailey home through much of her childhood, probably because of that.

Oh, Charlene wasn't the perfect mom. Far from it. She had actually been a little suffocating of Katrina because of the epileptic seizures her friend had suffered from when she was younger. Still, Charlene had always opened their home to Sam and treated her like another of her children.

The family had not been untouched by tragedy. First Katrina's older brother, Wyatt, had died in a winter storm after being hit by a car while working as a state highway patrolman. Then the family patriarch, John Bailey, the longtime police chief of Haven Point, had been gravely injured in a shootout, leaving him with severe disabilities for the short remainder of his life.

The two surviving brothers, Marshall and Elliot, and Katrina and her sister, Wynona, had become closer than ever through those hardships. She deeply admired the strength they had demonstrated and wished she could emulate it. Look at her. It had been nearly six months since her mother's death and she still felt like a mess inside, going all emotional over a birthday.

"I'm doing fine," she said now in answer to Charlene. "I've finally started to get used to not seeing her working the cash register at the store."

Charlene hugged her. For a moment, Sam was tempted to rest her head on the woman's shoulder and absorb the love and caring.

"I miss her, too," Charlene said.

"The town doesn't seem the same without Linda," added Barbara Serrano.

She could feel tears burn at her friends' compassion but blinked them away and sat down, taking a healthy sip of her secondhand wine.

"Since your mother isn't here, it's up to us to give you the third degree in her absence," Charlene said sternly.

"You don't have to, really. I'm good."

They ignored her, as she fully expected. "What's this we hear about you spending time with Gemma's brother?" Barbara teased.

"You have to watch out for those handsome men from over the pond," Lindy-Grace Keegan said with a laugh.

To her relief, Gemma and Margaret were busy talking with Julia Caine, Megan Bailey and Elizabeth Hamilton on the other side of the terrace, out of earshot of this embarrassing conversation.

"That one can cross my pond any time he wants," Eppie's sister, Hazel, piped up.

Sam caught Katrina's gaze and felt a giggle rise up. Hazel was over eighty, after all, and long a widow.

"Must you be so crass all the time?" her sister, Eppie, chided quietly. "It's quite unbecoming at our age."

She rarely heard such sharpness between the two of them. Usually they spoke in tandem.

"I'm so sorry to offend you," Hazel said, sounding not at all contrite. "I guess you've become a prude in your old age. I'd still like to know if there's something going on with our Samantha and Gemma's hunky brother."

"No," Samantha said quickly, her cheeks heating as Gemma and their mother approached their group.

It was clear immediately that Gemma, at least, had overheard the last part of the conversation. "That's not precisely true, is it, Samantha? She is going to the wedding as his plus-one," Gemma told the older ladies.

"Really?" Julia Caine asked, looking pleased.

Oh, Gemma had done it now. Her friends would hound Sam all night about Ian if she didn't figure out how to divert the conversation.

"Gemma, have you decided where you're going on your honeymoon?" she asked with steady determination.

Katrina gave her a sympathetic look and lent a helping hand to the effort. "Yes. Last I heard it was a big secret. But we need details. *All* the details."

"Josh has kept everything a big secret and I only found out myself a few days ago. I suppose I can tell you all now that the wedding is only a week away. Also, how can it be only a week away?"

For an instant, Gemma looked slightly panicked until her mother squeezed her arm, which seemed to steady her.

"Right. Well, he has a friend with a luxe cabin in Alaska. We're being flown in by a bush pilot, who will leave us for an entire week with a fully stocked refrigerator."

"Oh, wow. You had me at fully stocked refrigerator," Andie Bailey said with a laugh. "I'm so tired of cooking dinner."

"Right? Why do they need to eat every single day?" Devin Barrett said with a sigh.

"You didn't have to cook dinner tonight, though," Eliza said. "We've got a fabulous meal in store and then cake. So much cake. Shall we get started?"

By the time they finished eating under the globe lights strung across the terrace, Sam forgot she was ever reluctant to come to the shower. The evening had reminded her of all the things she loved about living in Haven Point. Laughter, good food, cherished friends.

Gemma seemed similarly touched. When she opened the gifts, many of them handmade, she even wept a little.

As people started preparing to leave, particularly some of the older women, she asked for a moment to address them all.

"You've all been so wonderful. Thank you. From the moment I came to Haven Point, you have all embraced and welcomed me and I am grateful beyond words. Thank you for the gifts. I shall use and cherish them all."

"Even the dishwashing scrubbers Eppie and I crocheted for you?" Hazel called out.

She laughed. "Even that. I'm sure Josh will put them to good use. When I took a job here at Caine Tech, I was running away from some fairly painful things in my past. It turns out that instead of escaping, I was really running *to* something beautiful. This is exactly where I belong, in large part because of the friends I've made here."

Sam sent a swift look at Margaret, wondering how Gemma's mother handled her daughter finding a new home and friends halfway across the world. Margaret seemed emotional, but Samantha somehow sensed she was also happy that her daughter had found acceptance and love here.

It was hard not to compare that to Linda's likely reaction under similar circumstances. Linda hadn't even been able to bear the idea of Samantha moving away for college in Boise, two hours away. How would she have endured if Samantha had moved to another country?

She would have pouted and thrown a tantrum for a week or two and then would have been accepted the inevitable.

It was a startling realization, another reminder that in

some ways she most likely had been too hard on her mother when Linda had still been alive. Her mother hadn't been completely unreasonable.

The shower began to break up after that. As she had been working and hadn't been able to assist in the decorating, Samantha stepped up to help clean up.

"You don't need to do that," Eliza assured her after Samantha carried a load of dishes to the gourmet kitchen. "The caterer has it under control."

"Is there something else I can do, then?"

"Gemma might need help carrying gifts out to her car," Eliza suggested.

Samantha filled her arms with gift bags, then headed around the house to the porte cochere out front.

As she approached, she heard Margaret and Gemma talking.

"I had a wonderful time," Margaret was telling Gemma. "All your friends are truly lovely."

"Aren't they?"

Samantha couldn't see her friend but could hear the happiness in her voice.

"I like them," Margaret replied. "Which makes me wonder why you're still hiding the truth from everyone."

Sam froze at Margaret's sudden sharp tone, so much like something she might have heard from her own mother before Linda would go on a tirade.

"Don't, Mother. Not tonight," Gemma said softly.

Margaret didn't heed her. "Don't you think it's only fair you stop hiding who you are?"

"I'm not hiding anything," Gemma said, her voice so low Sam almost couldn't hear it. "This is who I am now. I'm a computer nerd working for Caine Tech. And I'm happy to be that."

"That's only part of it. Try as you might to hide it, you're also Lady Gemma Summerhill. Daughter of the Earl and Countess of Amherst and sister to Lord Ian Summerhill, Viscount Summersby."

Sam almost dropped the gift bags. Her heart began to pound so hard she couldn't understand why Gemma and her mother didn't turn around at the sound.

"Nobody cares about that here, Mother," Gemma said firmly.

Oh, she was so very wrong. Samantha cared. The chasm between her and Ian had just widened until it now stretched farther than Lake Haven Valley.

He was a peer. His father was an earl. She knew enough about the peerage from the historical romance novels she loved reading to know that since Ian's older brother had died, he must now be his father's heir.

Why hadn't he told her? He had let her make a fool of herself over him, knowing all the time that any relationship between them was utterly impossible.

How could the future Earl of Whatever the Heck Margaret Had Said pursue anything with a dressmaker from a tiny town in Idaho?

What did it matter? This news changed nothing. So what if he was Viscount Summersby and would one day become a freaking earl? She was still exactly where she had been five minutes ago, before she found out the truth.

She had always known anything between her and Ian was impossible. This only confirmed exactly how impossible.

Sam wanted to cry suddenly. The tears burned hot and no amount of blinking them back could prevent one or two from slipping out.

Oh, she was stupid. No matter how mature she told

herself she had become, inside she was still Starry-eyed Sam, who fell in love with every guy who was nice to her.

Love. Who said anything about love? She wasn't in love with Ian. She was attracted to him, yes, and she liked him very much. But she couldn't possibly be in love with him.

So why did she feel shattered to learn exactly why they could never be together?

The two glasses of wine and the chocolate lava cake she'd had early in the evening seemed to churn through her and she thought for a moment she would be sick. She swallowed down the bile. This was silly. She was stronger than this.

Nothing had changed. Gemma was still her friend and deserved her support.

She slipped back inside the house. When she walked out a second time, she closed the door loudly behind her. Margaret and Gemma stopped their argument immediately, though she could feel the tension between them.

"Oh, darling," Margaret exclaimed when she saw her. "Thank you so much for helping us carrying things out. We were just trying to make room in the boot of Gemma's tiny little car. We should have thought things through and had Josh drive us in his big, macho pickup truck so we could carry everything home."

"I'm sure Eliza wouldn't mind if you needed to leave a few things here overnight," Sam managed with a cheerful smile as fake as Roxie Nash's lip implants.

"We can at least fit in these few things. Thank you for carrying them out," Gemma said.

Was that a searching look her friend was giving her? Was Gemma wondering how much of their conversation she had overheard? She didn't want to reveal that she knew the truth now. Gemma would tell them all when she was ready.

"You're welcome. I can take a load of gifts to your house, if you need help carrying things."

"We should be fine. I think I can fit most of it."

"Great. I'll wait before carrying out any more gifts until you figure out how much room you'll have."

"Thanks," Gemma said.

Sam hurried into the house. She wanted to find her purse and her car keys and slink away into the night but she knew her friends would find that behavior suspicious. As she slipped back to the terrace, she did her best to mask the sadness that had settled over her like a dingy cloud.

Nothing had changed, she told herself again. She only had one more reason to forget about her growing feelings for Ian Summerhill.

Everything suddenly seemed to make a grim sort of sense. She remembered their conversation the last time she had talked to him, the despair in his eyes as he had talked about moving closer to his parents and about helping his father with the family businesses.

He hadn't been talking about some kind of commercial endeavor. He meant all the assorted business that must come from being an earl.

The family must have land and holdings that needed care.

Some of her shock began to trickle away, replaced by a growing compassion. Poor Ian. He was a biology professor who loved his work and his students. He couldn't have feigned that. He didn't want to give up his research, but had talked about having no choice but to help his father.

He had seemed so sad the last time they had spoken.

And she had tried to offer advice about talking to his father about what he really wanted.

He couldn't do that. He was as trapped by obligation as she had felt all her life. Compassion seeped through her, along with lingering hurt.

He should have told her the truth. She would have understood. Knowing he was the heir to an earldom certainly would have kept her from spinning ridiculous fantasies she didn't even want to acknowledge.

CHAPTER THIRTEEN

HE DIDN'T WANT the summer to end.

Ian sat on what was becoming his favorite spot, the bench on the edge of the dock in Samantha's garden, watching his research boat bob on the small waves and listening to the night creatures hoot and splash around him.

Gemma's wedding was only a week away now and he and the children would be leaving a few days after that. Every time he thought about flying back to Oxford and packing up their things to move home to Summerhill House, he felt claustrophobic, as if he were drowning in those deep, dark waters of the lake, the air slowly seeping out of his lungs.

He sighed, forcing himself to breathe through the sensation until calm returned. He wasn't drowning. He was doing the responsible thing. The inevitable one.

A light came on inside Samantha's house, shining across the expanse of lawn through her windows.

That ache in his chest seemed to come back, the yearning for something he couldn't have.

For her.

Why couldn't Gemma have hired someone from England to design her wedding dress? Some matronly older woman with a squint and a pencil stuck behind her ear?

And why couldn't he have found another house to rent for the summer, somewhere far away from her? If he had never met Samantha Fremont, then he wouldn't have this ache in his chest at the idea of leaving her.

He couldn't blame Gemma or the real estate agent who had led him here for the feelings growing inside him. He could blame no one but himself. He had known she was trouble the first time he spoke with her and he had fallen headlong, anyway.

No sense brooding about it, Ian told himself. He stood to go back inside his own rental house when he saw Samantha's back door open. A moment later, she walked down her back steps with her little dog on a leash.

He knew the moment she spotted him. She stopped in her tracks and looked torn, as if she wanted to return to the house. After a moment, she seemed to reconsider and resumed walking toward the dock.

"We have a bad habit of meeting like this."

Was this the reason he had lingered out here, long after he should have gone back inside? Was he hoping she would come out to join him?

Yes, he admitted. He had missed her deeply these past few days and had thought of a hundred things he wanted to tell her when he next saw her.

Now all of those things seemed to have floated away across the lake like so much cottonwood fluff.

"How was the bridal shower?"

She gave him a long look that suddenly set him on edge. "Interesting."

"In what way? Or do I want to know?"

For a long moment, he didn't think she would answer. Finally she gave a small, almost imperceptible sigh and settled next to him on the bench.

The air was suddenly luscious with the scent of her, strawberry and vanilla and Samantha. The moon passed between clouds, gleaming on the water as small breakers lapped against the dock.

"I suppose there's no point in dancing around it."

"Dancing around what?" He had a sudden premonition of danger, though he couldn't have said exactly why.

She met his gaze. "I overheard your mother and Gemma talking. I didn't mean to eavesdrop. I was helping carry gifts out to the car after the party and they were talking. I don't think they knew anyone was there."

He couldn't imagine what his mother and sister might have said to spark this strange mood. "Is everything okay?"

She met his gaze. "You tell me, Lord Ian."

There it was, exactly what he had been dreading.

He sighed. "Ah."

"Yes. *Ah.* I thought you were simply a rather adorable distracted scientist. The classic rumpled university professor. Why didn't you tell me the truth?"

He stumbled for a moment, transfixed that she had called him adorable. Is that truly what she thought?

Not really the point, he reminded himself.

"I couldn't tell you, for a few reasons."

"From what I overheard, I'm guessing Gemma asked you not to."

"That was part of it."

"I don't understand why all the secrecy. Why would she think anyone in Haven Point would care whether she was Lady Gemma or plain old Gemma?"

"I think her reasons had more to do with herself than anyone here. She wanted to forget, I think. Make a new start. Our brother's death affected her more than any of us realized, beyond her obvious physical injuries. I was busy with Susan's cancer amid the ugliness of our divorce and my parents were battling with their own grief. None of us noticed how Gem was struggling until she announced she was taking a job overseas."

"Poor thing."

"Yes." He shifted, feeling guilty that he hadn't seen Gemma's pain because his own had obscured it.

"I gather she wanted to make a new start, unencumbered by her title. Apparently she ran into some professional difficulties at a previous job and chose not to use it here. She planned to tell everyone after the wedding but didn't want it to become any kind of issue beforehand. We discussed it as a family and opted to follow her wishes while we were here."

He wasn't sure if she believed him. The darkness made it difficult to tell.

Why did they always seem to meet out here on the dock at night? It had become their own private spot.

"The other reason I didn't tell you," he said honestly, "is because, like Gemma, I prefer to forget it myself."

Before David's death, as the second son to the earl, he had been the Honorable Ian Summerhill but had never used that honorific in his academic or professional career. Oh, it was hard to hide completely. Word tended to get around in most circles, but he wanted to think he had earned his place on his merits, on his scientific achievements, not on a bloodline that had been an accident of birth.

"That's the reason you're leaving science behind, isn't it? When your brother died, you became the heir to your father's title."

The sadness in her voice matched his own so perfectly that he had to fight the urge to pull her into his arms.

"I never expected to inherit and was always allowed to pursue my own interests. When David died, everything changed."

"Three years ago. I never made the connection. Did your brother die before or after Susan left?"

She was too clever for her own good. "You picked up on that, did you? After, if you want the truth. David died about six months after Susan had left me. When she learned I was now Viscount Summersby instead of plain Professor Summerhill, she tried to come back, said she'd made a terrible mistake and would I forgive her."

"I hope you told her to shove off."

He smiled. "Not in so many words. But I didn't take her back, of course. Not then, anyway."

"But you let her come live with you after she was diagnosed with cancer."

"What else was I to do? She needed care."

She was quiet for a long moment. When she spoke again, her voice was low. "You're an extraordinary man, Ian Summerhill. Or Lord Ian. Or Viscount Summersby. I don't know what to call you."

"Just Ian," he murmured. Though he now had a hundred more reasons not to do it, he couldn't help himself. He had to kiss her.

Unlike the urgency and heat of their previous kiss here, this one was soft, tender, but no less moving.

Each time he kissed her was a revelation, a new discovery of uncharted territory. He wondered if it would always be that way. Something told him it would, that he could spend a lifetime exploring different ways to kiss Samantha Fremont and would never grow bored.

This time, she was the one who pulled away.

"We have to stop." Her voice was thready, aroused.

He couldn't seem to gather his thoughts. He didn't want to stop, ever. He wanted to spend the rest of his life kissing her here in the moonlight.

Her head was obviously in a different space altogether. While he was still aching and aroused, she stood, breathing hard. She still had her dog's leash in her hand, he realized.

"I can't keep doing this with you, Ian. Surely you can see that. I have spent my entire adult life being an idiot where men are concerned. I fall for the guys who are completely unavailable. I can't believe I'm doing it all over again."

He was being altogether unfair to her. He had known it from the first time he kissed her.

He felt like the worst sort of ass.

"I'm sorry. I can't seem to help myself when I'm around you. All logic seems to desert me. I hope you know I wouldn't intentionally hurt you."

"I know." She gripped her dog's leash more tightly. "You're a good man, Ian. I… I wish things could be different. Why couldn't you simply be a rumpled biologist, obsessed with stinky fish?"

"That would have been much better," he agreed. While he might be embarrassed at her description of him, that didn't make him any less entranced by her. "I wish that were the case, more than I can ever tell you."

Her features softened. "I know," she murmured. Then, generous soul that she was, Samantha hugged him again, resting her head against his chest. She held him for a long time while the night settled around them.

Finally she lifted her head and kissed his cheek before gripping her little dog's leash and heading back into her house.

SAMANTHA HELPED BETSEY back into the room with the puppies, then couldn't resist sitting on the floor. Oscar and

Calvin immediately waddled to her, licking her until she picked them both up.

They were growing so fast. They were mostly weaned now, only turning to their mother when they needed comfort.

Samantha was the one who needed comfort now. She cuddled the puppies close, feeling their heartbeats.

Oh, she was such a fool. Had she learned nothing from twenty-eight years on the planet? How could she still be making such utterly stupid mistakes when it came to men?

She had known from the beginning that Ian Summerhill wasn't for her. The roadblocks had been obvious from the first. Any other woman would have been wise enough to stay away from him, to protect herself better. Not her. She tumbled headlong the first chance she had.

She hadn't changed a bit from the silly, immature girl who had told her high school boyfriend she loved him the first time he kissed her.

Hot, frustrating tears trickled out. Oscar tried to lick them away, which made her smile but didn't ease the pain in her heart at all.

For once, at least, she had given her heart to a man who fully deserved it. She ought to get a few points for that, right? Unlike many of the guys she had previously dated, Ian was mature, compassionate, dedicated to his family and passionate about his career.

Any woman would have been crazy not to fall for him.

She should have tried harder, though.

What was she going to do? He was a peer of the freaking British realm. He wasn't the kind of guy who would fall for someone like her, a seamstress from a tiny nowhere town in Idaho who had seen very little of the world.

She was destined for heartbreak, could see no way to avoid the train wreck headed her way.

The wedding was only a week away and then Ian and the children would be on their way back to England. Meantime, she would simply have to figure out how she would navigate the rest of her life without them.

So much loss. She hugged the puppies closer—yet another loss in her immediate future—and wondered where she would find the strength to endure it all.

CHAPTER FOURTEEN

THE DAYS LEADING up to Gemma Summerhill's wedding to Josh Bailey turned into some of the busiest of Samantha's life.

The store seemed constantly filled with customers. Samantha couldn't help any of them and had to leave their shopping to her assistants. She was too busy taking care of a flurry of last-minute alterations, orders for three more wedding gowns and fittings for two of the brides who were planning to marry in dresses she had designed.

At least the frenetic pace helped distract Samantha from the underlying heartache, but throughout her busy days and empty nights, she was aware of a dull, constant ache in her chest.

She hadn't seen Ian since those moments by the lake. She wasn't sure if they were simply on differing schedules or if he was purposely avoiding her.

This was the day Margaret had come into the store to pick up her altered dress and Sam waited with bated breath while she tried it on and looked at herself in the trio of full-length mirrors.

"Does it work for you?" she finally had to ask.

Margaret looked enchanted. "It's gorgeous. Utterly gorgeous. I can't believe it's the same dress. How on earth did you manage that particular miracle?"

"I had a good quality dress to start with. That helped

tremendously. The dress was fine at the outset. It had to be or you wouldn't have purchased it in the first place. It just wasn't quite right for you. I only had to make a few changes, really, to help it fit your style and body type better. I love the drape of the fabric and it's a beautiful color for you."

"Yes. I believe I shall wear this exact shade from now until eternity."

Oh, she liked Ian's mother so much. His entire family charmed her.

"What do I owe for your work?" Margaret asked after she had changed out of her dress and back into her slacks and white tailored blouse.

Samantha greatly disliked this part of running a store. If she had her way, she would sew for free and give everyone all the dresses. But she couldn't live on benevolence. She had dog food to buy.

She handed the invoice she had already prepared for Margaret. Ian's mother looked at it, then shook her head. "That little? That can't be right. Even with the horrible exchange rate, that's a steal."

"That's my rate, Margaret. Take it or leave it," she said, then suddenly remembered something she had been trying hard to forget. "Oh. I'm sorry. I suppose I should have been calling you Lady Margaret all this time."

Margaret raised a finely arched eyebrow. "That is a closely guarded secret here in Haven Point. More closely guarded than Barbara Serrano's red sauce recipe, and believe me, I've tried to get it out of her since I've been here. Did Ian tell you?"

She shook her head, embarrassed. "I overheard you and Gemma talking the night of the shower. I wasn't eavesdropping on purpose, I promise. It just happened. I'm sorry I invaded your privacy."

Margaret gave a dismissive gesture. "I think it's silly for Gemma to be concerned about people finding out the truth. Who cares about that here? But she has her reason."

"That's what Ian told me. Lord Ian, I suppose I should say."

She was afraid some of her misery must have filtered through her voice, especially when Margaret gave her a close look. "Yes. Lord Ian. Every time I hear that, I'm still shaken a little. None of us expected him to become Viscount Summersby, you know. His brother was always supposed to be the heir."

"That's what he told me. I'm so sorry for your loss."

Margaret's mouth tightened. "No parent should have to endure the loss of a child. It is against the natural order of things, pain beyond measure."

Sympathy welled up for the other woman and she couldn't help reaching out and squeezing Margaret's hand. The other woman surprised her by turning her hand over and gripping Samantha's hand in hers.

"All of us have been impacted in various ways. I'm not sure Henry will ever recover, to be honest. He misses David fiercely. Gemma suffered greatly, physically and emotionally, since she was driving and blamed herself, though it was no fault of her own. But Ian. He and David were very close. He not only lost his best friend but his way of life, really. His whole profession. He has to give up so much."

"Why does he have to? Can't Lord Henry find someone else to handle his business concerns and leave Ian to pursue what he loves?"

Margaret sighed. "I wish it were that easy. I truly do.

His father has given him as much time as possible during Susan's illness, even extending that for a year to help the children through their grief. But I'm afraid time is running out."

She gave Samantha a careful look. "What has Ian told you about his wife?"

She wasn't sure how to answer that question. Did his parents know the truth?

"He told me they were in the process of divorcing when she was diagnosed with cancer," she said carefully.

"I tried to love her, for Ian's sake and for the children. I truly did. She had her good points, though as time goes on it is becoming harder and harder for me to remember those. But I could never forgive her for hurting my son and my grandchildren. Even as she was dying, I couldn't forgive her. Does that make me a terrible person?"

"I think it makes you human," Samantha said. "I'm not sure I could, either."

Margaret was quiet for a moment, then finally released Sam's hand, leaving her feeling a little bereft.

"I don't know what your relationship with Ian is. I'm not going to pry, as he would be the first to tell me it's none of my business. But I must tell you that since he's been here, my son seems happier than I've seen him in years. He smiles more, he laughs, he even teases his sister. Something tells me that's down to you."

"Maybe he's just enjoying being here in Haven Point, working on his research."

"That could be part of it. The rest, I think, is you."

Samantha didn't know how to answer that. Couldn't Margaret see how impossible anything was between Sam and her son?

She supposed it didn't matter what Margaret saw or

didn't see. Samantha knew they could never be together. No matter how much she might wish otherwise.

THE SATURDAY OF Gemma's wedding looked as if it was going to be one of those absolutely perfect Haven Point June days.

The temperatures were mild, the lake breeze sweet and the sky was a pure, gorgeous blue, with only a few puffy white clouds passing across for contrast.

Sam spent the morning at the store, finishing a dress she was making for a bride from Shelter Springs, then left everything in the capable hands of Rachel Muñoz after lunch so she could go home and dress for the ceremony.

When she arrived, she found the puppies had somehow opened one of the drawers of her mother's sewing machine and pulled out all the spools of thread. They were now tangled in a brightly colored mess.

"Oh, no! You rascals," she exclaimed, and hurried for her scissors to cut them free.

The puppies were becoming so active it was hard to keep them contained in one room. They were completely weaned now and Betsey was spending more and more time away from them.

They were ready for their forever homes, but was she ready to say goodbye? That was the question, she thought as Coco snuggled against her leg while Sam cut away at green thread wrapped around her paws.

She didn't worry about their futures. Charlene Bailey was taking Oscar, Lindy-Grace Keegan wanted Coco for her boys and little Calvin was going to Ben McKenzie's mother, Lydia.

She knew they would all be loved and cared for in their

new homes but it didn't make the idea of parting from them any easier.

With the puppies settled once more and all the thread cleaned up, she finally closed the door and headed in to get ready for the wedding.

She had a date, after all.

The doorbell rang just as she was finishing her makeup.

Her stomach quivered with anticipation. If she had missed Ian and the children this much after only a few days, how would she cope once he was back in England and out of her life?

She checked her image in the mirror, feeling a little like a princess heading to the ball in her prettiest dress. Only she supposed she was the fairy godmother and the busy little mice, too, since she had made this one herself.

She had designed her dress to be elegant but understated, a simple column of the palest turquoise, tea-length with capped sleeves.

She had chosen to wear her hair simply to match the lines of the dress, in a French twist that accentuated her neckline and collarbone and showed her earrings to good effect.

Heart pounding, she hurried to the front door. She expected only Ian and was delighted to find Amelia and Thomas standing on either side of him.

"Hello." She managed a smile, though she felt slightly giddy.

"Hi."

He hadn't taken his eyes off her since she opened the door. Sam met his gaze and couldn't look away, trying not to shiver at his hot stare. She wasn't sure how long they stood in the doorway gazing at each other. Fortunately, Thomas broke the silence.

"Hullo," Thomas said. "We're here to take you to Aunt Gemma's wedding."

She managed to jerk her gaze away from his father to find the boy looking dapper in a charcoal suit just like Ian's, a miniature version that fit him perfectly.

"We're a few moments early," Ian said, finally finding his words. "Sorry about that but the children were dressed and clean for five minutes. Mrs. Gilbert suggested the best chance of keeping them that way was simply to leave for the wedding before they could mess things up again."

"I'm almost ready. I only need to grab my shoes and check on the puppies one more time."

Amelia made a tiny sound of excitement. "Please, Dad. May we say hello to the puppies?"

"If you look and don't touch. Gemma probably wouldn't mind dog hair all over you but the photographer she's hired might."

"We'll be careful," Thomas promised.

Samantha took them to the sewing room and opened the door, keeping the gate in place. All the puppies yelped in greeting, dancing and writhing around, to the children's delight.

"I love these puppies," Amelia said with a sigh that sounded as if it came from deep within her soul.

"I do, too," Thomas said, his voice wistful. "I so wish we could take one home with us."

"We're leaving on Wednesday next," Amelia said. "I wish we didn't have to go."

She sounded so sad that Samantha wanted to kneel down right there and wrap her arms around her.

"What about all your friends at home? You told me about your friend Christine, who was going to Barcelona this summer with her family. Won't it be nice to tell her about your trip to Idaho?"

"That will be fun, I suppose. I've sent her pictures of the puppies and she's so jealous. She adores puppies."

"There you go."

"Still, I'll miss the puppies. Pictures aren't the same as hugging them."

"They'll be going to their new homes next week, anyway."

"Will Betsey be sad about not being with her babies anymore?" Amelia asked, suddenly looking stricken.

"She might be sad for a day or two. But she'll be all right."

"Will *you* be sad?" Thomas asked.

"A little. But I'll be all right, as well."

"I'll miss you," Thomas said, his voice a little shy. She could almost feel her heart shatter.

This time she did kneel down, as hard as it was in her dress, and hugged both children.

"I'll miss you both, too. You'll be sure to write me, though, won't you?"

"Yes. Would it be all right if I colored a picture for you?" Thomas asked.

"Definitely."

"Maybe we can FaceTime, too, on Dad's computer," Amelia suggested. "That's what we do with Aunt Gemma."

"I would like that very much," she said.

When she stood again, she found Ian in the doorway to the living room, watching the interaction with an expression she couldn't read.

He cleared his throat. "We really should be going. We wouldn't want to be late for Gemma's wedding."

"No. Of course not. I only need a moment."

She slipped into her bedroom for her shoes and evening bag and then returned to the living room. "Ready."

She might be ready for the wedding, she thought as they all headed for Ian's vehicle. But she was certainly not ready for everything that would come after.

How would he possibly be able to keep his hands off Samantha through the entire evening?

The evening was one thing. He could endure anything for one night. But how would he be able to walk away from her to fly home in only a few days?

She had become infinitely precious to him during the short time he had been in Haven Point. He pictured her there as she had been a short time ago in the hallway of her home, holding both of his children and looking as if she was about to weep. His chest ached.

How had she become so very important to his world?

She brought sunshine and joy into a world that had seemed dark and cheerless for a long time.

The children chatted all the way to the house of Gemma's friends where the wedding would be held. As soon as they walked to the backyard, which was decorated with garlands of entwined ribbons and lush, brightly colored flowers, his mother headed straight for them.

"Thank the lord you're here," Margaret exclaimed.

"What do you need me to do?" Ian asked immediately, afraid he had forgotten some kind of wedding responsibility.

"Not you. *Her*." She pointed to Samantha. "We're having a wardrobe malfunction. The mother of the groom is wearing a dress that just ripped at a fairly important seam and she's quite literally frantic. She's crying right now in the room off the kitchen we've all been using as a dressing room. Is there any chance you could possibly work your magic and repair it?"

Samantha didn't hesitate. "Of course. Show me where to go. I have a spare needle and thread in my bag."

Ian had to blink, wondering what sort of woman carried a spare needle and thread in an evening bag little bigger than a credit card.

"Let's go see if there's anything we can do to help outside," he said to the children after his mother and Samantha hurried away.

"Is Mrs. Gilbert here yet?" Amelia asked.

He looked around. "I don't see her. But she'll be here."

They walked around the expansive lawn overlooking the lake where chairs had been set up under an awning for the wedding ceremony.

Ian wasn't normally the kind of guy who noticed that sort of thing, but even he could tell this was a stunning setting for a wedding.

A quartet of musicians with stringed instruments was setting up on one side, tuning their instruments as a few guests started to arrive.

Already the low hum of conversation and laughter filled the afternoon.

He refused to draw comparisons between this joyful event with his somewhat stiff, formal wedding to Susan. The past was past. His marriage might have been a mistake but he had gained two amazing children out of it, so he couldn't regret any of it.

He spotted his father rearranging chairs with McKenzie Kilpatrick and Eliza Caine and immediately headed in their direction.

"We're here to help. Three Summerhills reporting for duty. What can we do?"

McKenzie threw him a look of vast relief. "Thank you! We had a bit of a crisis when one of the dogs escaped from the garage and came barreling through. I'm afraid he messed up the garlands on the chairs."

"I'm so sorry," Eliza said. "Boomer can be such a rascal."

"No harm done," McKenzie said. "We can fix it."

"We can help you put the chairs into their correct positions," Thomas said, looking serious and concerned in his adorable little gray suit.

She looked down at him with a broad smile. "That would be extremely helpful, kind sir."

He and the children helped set the chairs back into rows while McKenzie rearranged the garlands. After that, they carried out more flowers to put on the guestbook table and even helped usher people to their seats.

They were so busy he didn't have the chance to see Samantha again until just prior to the ceremony, when he and the children were finally seated and most of the guests had arrived.

He had saved the seat next to him for her and was relieved when she slid into it, a bit more disheveled than she had been when they arrived.

Somehow her slight disarray only managed to make her look even more glorious.

"Everything okay?" he asked in an undertone.

"It is now. I had to sew like the wind to make some major repairs on the mother of the groom's dress. I hope I never have to do that again," she said vehemently.

He spotted the woman in question walking in on Josh's arm. She looked lovely in a rose-colored dress that perfectly matched some of the flowers in the garlands draped on the rows of chair.

Even looking at her dress closely, he couldn't see any evidence of Samantha's handiwork.

"I'll assume she didn't buy that dress from you," he said.

"No. She ordered it online apparently, without even trying it on. First they sent the wrong size. Then, because of a shipping delay, this one didn't arrive until yesterday. It needed a slight alteration in the bodice but the person who worked on it last-minute did a slipshod job of it. I think she should be good now. It should hold together, as long as she doesn't go crazy on the dance floor later."

"Once again, you save the day."

She gave him a grateful look, but before she could answer, Josh and the woman who would be marrying them whom Ian had met the evening before at the rehearsal dinner, the reverend at the church Gemma attended in town, moved to the front. A moment later, the quartet began playing the music his sister had chosen for her bridal processional.

Ian held his breath as Gemma came gliding down the aisle on his father's arm, alight with happiness and stunning in the dress Samantha had made. It was perfect for her, as if the dressmaker had somehow managed to bottle her personality and weave it into cloth.

He heard a sigh coming from Amelia and looked down to find her hands clasped together, pressed tightly to her chest, as she watched her aunt make her way down the aisle, her arm tucked through their father's.

Hardly showing any sign of her limp, Gemma glided toward her groom, who stood with eyes suspiciously moist as he watched her.

The moment was profoundly perfect, as lovely and romantic as he could ever imagine a wedding.

Beside him, he saw Samantha wipe away happy tears. He reached for her hand and held it in his, not caring who might see.

CHAPTER FIFTEEN

SAMANTHA ALWAYS SHED a tear or two at weddings, caught up in the romance and the beauty of two separate lives combining to become one. This one, though, seemed to hit her particularly hard.

She found a sweet tenderness in watching the stunned joy on Josh Bailey's handsome face as he watched his beautiful bride make her way down the flower-strewn aisle toward him.

Gemma must have been crying a little, too, though Samantha couldn't see it. She only guessed it when Josh pulled a handkerchief out of the inside pocket of his tuxedo jacket and pressed it with heartbreakingly gentle care to one of Gemma's eyes and then the other.

The gesture was so tender and emotional it stole her breath.

Sam didn't have anyone to wipe her tears away. That was suddenly, starkly apparent. If she wanted to see the world clearly, it was up to her to wipe her own blasted eyes.

She reached into her trusty bag for the lace hanky she had brought along. She sniffled a little, dabbing at her eyes, when she suddenly felt a hand on hers.

Ian.

He didn't look at her, his gaze focused on his sister and her groom, but his fingers curled around Samantha's, warm and comforting.

Her breath caught, her heart pounding, and she wanted

this moment to continue forever, frozen in her memory. A beautiful bride and groom, many of her friends and neighbors filling the seats around her and Ian and his children next to her.

She loved him. The undeniable truth of it poured through her like that fading sunlight on the water.

She had suspected as much for a long time, probably since that first kiss that had left her so shaken.

There was no denying it now, when he held her hand with such gentleness that she felt more tears spill out.

This wasn't like anything she had felt before. It was raw and painful, as if her heart had been flayed open.

She loved him more than she imagined it possible to love another person. He was a good, kind, honorable, *wonderful* man who treated her with respect and concern and who cared deeply about his children and his family.

How could she *not* love a man like him?

His thumb rubbed against hers and she closed her eyes, trying to absorb every sensation of this moment to sear into her memory.

He was leaving in only a few days. How would she bear it?

This time, she feared, Starry-eyed Sam would never be the same. Impending heartbreak loomed on the horizon like a dark cloud filled with devastation.

She couldn't stop him from leaving. The only thing within her power was right now, this moment. She would simply have to do her best to enjoy the rest of Gemma's wedding activities.

Tomorrow would be soon enough to begin processing the pain.

SHORTLY AFTER THE CEREMONY—after vows and rings had been exchanged, a tender kiss had sealed the union and they had embraced nearly everyone there who was eager to offer congratulations—the chairs were moved to the edge of the large white awning to clear a space for dancing.

While Ian and his children helped move furniture, Samantha hurried toward the refreshment table to see if she could help with anything.

"The caterers seem to have everything under control," Eliza assured her. "Just go enjoy yourself."

She felt a raw, almost hysterical laugh score her throat at that advice. How could she enjoy herself with the heavy weight of impending sadness bearing down on her?

She grabbed a flute of champagne and took a sip just as Margaret approached her and grabbed her free hand in both of hers.

"That dress. Oh, Samantha. Thank you. My baby girl was the most beautiful bride. I can't tell you how many people have mentioned her gorgeous gown to me."

"Gemma would have been beautiful, no matter what she wore."

"But that gown put everything over the top. You should know I consider you the heroine of this wedding. You not only designed Gemma's gown, you altered my pitiful dress into something completely perfect and now you've turned Sally's wardrobe disaster into a triumph. What would we have done without you?"

"Probably found another seamstress," Samantha said.

"No one as good as you," Margaret insisted staunchly. "You're amazingly talented."

"Thank you." She couldn't help but be honored and touched at the praise.

"You're welcome. Look, I know this isn't the time to discuss this, in the middle of the celebrations, but I feel I have to say this now while I'm thinking about it. Who knows when I'll have another chance to talk to you. You really must consider expanding your operation."

She stared, astonished at the unexpected suggestion.

"I'm quite serious about this, darling." Ian's mother beamed. "I consider you my own personal discovery. Well, technically Gemma discovered you but that's neither here nor there. The point is, I have friends in the London and Paris fashion industry, friends who would be very excited about someone with your talent. I would love to connect you with them. What do you think?"

Samantha nearly dropped her champagne. "You want to connect me with designers in London and Paris?"

"Well, I have a few contacts in New York but I'm afraid most of my friends in the business are overseas. I promise, once I start posting pictures of Gemma's gown, they'll be begging me to tell them who designed it. If you're strategic, you could leverage those contacts into entirely new markets."

New markets. She could barely handle the dress orders she already had. How could she even think about expanding?

She could hire other seamstresses. It wasn't a new idea but perhaps she had to consider it more seriously now.

She knew many talented seamstresses who would be eager for the work. She could focus on designing and let someone else handle the work of taking those designs and bringing them to life.

The possibilities started wildly spinning in her head. For a moment, she felt giddy, imagining it.

Just as quickly, she drew a breath and yanked down the curtain on the images.

She knew exactly what her mother would say if she were here. She could almost hear Linda's echoing in her head.

Don't get ahead of yourself, Samantha, and go all starry-eyed again. Why would she make you an offer like that? What's in it for her? Anyone can promise you anything. But when it comes down to the nitty-gritty, will they deliver? Most of the time, no, and you'll only end up hurt for dreaming too big.

What would she possibly be able to offer designers in Paris and London, a small-town boutique owner and wedding gown designer like her?

She was about to thank Margaret for her enthusiasm but tell her no thank you, that she had a safe, comfortable business here in Haven Point, where she knew her customers and could design bespoke gowns for them on a smaller scale. Before the words could come out, she caught herself.

What was she thinking? How could she turn down such an offer?

This could quite possibly turn into an incredible opportunity for her and she was about to close the door on it, simply because of what she could imagine her mother saying.

Linda was gone. What she might or might not have thought about Samantha expanding her dressmaking business didn't matter anymore.

Sam had spent her entire life trying and failing to make her mother happy. Maybe, just maybe, it was time she focused more on doing what was necessary to make *herself* happy.

She felt as if an earthquake had just ripped through, shaking the foundation of everything she believed about herself.

She was talented. No matter what her mother might have said about dreaming too big, she wanted to take this chance.

More than likely, it wouldn't lead to anything. So what? If she tried and nothing happened, she wouldn't be any worse or better off than she was right now. She would still be in exactly the same situation, running a very successful boutique and creating custom gowns for a few select brides.

Margaret could clearly see her emotional turmoil. She squeezed Sam's hand again. "You've been given a gift, my dear. I would never say you're wasting it here because I don't think that at all. You do wonderful work. But imagine what you might do if you looked outside of Haven Point!"

"You could be right," she said warily.

"I am right. If you send me photos of a few of your favorite gowns you've created, I can deliver them to some select, well-placed friends. I can't make any promises but I would utterly love the chance to help you try wedging a foot in the door."

"Thank you. I would appreciate that very much," she said before she could talk herself out of it.

"Oh, hurrah." Margaret gave an exultant laugh and hugged her, champagne and all. Samantha gripped it aloft tightly so she didn't spill all over Margaret's dress, which she had worked so hard to alter.

"Before we leave town, we have to exchange contact info. I'll be in touch as soon as I hear anything."

She would at least have some connection with his family after they returned to England. She wasn't sure if that would make things easier or harder. She cared about Ian's family as much as she cared about him.

How had they all become so precious to her?

Henry came over just as Margaret released her.

"There you are," he said, looking at his wife with so much love it made Samantha want to cry.

"Yes. Here I am. Is there a problem?"

He took her hand. "No problem at all. They're about to start the dancing, that's all. I'll be taking our girl out for the traditional father-daughter dance and thought you might want to be there when I do. After that, of course, I'll be looking for my favorite dancing partner."

Margaret rolled her eyes a little. "With my bad knee, you know I can't dance the way I used to."

"I can't, either. Which makes us perfect for each other," he said, squeezing her hand.

To her chagrin, Samantha felt more tears gather at the sweetness between the two of them. It was a very good thing she had used waterproof mascara.

She had seen too few examples of seasoned romance in her life. Certainly not in her own childhood. She had very few memories of her own parents demonstrating love for each other.

She could recall her mother's deep grief after her father killed himself but it seemed to have quickly shifted to anger and betrayal. Only a few months after her father's death, her mother didn't like to hear his name from anyone, especially Samantha.

Margaret and Henry were clearly still in love, despite having children in their thirties and despite the shared pain of losing one of those children. She found it sweet and tender but somehow edged with a bittersweet rind, like orange peels.

She desperately wanted this same kind of relationship with their son, something that would last through generations.

Instead, she had only a few days to savor her time with him. After that, all of them would be gone.

"I do hope you'll save a dance for me," Lord Henry said with that warm, fatherly smile she was coming to adore.

"I would be honored," she told him. "For now, you should probably go find Gemma. She'll be waiting for you."

"I meant what I said. You're going places," Margaret told her as Henry started leading her toward the dance floor. "Send me those pictures."

"I will," she promised.

She might not be able to have Ian but she had other dreams that might still come true, with enough work.

It was small consolation, but consolation nonetheless.

HE COULDN'T REMEMBER a wedding he had enjoyed more. His own would certainly not even make the top twenty.

Ian moved around the dance floor with his daughter, savoring the night and the stars and the music.

Everything about the event was magical, from the setting to the flowers to the company.

He was beyond happy Gemma had found a man who fit her so perfectly and brought out the best in his sister. She had been through so much and deserved every ounce of happiness she had found with Josh Bailey. He foresaw a future of joy and contentment for both of them.

"Dad! You're not counting right." Amelia sounded more exasperated than annoyed.

"Sorry. You know I'm not much of a dancer. When I have to dance, I mostly stand in one place and sway, I'm afraid. If you want true dancing, you may have to stick with your little brother. He seems to be slaying it."

They both turned to admire Thomas, who was currently dancing with Samantha. Ian's son was gyrating his little heart out while she mostly stood by and watched him with a delighted smile that seemed to arrow straight through to Ian's own heart.

He adored that she seemed to love his children. He could tell it was genuine, too, not an act she was putting on in an effort to impress him.

"Weddings are fun," Amelia said with a happy sigh. "Can we go to another one sometime soon?"

"I am afraid we don't know anyone else getting married any time soon. At least not that I can think of right now. Most of our friends are already married."

Amelia didn't appear bothered by that. "We could always go to weddings for people we don't know."

"That's not the way it works, usually," he said, trying to keep a straight face.

He imagined dressing up in wedding finery with Amelia and crashing weddings of people he didn't know, simply for the fun of it. The idea made him smile as he twirled his daughter past his parents on the dance floor. Margaret and Henry looked perfectly matched, as always.

The music ended at that moment and his father dropped his arms from his wife. "I believe I would like to cut in, if you don't mind," he said to Ian. "I've been waiting for a chance to dance with my granddaughter. Though I must say, she looks entirely too grown up tonight. When did you become such a lovely young lady?"

Amelia giggled, clearly pleased. "I don't know," she said.

"Stop growing," her grandfather ordered. Unfortunately, for all Lord Henry's influence and power in certain sectors, he held no sway when it came to the inevitable progression of time.

Soon enough, Ian would be the father of the bride at Amelia's wedding. He stood watching his daughter whirl off with his father, a little bereft to think about her one day dancing with her own bridegroom.

His mother cleared her throat and he realized with some dismay that she was waiting for him to do the polite thing and ask her to dance since her partner had just deserted her.

"Mother, would you like to dance?" he said instantly.

"You don't have to do that," Margaret said, eyes twinkling. "Especially since I imagine there's someone else here you would rather be taking out onto the dance floor."

Ian felt his cheeks heat and had to force himself not to look for Samantha, whom he could see on the periphery of his vision still dancing with his son and apparently enjoying herself immensely.

"You are the only one I want to dance with at this moment," he said chivalrously, though he earned only a disbelieving harrumph in return.

His mother didn't move with the grace he remembered from his youth, afflicted with arthritis that she never complained about. She needed a knee replacement but had been postponing it for months.

He didn't like thinking about either of his parents growing older, any more than he wanted to think about Amelia some day marrying some nameless, faceless man who had best treat her right.

"It's been an unforgettable day, hasn't it?" Margaret said softly.

This time he couldn't help his gaze from shifting to Samantha. She was still dancing with Thomas and was laughing at something his son was saying. The lights strung around the lawn lit up her features like a Raphael Madonna.

His chest tightened and he stumbled a little, missing her already.

"She is delightful," Margaret said softly, following his gaze.

"Yes. I agree." Ian did his best to keep any emotion out of his voice and expression, though he had a feeling it would do him no good. His mother always had an uncanny knack for mind reading, often before he had figured out his own thoughts.

"What are your plans after next week?" Margaret asked, giving him a searching look. "I assume you'll stay in touch with her."

Yes, his mother knew him entirely too well. What could she see in his expression? Could she tell he was in love with Samantha?

He stopped dancing altogether as the truth of it poured over him like water gushing from Bridal Veil Falls.

Love.

He couldn't be in love. He had only known her a few short weeks. Infatuation, maybe. Certainly lust. But love?

The more he thought of it, though, the more he realized that was the only possible explanation for everything in his heart and his mind. This tenderness was far more than infatuation and lust.

He was in love with her.

Somehow during his short time in Haven Point, Samantha Fremont had become infinitely dear to him.

He loved her smile, her talent, the sweetness she showed his children. He had come to cherish a hundred things about her.

The realization should have filled him with joy. Instead, he ached at the impossibility of it.

"After next week, the children and I are packing up the

Oxford place and moving to Summerhill, where I plan to throw myself into helping Father and learning everything there is to know about the earldom."

A twinge of pain tightened her features and he regretted his flat tone immediately. His parents knew well that he had never wanted to be heir. He didn't need to remind them of it, like a petulant child who couldn't have the toy he wanted in the market.

"What about Samantha?" his mother pressed.

Something else he couldn't have. "What about her?" he asked, this time careful to keep his expression free of the torment stirring beneath the surface.

"Are you making plans to visit her again? I've heard fall is a beautiful time here at the lake. Or will you invite her to visit Dorset once you're settled?"

He could clearly picture how wonderful either of those things might be. He would love to show her the river Amherst, his childhood swimming hole, the picturesque village near the estate that reminded him a great deal of Haven Point.

He could imagine showing her the kissing bridge over the stream at Summerhill, the Roman ruins nearby, the hills he and David used to hike.

He also knew he could do none of those things.

"What would be the point?" he asked, his voice brusque.

She stared at him, clearly astonished at his tone and his words. "The point? The point is she's a wonderful woman. You have feelings for her and should see where they lead."

He didn't want to talk about this right now and certainly not with his mother. He wanted to go somewhere alone, somewhere near the water, where he could try to process the tumultuous shock of realizing he loved a woman he could never have.

Short of abandoning his mother on the dance floor, he couldn't see a way to avoid the conversation, especially when Margaret's face was twelve inches away from his and she was holding him tightly.

"My feelings, such as they are, won't lead anywhere because I don't intend to act on them," he answered, his voice low but firm.

She angled her head, studying him so intently he finally had to look away from her scrutiny. After a long moment, she sighed. "I am your mother and love you more than words. But I think it's fair to say there are times I don't understand you in the slightest. This is one of them."

"Because I don't see the point in causing inevitable pain in two people by pursuing something with no possible future?"

She stared at him. "No possible future? Why ever not?"

"Samantha and I have completely different lives separated by five thousand miles. There's no way to reconcile that. I see no point in dragging things out, prolonging the inevitable."

"Nothing is inevitable except that we're all going to leave this life at some point."

"I've been through this once, Mother. You know what a disaster I made of that."

Margaret said nothing for a moment as the music continued, a soft, romantic ballad that only seemed to heighten the ache in his chest.

"Now that sounds like an excuse to me if I've ever heard one. Please forgive me for saying this," she finally said. "But Samantha and Susan are completely different women."

He knew that, entirely too well. He wasn't sure they could be more different.

"Agreed."

"You were married to Susan for five years and I never once saw you look at her the way you look at Samantha. As if she is your sun and your moon and all the stars in your sky."

Could everyone at the wedding see how he felt? He sincerely hoped only his mother was this observant.

He purposely avoided her gaze. "How I look at her doesn't matter."

"How can you say that?"

Ian sighed. "It's impossible, Mother. You have to see that."

"I see no such thing."

"I made a horrendous mistake with Susan. Despite that, two amazing children came out of that union. They are my priority. I can't risk them being hurt, especially after everything they've been through with their mother these past few years."

"You're older and far wiser now, son. Hard experience has given you a discernment that few others ever achieve. I know you have the good sense to make a far different choice now than you might have a decade ago."

He couldn't disagree. He had made some very ill-considered decisions in his youth.

"Anyway, Susan wasn't really your choice," his mother said softly. "You wouldn't have married her if she hadn't told you she was pregnant with Amelia, would you?"

He closed his eyes, remembering how trapped and helpless he had felt when Susan had told him the news of her pregnancy.

He hadn't wanted to marry her or anyone at that point in his life. In fact, he had been about to break off their relationship, which had begun as more of a convenience because their mutual friends were dating each other.

"I married her, though, didn't I? And had a second child with her."

Their marriage hadn't been completely terrible. Sometimes he tended to forget that part. She had been a loving mother and they had tried to build a sturdy base for Amelia and later Thomas.

"I tried to care about Susan, for your sake and the children's," Margaret said. "Despite all my efforts, we never quite clicked, which I think was as much my fault as hers."

"I can't believe that." As he recalled, his mother had been extraordinarily kind to Susan, generous to a fault. He could remember many times when she had taken her shopping or to one of her charity events where Susan had loved being the daughter-in-law to the Countess of Amherst.

"I am only mentioning that to make the point that your father and I already adore Samantha. We both said earlier today how happy we were that you were bringing her here as your date to the wedding and that we hope you continue seeing her."

"How can I? It's impossible," he said again. "Samantha's life is here in Haven Point. She has friends, a dog, a business she loves. Suppose we date long-distance and eventually decide we want a future together. She would have to give all that up and move to Dorset with me. You and I both know I no longer have the freedom to live anywhere I like. I am tied to Summerhill."

They had stopped dancing some time ago, without Ian fully realizing, and were standing on the edge of the dance floor. His mother, with her discerning eyes, placed a cool hand on his cheek, as if her touch could calm the turmoil inside him.

"Oh, son. You say that like those are your only options, that you must either abandon the estate and move here or she must abandon her business and move to England with you."

"What else is there?"

She looked sly suddenly. "For your information, I've been talking to the lovely Ms. Fremont about expanding her reach, moving into new markets with her dress designs. Why couldn't she hire someone to run her store here, which would give her the chance to focus on her designs?"

He remembered Samantha saying she would be a designer, if she had her choice. Would she seriously consider such a drastic step?

"I can't ask her to completely change her life like that," he protested.

Margaret gave him a pitying look. "Why not? Every woman has to radically change her life when she marries. Just like every man does, as well. Even if they don't move across continents, they must make concessions and adjustments. If Samantha cares about you, she won't mind."

"I have no idea how she feels," he said.

His mother smiled softly. "Remember I told you that you look at her with your heart in your eyes? Here's the funny thing. When you're not looking at her that way, she's looking at you with the exact same expression."

He couldn't help himself, he shifted his attention from his mother to Samantha. His gaze met hers across the dance floor and she immediately looked away, color seeping into her cheeks.

Ian could feel his heartbeat accelerate. Was it possible? Could she share his growing feelings? Would she consider the possibility of someday making life changes that would enable them to be together?

How could he possibly ask that of her? It seemed grossly unfair.

He had never felt more trapped by the constraints placed on him now as his father's heir. What if he could walk away from his life in England and move here with the children and study salmon to his heart's content?

No sense dealing in rhetorical questions. He couldn't. Just as he had married Susan when he found out she was expecting his child, he could not walk away from his responsibilities as heir to Amherst.

How much more bearable would those responsibilities be if he had Samantha at his side?

The idea tantalized him as much as it tormented him.

"You're my son and I love you. But if you have feelings for Samantha and do nothing about them, I would be gravely disappointed in you," his mother said. "I would hope no son of mine would throw away something that could be wonderful because of fear."

She was right. He loved Samantha. She filled his heart with joy and color and texture and he didn't want to imagine a future without her in it.

Yes, he had made mistakes in the past. His marriage had been a disaster. But Susan had never been the right choice for him.

Something told him Samantha was that and more. No. She was the *only* choice. If he didn't act on his feelings for her, Ian suspected he would spend the rest of his days alone and unhappy, living a life he didn't want and aching for a woman he couldn't have.

Gemma Summerhill's wedding to Joshua Bailey would always have a place in Samantha's memory as one of the most romantic and yet most difficult she had ever attended.

She had found moments of pure joy, like dancing with Thomas and laughing at his free-spirited delight. Sitting beside Ian and holding his hand when Gemma and Josh had exchanged vows. Catching up with friends she hadn't had the chance to see in too long.

Twisting through the bright spots of the event was the inevitable knowledge that this evening was a watershed moment and only brought her one step closer to the day when Ian and his children would fly out of her life.

"Everything okay?" Bowie asked, settling his sleeping daughter, Gabi, more comfortably in his arms. "You don't seem like your usual happy self."

They sat at one of the round tables placed around the dance floor, where she had stopped to talk to Katrina a short time earlier, just before Kat had promptly been dragged away to dance with Milo.

She sighed. "I love weddings. Don't get me wrong."

"That's probably a good thing, considering you design wedding gowns."

"Right?" She managed a smile. "They're almost always joyful occasions. This one is, absolutely. Gemma and Josh are perfect for each other."

"But?" Bowie pressed.

"I don't know. Despite my happiness for them, sometimes at weddings I can't help feeling a bit of melancholy."

It had nothing to do with her own marital status or that she didn't have a family of her own, which might be the logical assumption.

Weddings opened many doors but inevitably closed others.

"Were you melancholy at ours?" Bowie asked. "If you were, I don't think I noticed."

"I was sad to lose my best friend," she admitted. "But I

got over it quickly, especially once I accepted I was gaining another good friend in you, along with two adorable children."

"There you go," he said with a smile.

She didn't have time to respond because Ian chose that moment to come over with two glasses of champagne. He handed one to her, which she took even though she knew she'd already had three, which was about two past her personal limit.

"I'm the worst wedding date. I've hardly seen you all evening," he said on an apologetic note.

She had almost forgotten he was her date for the wedding— and also her ride home.

"Ian, have you met Bowie Callahan? He's lucky enough to be married to my best friend, Katrina. Bowie, this is Ian Summerhill. Gemma's brother."

"I would shake your hand but I'm afraid mine are full at the moment," Bowie said.

"No worries." Ian smiled easily. "I've been there myself. I'm fortunate enough to have a nanny, who only ten minutes ago took the children home, since my son was falling asleep on his feet and my daughter wasn't far behind."

Samantha was sorry she hadn't had the chance to say good night to the children before Mrs. Gilbert took them home for the evening.

They made small talk for a few moments, before Ian turned to her. "The champagne was a pretext," Ian admitted. "In actuality, I was wondering if you might have a dance free for me."

Something about his solemn expression sent butterflies twirling through her. "Yes," she said softly. She wanted to tell him he could have all the rest of her dances forever, but couldn't seem to find the words, even if such a thing were possible.

Leaving the champagne on the table, she took his hand and he led her out to the dance floor.

She didn't want this moment to end. She wanted to remember it for the rest of her life, dancing with the man she loved under a sky peppered with stars.

"The moon is beautiful on the water here, isn't it?" he murmured.

She told herself it was the champagne that left her breathless, light-headed. "I've always loved the view from Snow Angel Cove. The lake and the mountains are the same but the perspective seems so different. There's a beautiful spot down by the water where you can see all of Haven Point, and some of Shelter Springs, too."

"I would like to see that."

"It's just through the trees there." She gestured vaguely in the direction, though she couldn't seem to take her gaze away from the intensity of his expression. Something was happening here. Something significant she didn't understand.

"Do you mind missing the rest of the dance?"

She would much rather walk along the lakeshore with him, holding his hand and trying to pretend he wasn't leaving in a few days.

"I don't mind," she said.

"Lead on," he said.

They slipped away from the dance floor, away from the lights and the crowd. The crushed gravel path was illuminated by small globes, their lights spilling down in small half circles.

She was intensely aware of Ian walking beside her silently, his features veiled in darkness but his hand warm and comforting in hers.

Finally the pine and spruce opened up a little, revealing a little hidden cove on the lake. They weren't far from the wedding festivities but might as well have been in their own private world here. She couldn't see the lights through the thick trees and even the music seemed muted.

"Wow. You're right. This is stunning." Ian walked to the water's edge and gazed out across the water at the lights of Haven Point and Shelter Springs gleaming in the distance along the lakeshore.

She imagined Eliza and Aidan must come here often. A small cushioned bench had been thoughtfully provided, angled just so across the water to take in that view of the lights and the mountains. It would make a lovely place to sit on a summer afternoon and read.

She sat down, tucking her dress around her. She shivered a little, wishing she'd brought along the wrap that went with the dress. The air was cooler here in the trees, especially with the breeze blowing off the lake.

"You're cold," Ian said. "I'm sorry. I can take you back to the party."

"I don't want to go back," she admitted softly. "This is nice."

"It is, isn't it? The least I can do is warm you a little."

He sat beside her and pulled her against him, her back nestled against his chest. Everything inside her seemed to sigh as his arms came around and held her close.

This. She never wanted to move from this spot.

They sat for a long time, listening to the sounds of the night and the muted music while all the emotions she had been fighting since Ian came to town with his children seemed to bubble close to the surface.

She thought she felt his mouth brush the top of her head but told herself she must be imagining things.

"I wish we could stay here all night in exactly this spot," he said gruffly.

"I was thinking the same thing but I'm afraid my dog and her puppies would wonder what happened to me."

"When will their new owners be coming for them?"

She didn't want to think about the other impending loss in her world. How would she find the strength to endure it?

"I was going to deliver them all to their new homes Monday but I've decided to wait until the weekend. After... after you and the children leave."

She wanted to wait a month so she could at least have puppy cuddles to comfort her but knew everyone taking a puppy was anxious for their new arrival.

She dreaded the coming week, on so many levels.

"I was thinking it might be easier on Amelia and Thomas if I took the puppies to their new homes after you're all on your way home. They will still have to say goodbye to the puppies but not one at a time."

His arms tightened around her. "I'm going to have to check their suitcases carefully. I think Thomas would pack all three of the puppies in there, given half a chance."

She smiled a little, though her throat felt raw and achy with emotions.

"I'll miss them," she said. "The puppies and...and Thomas and Amelia. So much."

That was it. Her emotions bubbled over and she drew in a sharp breath, trying to close the floodgates before the tears could start.

"I'm sorry," he murmured near her ear. "So sorry."

She turned her head slightly, just enough that his mouth could slide to hers.

Ah. She had been waiting all night to kiss him again. His mouth was deliciously warm and tasted like champagne and strawberries.

The kiss was gentle, slow, with an aching tenderness that made more tears spill over.

She wanted to dash them away before he saw them but he must have caught the glimmer in the moonlight.

He drew away, concern in his eyes. "Are you crying?"

"A little. I'm sorry. Don't mind them. I just... I wish you didn't have to go so soon."

He pulled out a handkerchief and in an echo of the sweet gesture she had seen Josh do to Gemma during the wedding ceremony, Ian gently dabbed at her eyes. "I'm going to make a mess of your makeup, I'm afraid."

She was lost. Completely, hopelessly, utterly lost. "I don't care about my makeup," she murmured. "I care about you."

There. The words were out and she couldn't call them back.

"Do you?" he asked, his voice and his expression strangely intense. There was a vulnerability there she wouldn't have expected.

How could he possibly doubt her feelings when they seemed so very obvious to her and she suspected everyone else who had been at the wedding?

"Oh, Ian. You must know I do." Through the emotion choking her, she gave a raw laugh. "I might as well be honest. I'm in love with you."

"You're...what?"

"I didn't want to be. I tried everything I could think of to protect my heart, but you basically made it impossible for me to do anything else but fall in love with you."

He said nothing, just continued to gaze at her with

shock and something else in his expression, something she couldn't identify.

"You don't have to say anything. I've been through this before and can assure you I'll survive."

It was a lie. She had never been through anything like this before. All those times she thought she was in love before seemed so completely ridiculous and small in comparison to this, like the difference between a puddle of water and the vast ocean that would soon separate them.

"What if I don't want you to get over it?" he asked, his voice rough. "It seems only fair that you suffer a little, too, considering that I'm in misery. I fell for you hard. Maybe not the first time we met but certainly by the second, and I've been trying to talk myself out of it since then. Without success, I should add."

She gazed at him, her throat tight and her heart pounding. He couldn't mean what she thought she heard him say. Could he?

"You didn't."

His laugh was low, rough, and he reached to wipe another tear she hadn't realized had trickled out.

"Tell that to my poor salmon. I've been too distracted to finish my project. I'm afraid I'll be going home with incomplete research."

"Oh, no. Does that mean you'll have to come back?"

"I imagine so. Again and again, as long as it takes until I can convince you to spend the rest of your life with me."

Okay. This really couldn't be happening. She stood up, needing to feel the ground under her feet to make sure she wasn't lost in some champagne-induced hallucination.

"Sorry. What did you say?"

He sighed and rose, as well, taking her hands in his.

"I'm jumping ahead of things. That's not where I meant to start."

"Where…where did you mean to start?"

"By telling you I love you. When we came here for the summer, I never expected to fall in love. I've told myself love wasn't in the cards for me anymore. I made such a mess of my marriage and now I have the children to think about. They're my priority. But they fell for you first and I was close behind."

She kissed him then, unable to help herself. He gave a rough-sounding laugh and pulled her close, his mouth firm and hard on hers. They kissed for a long time, there beside the lake, while an owl screeched overhead and lake creatures splashed offshore.

"I should probably make it clear I'm a poor bargain," Ian said after long, delicious moments. "I get distracted by the oddest things and I can be a little obsessed with my research."

"I like that about you," she confessed. "I can be the same way when I'm struggling with a design."

"Then there's the whole peerage thing. I never wanted to be the Earl of Amherst, as I told you. But I do believe I can endure it, especially if I have you by my side."

This couldn't be happening. Ten minutes ago, she had been devastated at the thought of living without him and his children. Now he was talking about a future together.

A future that included a title. In England!

She eased away a little as a thousand questions crowded through her head. "What about my shop?"

He sighed. "That's the place where I really should have started, I suppose."

He took her hands again, that vulnerability back in his eyes. "Unlike Gemma, I can't leave everything behind and move here with you, much as I would love that. My family needs me."

"I know," she said softly.

"I understand that you have a life here. A life you love, with friends and your business. I don't know how to ask you to give that up."

Ask, she wanted to beg. *Please ask.*

"I was wondering, would you ever consider hiring someone for the day-to-day work and running things yourself from a distance? You could come back as often as you like and could certainly design gowns from Dorset."

"You want me to move to England with you. Leave my friends. My…my home."

"Not straightaway, certainly. But eventually, perhaps, if you decide you want to consider a future with me."

There was nothing to consider. Not really. She loved Ian and his children with all her heart. Any future without them would be gray, empty, lifeless.

The man she loved with all her heart was offering her everything. The family she had dreamed about, a chance to pursue her dreams of becoming a designer, a life filled with joy and laughter and love.

She said nothing, considering just how to answer him. At her continuing silence, he eased away a little.

"It's too much to ask of you. You would have to surrender everything you have built here. Everything familiar and comfortable. I understand if it's more than you're willing to compromise."

She took his hands in hers, facing him with all the love in her heart.

"Leaving Haven Point would be a huge sacrifice for me," she agreed. "I would miss my friends most of all."

She would feel a little lost without a regular dose of the Haven Point Helping Hands.

"I know. I'm sorry. You could come back whenever you wanted, though. We could even make it an annual or semi-annual thing. Gemma will be here, after all."

She wanted to cry again at his concern. No man had ever worried so much about her happiness and she didn't quite know how to respond.

"It would be a sacrifice to leave my home behind," she went on. "But the payoff—a life with you and Thomas and Amelia—would be joy beyond my wildest dreams."

The air seemed to leave him in a rush and then he lowered his mouth again and kissed her with fierce emotion.

She laughed a little, kissing him back with everything in her heart.

All of her life when she had been dreaming of a handsome prince, she had really been waiting for Ian. A distracted, slightly rumpled, too-serious biology professor who also happened to be Viscount Summersby, the future Earl of Amherst.

And the man she loved with all her heart.

EPILOGUE

One year later

"ARE YOU READY for this?"

Samantha looked over at Lord Henry, who had become so very dear to her over the past year—dear enough that she decided to break convention and had asked him to walk her down the aisle to marry his son.

He might be a bit gruff but his heart was as soft and gooey as the saltwater taffy he loved, especially when it came to his children and his grandchildren. She considered herself incredibly fortunate that over the past year he and his wife had opened their hearts to her.

"I'm so ready," she said.

He tucked his arm through hers. "You look stunning, my dear."

She had to agree. A woman shouldn't need to be modest on her wedding day. The dress she had created for herself, the one she had been dreaming about wearing since she was old enough to make doll dresses out of hair ties and discarded fabric, was the hardest dress she had ever made.

She had struggled with it for months and had almost postponed the wedding until she was able to get it just right.

She wanted to think it was a masterpiece. There were no ruffles, no lace, no long, flowing train. This dress was elegant, simple, understated. Not attention-grabbing but unmistakably beautiful. It was perfect for the woman she had become.

She wasn't sure if she would offer this in the new catalog she was developing under her new fashion label or if she would keep this particular design all to herself, her own unique, one-of-a-kind dress for this unforgettable day when her dreams came true.

Her heart pounded as she walked down the aisle of the little church in Haven Point where she had attended every week with her mother.

She looked toward the pew where they had always sat together and felt a little pang that Linda wasn't there today.

Over the past year, she had achieved some measure of understanding over the thorny relationship she'd had with her mother.

Her mother had been a difficult, critical woman, unhappy with her life and circumstances. She had taken out her own discontent on those closest to her, particularly her daughter.

Samantha couldn't forgive her for some of those wounds that had been etched deep into her heart. But Linda was gone now and Sam had decided dwelling on the pain would only allow it to continue to fester.

Today she would remember the good times with her mother. Learning to sew at her first portable machine, laughing at a show they enjoyed together, talking about a book they had both read.

She might not have actual family here but the chapel was filled with those she loved. Her family in spirit. Katrina was there with Bowie and their children, including the new little one, a girl Kat had named Isabella.

Elsewhere in the chapel, everywhere she looked, she

saw people who had supported her and embraced her on her journey toward becoming a woman of strength. Barbara Serrano. Charlene Bailey. Wynona, Julia Caine, Megan Hamilton Bailey. McKenzie, Devin, Lindy-Grace, Eppie and Hazel. And scores more.

She loved them all and was deeply grateful to have these people in her life.

Finally, her gaze went inexorably to the altar where Ian stood, looking every inch her handsome prince. His dark wavy hair was slightly messed in front but his collar for once was straight.

Thomas stood to one side and Amelia on the other, both of them beaming at her.

Her heart seemed too full to contain all the love inside it. She was the most fortunate of women and couldn't wait to become their stepmother.

Yes, she had made sacrifices. After much personal angst, she had finally sold Fremont Fashions to her worthy assistant, Rachel Muñoz, who had promptly rebranded it. She had stopped in the day before and been thrilled at the changes.

After selling the store, she had moved to England with Betsey, taking a small flat in a row of cottages that had once housed textile workers employed by Ian's ancestors.

When they married, she would move in with Ian and the children to the dower house on his father's sprawling estate. The dower house alone was a gorgeous seventeenth century structure about three times the size of her house in Haven Point, with a beautiful view overlooking the river Amherst.

In a few months' time, she would be opening the showroom for her bridal designs and she already had orders to fill the next year.

She was excited about all the changes in her life, but she was most ready for this one. To marry the man she loved. She looked at Ian waiting for her, his gaze locked with hers and filled with vast emotion, a deep love that had filled all the empty spots in her heart.

She gripped Lord Henry's arm and glided down the aisle past all the people who had shaped her into the woman she had become, toward Ian and the future they would build together.

* * * * *

A HAVEN POINT BEGINNING

CHAPTER ONE

THIS WAS A mistake of epic proportions.

Gemma Summerhill gripped the steering wheel of the hybrid SUV she had purchased six weeks ago, when she first came to the States. She was going only about five miles per hour but that still seemed entirely too fast as she steered through treacherous conditions with giant snowflakes slapping against the car with astonishing force.

She shouldn't be here. She should be safe and dry in her charming rented cottage beside Lake Haven, sitting by the fire with a cup of tea at one elbow and a good novel on her lap.

Whose crazy idea was it to go into the mountains today, with a storm coming on?

Hers. She sighed. She should have checked the weather report more carefully and shouldn't have relied on one app that had promised a beautiful fall day.

In her defense, the October day had been lovely when she set off that morning for an easy hike, all warm sunshine, clear skies, comfortable temperatures. Oh, how quickly conditions could change. Now the Idaho mountain road was slick, precarious, and the rain that had hit with ferocious strength about twenty minutes earlier had shifted just as quickly to snow.

Gemma peered through the windshield. With the sun quickly setting and those wildly churning snowflakes coming at her, she felt as if she were driving at warp speed through a galaxy far, far away.

A song came on the radio, a country ballad about a woman who made one bad choice after another. Gemma wanted to roll her eyes. That could well be her anthem right about now.

She had so been looking forward to exploring the backcountry. She had been in Haven Point for six weeks and had mostly hiked around the lake. This had been her one time to see more of the countryside.

It had been spectacular, Gemma had to admit. The aspens were a beautiful golden color and the other trees provided contrasting colors in reds and oranges. As she had hiked the route McKenzie Kilpatrick had told her about, an easy trail to a beautiful alpine lake, she had felt good. Her leg had bothered her, as it always did when she pushed it too much, but the gorgeous setting had helped distract her from it.

Once she reached the lake, she had the place all to herself and had sat for a good hour, in awe that she was there. She had been thrilled to see two moose in the distance as well as a handful of elk.

This was exactly why she came to Idaho and took the job with Caine Tech—the chance to experience beautiful settings like that one, as far removed from their neatly manicured home in Dorset as she could imagine.

And then everything went wrong. The trail back to her vehicle should have been easier but she had found even slightly downhill terrain more difficult to navigate with her bad leg. And then she had stumbled on a rock when she was about a half mile from her vehicle, twisting her ankle enough that she'd had to hobble the rest of the way.

The snowflakes seemed to whirl and dance with increasing intensity now and her tires fought for traction on the road. If she went out of control, she would plunge down the mountainside with only trees to block her fall. There were no guardrails on this backcountry dirt road, no warning signs. Only darkness that plunged down for hundreds of feet.

What if she couldn't make it down the road the rest of the way? What if she was stranded here on the mountainside? She had passed a few ranches on the way up. Surely she could find someone who could give her shelter until she could make her way home.

She shouldn't have come alone. Gemma knew the rules about never hiking into the backcountry without a buddy. The salesperson at the sporting goods store in town had been firm on that.

She had figured she would be going only on a short hike and would be fine on her own. While she had made friends since she came to town, she didn't know any of them well enough to call them on a whim on a Saturday afternoon and ask if they would like to go hiking with her.

Anyway, she had stocked up on survival supplies at the sporting goods store, extra rations in her backpack, even bear spray.

None of that would do her any good if she slid down the mountain in her car.

She should have heeded the warning signs that a storm was coming. Clouds had been gathering all afternoon. She had thought she might have to deal with one of the regular squalls that hit the area in the afternoons. She just never expected the rain to turn to sleet and now full-on snow.

What had been her big hurry, anyway? She could have saved her exploring for the following spring and summer, when the weather would be nicer and she wouldn't run the risk of frostbite. She was in Haven Point for the long-term. This was a life choice she had made, a chance to start over away from her family's loving but suffocating influence.

The vehicle slid again on the slick road. Gemma gasped, her hands sweaty and her stomach in knots. From the depths of her subconscious, memories clawed to the surface.

A screech of tires, shattering glass, the sickening, horrible silence afterward as she cried out her brother's name and received no answer in return.

Her right leg ached a vicious echo of her thoughts, a constant reminder of that horrible day.

As she had been trying to do for three years, she attempted to push away the memories so she could focus on the crisis at hand. They never entirely left her, always hovering just on the edge of her awareness.

This wasn't at all the same situation. She was in full control, even when the tires were sliding. The car's all-wheel drive and traction control were doing their job. An out-of-control lorry was not about to run through a stop sign and plow into her.

She had only to drive slowly, carefully, down the mountainside to her cottage, where she could turn on the gas fireplace, change into dry clothes and drink something hot and comforting.

The sun seemed to set extraordinarily quickly. One moment she was driving through murky, snowy twilight, the next it was full dark.

Only a little farther. She had to be close to where the dirt road changed to pavement. A few more moments. She could do this...

She heard a rumble outside the car, distant at first and then growing louder. The trees on the mountain side of the road seemed to tremble and then the next instant, before she realized what was happening, a river of mud and rocks and debris poured across the roadway directly in front of her.

She slammed on her brakes and felt the vehicle's rear tires fishtail. She had braked too fast, too hard. The car was out of control now, heading for the trees on the downward slope. This couldn't be happening. Not again. She couldn't die in a car accident, after all the work it had taken her to survive the last one.

She hit the brakes again and somehow, miraculously, the car bumped gently into the trunk of a pine tree and came to a shuddering stop just inches from plunging down the mountain.

She wasn't dead. How was she not dead?

Gemma could feel herself shaking violently. What the bloody hell had just happened?

Her mother would die if she heard such unladylike language coming from her. But Margaret wasn't here, was she? She and Henry were safe and sound at Summerhill.

A wave of homesickness washed over Gemma and for a wild moment, she wanted to be with them, even though their overwhelming concern had been strangling the life out of her.

She sat for another moment, trying to calm her racing heartbeat. How was she going to get out of there? She checked her phone. While she had some remaining battery life, she didn't have a signal, something not uncommon, she had learned, in the mountains surrounding Lake Haven.

So she couldn't call someone to rescue her. She would just have to find help. She thought of those ranch houses again. Maybe someone would be home at one of them and she could call for a tow—though how a tow truck from Haven Point would cross that mountain of debris that was taller than she was, Gemma had no idea.

Still shaking, she opened her vehicle door and started to climb out. The snow immediately soaked her coat, cold and merciless. She needed supplies and her backpack was in the rear seat. She carefully made her way there and had just started to open the back door when her stupid bad leg decided to give out. Gemma had to grab hold of the door frame so she didn't end up in the mud.

She reached in for her backpack. When she stood again, she saw a huge creature emerging from the darkness, heading straight toward her.

Gemma screamed. She couldn't help herself, afraid she was about to become dinner for a bear or a cougar. The creature faltered for a moment but then kept coming. She aimed the torch she instinctively grabbed out of her pack at it and realized it wasn't a mountain lion, it was a happy-looking chocolate Labrador retriever wearing a red collar.

"Where did you come from?"

The words were barely out when an even larger creature emerged from the darkness. It took her several seconds to realize it was a man on horseback wearing a cowboy hat and an oiled slicker against the elements.

"Hey there. This looks like trouble."

Gemma knew that voice, with its slight Western drawl. She narrowed her gaze and then recognized Joshua Bailey, who owned the outdoor supply store in Haven Point where she had bought her backpack and other hiking items. She had met him several times since she came to town, as she was friends with cousins of his, sisters Katrina Callahan and Wynona Emmett.

She didn't know him well but had the impression he

was the kind of man she generally despised, the sort who thought he could charm his way into any woman's bed, that every female should come running when he crooked his finger.

She couldn't have said why she thought that. Maybe because of that drawl or that wide smile he freely bestowed on women of all ages or maybe because he was so extraordinarily good-looking.

Or perhaps because of the intense way she had caught him looking at her a few times since she came to town.

"Oh. It's you."

"The one and only." His teeth flashed in the darkness as he dismounted from the horse with a grace she tried not to resent.

"You look like you're in a pickle, Miss Summerhill. What happened?"

"I was driving along, minding my own business, when half the mountainside fell away."

She seemed to be shaking more in delayed reaction. She would be having flashbacks to that slide for a long time.

The dog nuzzled her hand and she reached down to pet its wet fur, finding an unexpected comfort from the warmth and protective stance.

"I was afraid that would happen with the first hard rain. A couple acres on that mountainside burned up in a wildfire a few months ago, leaving it prone to mudslides without the trees and undergrowth to anchor all the rocks and dirt in place. I hope you weren't hurt."

"I was able to swerve at the last minute and ended up hitting the tree. Not so much hitting it as bumping it, I suppose. I wasn't even going fast enough for my airbag to deploy."

He frowned. "What were you doing on the mountain? Seems like a nasty day for a picnic."

"It wasn't a nasty day when I started out. This only started about an hour ago. I went on a little hike and was trying to make it home."

"You're lucky you weren't a few seconds earlier or the mudslide would have carried you over the side of the mountain."

She could have died.

Was she cursed somehow? Other people went their entire lives without near-death experiences. She had now experienced two.

She looked at the debris field and then at her car, her head spinning and her knees weak. She felt dizzy and sick. She sagged against her car for support—and the next thing she knew, Josh Bailey was next to her, his arm around her and his face close to hers.

"Easy there. Easy. You're okay."

How had he made it to her side so quickly? "What… happened?"

"I'm not completely sure. You were talking to me one minute then slumped against your car, unresponsive, the next. If Toby hadn't been there to prop you up, you would have fallen to the ground. I think you may have passed out for a few seconds. Are you sure you didn't bump your head somehow when you hit the tree?"

"No." Not this time, anyway. One other fun side effect of her accident three years earlier was an unfortunate propensity to faint in times of great exertion or emotion. It never lasted long. Doctors thought it might be a result of the head injury she had sustained.

"I'm fine. I'm sorry. It…it must have been stress." She didn't want to move. He was warm and smelled delicious, rugged and masculine, and she felt safe for the first time since the rains started.

Longer than that, if she were honest.

She frowned. They were both drenched, the snow was piling up and she had to figure out a way to get home.

Anyway, she was a perfectly capable woman, a smart, innovative computer programmer who didn't need a man to make her feel better. Especially a man she didn't know and didn't particularly like.

But, oh, it had been so very long since someone had held her.

She knew exactly how long. Three years, since the accident that had changed everything. Facing months of recovery, she had pushed away Kevin, the man she had been dating at the time.

She hadn't known what else to do. Doctors hadn't known if she would be able to walk again and as she and Kevin had only started dating, she hadn't been willing to subject him to the uncertainty and turmoil.

Kevin had let her push him away, with depressing willingness, and was now married with a toddler.

"I'm sorry," she said now, forcing herself to move away from Joshua Bailey and his sweet dog. "I don't know what happened. I can't believe I passed out. I'm usually not such a baby."

"You've had a shock. Your reaction is totally understandable. I don't think you're a baby at all."

The sincerity in his tone went a long way toward easing her embarrassment. Maybe she had misjudged him in their previous encounters.

"I need to call for help. I have no idea how I'm going to get my car out of here."

"I'm sorry to be the one to break it to you but that car

isn't going anywhere anytime soon. It's going to take considerable work to clear those boulders and debris. Also, I'm afraid cell phones don't work on this stretch of road. We're in a weird gap between cell towers."

She had found out the same thing. What was she going to do?

She shivered and tried not to panic. She could perhaps sleep in her car.

"Here. Don't pass out again on me."

"I won't. I'm fine."

He looked doubtful. "First thing we need to do is get you out of this weather. My ranch is about a quarter mile back up the mountain. I do have cell service there. Why don't we head back that way, get you warmed up and I'll make some calls so we can figure out how we're going to get down the mountain?"

He was a virtual stranger. How could she just go with him to his house?

On the other hand, she couldn't stay here. Who knew how long it would take for help to arrive?

While she didn't know him, she did know his aunt and his cousins. She had quickly learned the Bailey family was well respected and well liked around the area. His cousin Wynona was the wife of the Haven Point police chief.

Some of her hesitation must have shown on her face. He looked rueful. "You don't know me and don't want to go home with a man who is a stranger," he said, accurately guessing at the reason for it. "I get that and applaud your caution. But I can't leave you here at night in the snow. I would be kicked out of the Good Guys club."

When she continued to hesitate, not sure what to do, he grinned, his teeth gleaming in the darkness.

"How about this? I know you bought bear spray when

you were in my store the other day. I assume you took it hiking with you, right?"

She nodded, not sure where he was going with this.

"Bear spray works even better on people. Bring it along. If I try anything funny, you have my permission to blast me in the face with it."

She didn't see that she had much choice. The snow seemed to be falling harder. They needed to get help and couldn't do that here with no cell service.

Anyway, he had a sweet dog and a beautiful horse.

After a moment, she grabbed her backpack, found the bear spray and quite pointedly put it in her jacket pocket.

"How are we to get to your house?"

He gestured to his horse. "Ollie can carry both of us. He's a strong guy."

She looked at the horse and felt a fierce tug of longing. "I…haven't been on horseback in a long time. I'm not sure I can mount up, with my…my bad leg."

It was a humiliating confession that earned her a compassionate look.

"Sorry. I should have realized. I can help you. Can you raise your leg enough to put it in the stirrup?" he asked. The kindness of the question made her throat ache.

"Of course," she snapped. She hated feeling so weak. She put the foot of her mangled leg into the stirrup and grabbed hold of the pommel on the saddle.

"Sorry if I have to get a little, er, personal here," Josh said. Next thing she knew, he had boosted her up by her rump and helped her swing her leg over.

"I'm sorry to ask but can you scoot behind the saddle? I could walk you and Ollie home but we'd get out of the storm faster if we both rode."

She nodded, feeling ungainly and stupid, and managed

to shimmy her body back, pulling her leg out of the stir-rup so he could use it.

Her poor abused leg, already sore from the exertions of the hike and that stumble, throbbed at the long-unaccustomed position. She ground her teeth and held on to the back of the saddle, doing her best to ignore the pain.

Whenever she found herself wallowing in self-pity about the limitations from the accident, she reminded herself it could have been much worse. For her brother, it had been.

The saddle shifted a little as Josh climbed onto the horse but she managed to keep her balance.

"Hold on," he said. "Ollie is the greatest horse in Lake Haven County but even he might slip in these icy conditions."

She didn't have anything to hold on to but Josh. Gemma frowned, reminding herself she had no choice, and wrapped her arms around his waist.

He urged the horse forward and the big bay obediently started trotting through the falling snow, the dog following close behind, a dark blur in the snow.

Her rescuer's body blocked most of the wind but temperatures had plunged and her clothes were still wet. She couldn't help shivering and buried her forehead against his back to keep her face out of the cold.

"We'll be there in a minute." He had to raise his voice to be heard over the wind. "I've got a fire already going inside and we can get you warmed up in no time."

She held on to the idea of warmth as they trudged through the storm, taking a turnoff she barely saw and heading up a long, twisting driveway until they reached a sprawl of outbuildings and a sleek glass-and-cedar house.

He rode to the front door, swung off the horse and reached to help her down.

Gemma managed to swing her good leg over the saddle but hesitated to dismount, not at all sure her bad leg would be able to support her.

"I've got you," Josh assured her. His words comforted her in a way she couldn't have explained. She hopped down and he did indeed catch her, his muscles strong and capable as he helped her to the ground.

Was it her imagination or did he hold her just a smidge longer than necessary? She tried to ignore the little burst of heat that flared inside her.

He led the way up the porch and opened the door for her. A blast of warmth enveloped her and she wanted to cry, suddenly feeling as if she had been cold forever.

"I need to go take care of Ollie. Make yourself at home. Toby can keep you company. The fire should still be going and there are warm towels in the dryer. You need to get out of those wet clothes first. There are clean clothes in the laundry room. Feel free to change into anything dry you can find."

Her teeth were chattering too hard for her to do anything but nod.

Josh gave her a look of concern. "Are you okay? Ollie can wait a minute or two, until I get you settled."

"I'm f-f-fine," she assured him, though she was quite certain the chatter of her teeth said otherwise. "Go take care of your h-horse."

"I'll be back in fifteen minutes."

She nodded and with the dog leading the way, she went toward that warmth.

His house was beautiful, with comfortable-looking furniture, muted colors and Western decor that seemed just right.

"Where's the laundry room?" she asked Toby. She could swear the chocolate-colored dog cocked his head toward a hallway where she could hear a low hum.

"Thank you," she said. The dog followed her as she limped in that direction, ignoring the ache in her leg, and opened a solid wood door. It was indeed a laundry room, warm and steamy and fragrant.

She opened the dryer and found it loaded with dark green towels nearing the end of their dry cycle. She pulled two out and used one to drape over her shoulders and the other to dry off the dog so he didn't continue to drip on the floor.

A little more searching unearthed a pair of baggy sweats folded on the counter of the laundry room as well as a frayed hoodie that read "Camping. It's In Tents" with the logo of his sporting goods store.

She scooped them up. "Powder room?" she asked the dog, hoping for further guidance.

This time, Toby merely gave her a quizzical look. Apparently she was on her own for that one. She opened a few doors until she found a bathroom decorated in sage greens and browns.

Leaving the dog in the hallway, she closed the powder room door and quickly changed out of her wet things and into her borrowed finery. Oh, if her mother could see her now, Gemma thought with a slightly hysterical laugh as she looked down at the baggy sweats and the disreputable hoodie.

After hanging her clothes to dry on the shower rod, she opened the bathroom door. Still no sign of her host but the dog was waiting by the door.

She smiled and petted his fur, already mostly dry.

She followed the irresistible lure of the fire crackling in the other room. The living room had vaulted ceilings and massive windows. She could see the lights of Haven Point sparkling below and imagined the view would be spectacular in the daylight.

As she sat by the fire, the stress of the past hour seemed to catch up with her. She closed her eyes, her head sagging against the cushion of the chair, so very grateful to be safe and warm and alive.

CHAPTER TWO

JOSH MADE HIS way back to the house through the driving snow that made it difficult to see more than a few feet ahead of him. At least the lights of his house glowed a welcome through the storm.

He had lived in this area of Idaho his entire life except for the years he played college baseball in California but the intensity of fall and spring storms could still take him by surprise, especially when they seemed to come out of nowhere.

Kind of like his unexpected visitor. And not just today but six weeks earlier, when she showed up one day in Haven Point with her big green eyes. He had known who she was at once and had almost blurted it out but caught himself when his cousin Katrina had introduced her as the new hotshot programmer working for Bowie, Kat's husband.

He had been so astonished to see Gemma here in Haven Point, straight out of his memories and his imagination, that he hadn't known what to say. He had a feeling he had been a jerk that day at Kat's barbecue, fumbling over his words, staring at her too long, saying all the wrong things.

Whatever he'd done, they seemed to have gotten off on the wrong foot. While Gemma had been warm and approachable to everyone else in town, she seemed to turn standoffish and painfully polite around him whenever they encountered each other.

Josh had no idea how to get past the prickly barrier she had erected between them. He only knew she was rapidly becoming an obsession with him, which wasn't at all anything he had ever experienced.

Josh knew he had a reputation, not completely unearned, as a guy who shied away from anything serious.

He had always figured he had plenty of time to decide what he needed and wanted out of a relationship. His two older brothers each had married young, right out of high school in one case and college in the other, and both were now divorced and entangled in ugly custody fights.

Josh had decided he needed to grow up first and figure out the best kind of man he could be before he found that someone special.

And then Gemma Summerhill had moved to Haven Point and shook his entire world.

It was ridiculous. He had spoken with her exactly three times at various social occasions in Haven Point. Four now, he supposed, counting the past half hour. None of those encounters seemed to have done anything to soften her sharp edges around him.

He never struggled to talk with women. Ever. He was usually completely comfortable with them.

So why did she leave him so tongue-tied? She was smart, for one thing. Bowie Callahan, Katrina's husband, had mentioned at that first meeting that Gemma had genius-level tech skills and that he and Aidan felt extraordinarily lucky to have her on their team.

More than that, Josh knew the truth, the secret she had apparently decided not to share with the rest of Haven Point. Keeping it was becoming increasingly difficult.

Maybe today, the first chance he had to talk to her alone, might offer him an opportunity to clear the air between them and start over.

With that spark of optimism, he walked into his house. He took off his coat and Stetson, listening for some sign of her. All he heard was Toby snoring.

Concern flared and Josh wanted to kick himself. He was an idiot. She had fainted for a few seconds earlier. He had been so busy worrying about getting her warm and safe through the storm that he hadn't remembered that until now.

He should have made she sure she was settled before worrying about Ollie. His horse could have handled standing out in the snow for a few minutes. What if she'd passed out again and hurt herself?

As soon as he had the thought, a reassuring calm quickly followed. If that were the case, if she had fainted again or were in trouble, Toby would be whining or pacing to raise the alarm.

Still, Josh hurried through the house and stopped dead when he reached the fireplace where he saw the fire had burned down to embers and needed a log.

Toby was curled up on the floor, keeping a watchful eye on a blanket-covered figure asleep on the sofa.

She looked fragile, delicate, skin almost burnished translucent in the fire's glow. Everything he knew about Gemma Summerhill told him that was an illusion. She wasn't fragile *or* delicate. She had been through a terrible ordeal and had the scars to prove it.

He wanted to stand there all evening, drinking in the sight of her, but that was a little too stalker-ish for him. Not wanting to startle her too much, he cleared his throat quietly.

"Gemma? Miss Summerhill?"

She stirred a little but didn't awaken. He was torn between his instinct to let her continue sleeping and his conviction that she wouldn't be happy with him if he did.

Now that he knew she was safe, he could give her a few more moments while he changed out of his wet clothing and made a few phone calls, he decided.

Those few moments turned into twenty by the time he returned to check on her. By then, he had stoked the fire in the great room and the two ground-floor bedrooms in case the power went out, made a couple of phone calls to find out the status of the mudslide cleanup areas and pulled a ready-to-heat minestrone soup out of his freezer.

They wouldn't starve, at least. He had a freezer filled with meals, both from the gourmet service he used and from relatives and friends who were always bringing him a plate of this or that.

He and Gemma had enough provisions to spend the entire winter hunkered down here in the mountains while the weather howled outside.

The idea was far more appealing than it should have been.

Toby rose and padded to his side. The dog's movement seemed to pierce her subconscious, waking her where his voice hadn't been enough. He watched her eyes flutter a little then open the rest of the way.

"Oh," she said, her cheeks turning rosy. "I think I must have fallen asleep."

"I believe you did." He was enamored with her accent and wasn't ashamed to admit it to himself.

"I'm so sorry." As she stretched a little, the blanket fell down, revealing that she wore his favorite hoodie and a pair of his sweats. She reached down to pet Toby and he tried not to be jealous of his dog.

"What time is it?" she asked. "Have they cleared the debris so that I can drive home?"

"No. I'm sorry. I've just been on the phone with a friend who works for the county road crew and he says they won't be able to make any headway on the slide until morning. Apparently another rockslide is blocking the road between Haven Point and Shelter Springs, which has to take priority because of the volume of traffic that uses that road and the proximity to the hospital."

She looked stricken. "Oh dear. Is there another way I can go home tonight? Surely there's another road off the mountain."

He pointed out the window. "The storm is still going strong. We've got six inches of snow. By morning we could have a foot. I'm afraid we're not going anywhere tonight."

"I can't possibly stay here."

She didn't need to sound so aghast at the very idea.

"I'm sorry, Miss Summerhill, but I'm afraid you don't have a choice. It's not the end of the world. I've got plenty of food, even if we were stuck here for several days."

"We won't be, will we?"

Maybe if they were here longer, he could figure out how to talk to her without stumbling over his words. It was unlikely, unfortunately.

"My buddy promised they'll be able to move the slide away by noon tomorrow."

"I'm supposed to work tomorrow. I'll have to let Bowie Callahan know I won't be able to make it to the office."

He could put her mind at ease about that, at least. "I already called to tell him about the slide. He offered to send a helicopter for you as soon as the weather breaks."

She looked momentarily hopeful, then shook her head. "That's kind of him but unnecessary. I can take a day away from work. I suppose the research and development department won't fall apart without me."

"From everything I've heard, you've already made yourself indispensable."

She looked astonished and pleased. "I don't know about that."

"Bowie has nothing but good to say."

"That's lovely to hear. Working for Caine Tech is the best job I've ever had."

"Are you hungry? I'm heating some soup."

She sat up and pushed the blanket away. He tried not to stare as she revealed a little sliver of skin below the hoodie. "I am a little hungry. How can I help?"

Heating soup in a microwave didn't really take a committee but he sensed she needed something to keep her mind of her situation. "Would you mind setting the table?"

"Not at all." Limping a little, she followed him into the kitchen, which was now redolent with the creamy tomato smells from the soup. He pointed to the cabinet with the dishes and they worked together for a few moments while Toby watched from the sidelines, ever hopeful that Josh would drop a morsel of food on the ground.

He ladled soup into bowls and sliced some French bread he'd bought at the grocery store in town earlier that day.

"This looks delicious," she said. "Did you make it?"

"I wish I could say yes. I can cook but usually don't have time. I have a personal chef service in Shelter Springs that supplies me with several meals a month for my freezer that I can cook on the fly."

"What a good idea," she exclaimed. She tasted the soup and gave an appreciative nod. "That's delicious. A really good flavor. You'll have to give me their number. I enjoy cooking but find I'm so tired at the end of the day after working that I usually choose something easy that I don't have to think about. Sometimes I cook on the weekends and then eat leftovers all week."

"I've done the same but weekends are often the times I visit my stores."

"You have more than one?"

"Six," he said. The number still astonished him. "And we're hoping to expand into Utah and Wyoming within the next few years."

"That's impressive."

"My goal is to make the outdoors more accessible to everybody. Quality equipment, a wide selection and competitive pricing. That's our business model."

"It must be working for you."

He was immensely proud of how much Bailey Outfitters had grown over the past five years, since he had taken a small sporting goods shop and expanded it into multiple locations with a strong vision and loyal customers.

He could talk all night about it but he was far more interested in Gemma Summerhill. "So. What brings you to Haven Point?"

"I had a job offer for my dream company. I couldn't say no."

"Is that all there is to it? You're not escaping a bad relationship or running from the law in England?"

She laughed. "Neither of those things. Though what would you do if I said otherwise?"

"If it was the second part, I would probably ask if you were dangerous."

"No, except perhaps when I have a laptop in front of me."

He smiled. "I'd better lock mine down, then, so I don't take any chances."

"You're safe with me," she said. "I've only used my skills for good since I was a teenager."

"That's a relief," he said. He liked the implication that she might have been a bit wild in her youth. Okay, he liked everything about her.

"As for fleeing a bad relationship," he went on, "I would probably say that anyone stupid enough to let you go deserves the loss."

As soon as the words were out, he wished he hadn't said them. She stared at him, for several seconds, eyes wide.

There he went, saying the wrong thing again. What *was* it about her?

"If you weren't running from a relationship or the law, what other reason compelled you to take a job in a little town in Idaho? Was working for Caine Tech really that compelling?"

She appeared to give his question serious thought. "No one really compelling reason, I suppose, but a hundred little ones. I had a good job in London. I had good friends there, my family, and was on track for several big promotions over the next few years. And then one morning I woke up and realized I dreaded waking up in the morning and facing my day. I wanted something else but I wasn't even sure what that was."

She set down her spoon. "That very day I received an email from Aidan Caine. A few weeks earlier, we had met at a conference and he had asked for my card. I assumed he was only being polite, but apparently he had been researching some of the projects I'd worked on. Out of nowhere, really, he emailed me asking if I would consider taking a temporary job here in Idaho heading up a new project in the research and development department."

"Wow. You must be amazing at your job, if Aidan would make that kind of ask on a short acquaintance. He's known as a discerning kind of guy."

She looked flattered. "It was certainly unexpected. I turned him down."

"You what?"

"Yes. Quite firmly. I told him I would only consider if he would make the offer permanent."

Oh, he liked her. Gemma Summerhill was a complicated, intriguing woman who fascinated him more than any woman he could remember. He wanted the storm to go on forever so he might have the chance to learn everything about her.

"Would you like more soup or bread?" he asked.

"No. Thank you. What about you? Have you always wanted to do what you're doing now?"

He smiled a little ruefully. "Not even close. When I was young, I wanted to be a professional baseball player, probably like most other boys my age. I was a pitcher. At one point, I had a ninety-mile-per-hour fastball."

"I'll admit I'm not that familiar with the sport but that sounds impressive." She rose and carried her bowl to the sink.

For the next few moments, they worked together to clear the table.

"I played college ball," he told her as he loaded the dishwasher. "In the last game of my university career, a couple of pro talent scouts came down to take a look at me. I was pitching a shutout and had batted a double and a triple. In the top of the ninth, I was sliding into home and had a bad hit with the catcher and injured my shoulder."

"Oh no!" she exclaimed.

"Yeah. It was a catastrophic injury. My big pro ball career was over before it ever began. After two surgeries, I tried to work back to the level I'd been before but something had changed. I just didn't have it anymore and was quite sure I never would again. I knew I needed a plan B so came back and went to work for the local sporting goods store in Shelter Springs, which happened to be owned by an uncle. A year later, he asked if I wanted to buy him out. Two years after that, Bailey Outfitters expanded and we opened five more shops throughout the region. And here we are."

"And still growing."

He had big dreams, yes. Right now, all of them seemed to involve the woman in his kitchen.

He wanted to kiss her. She was standing only a few feet away. It wouldn't take anything to take a step toward her, grab her hand and tug her into his arms.

And what a disaster that would be. He sensed she was nervous enough about having to stay overnight in an isolated mountain cabin with a man she didn't know.

The power flickered suddenly, once, twice, then went out.

She gasped a little as the room was plunged into darkness except for the glow from the fire in the great room. He saw Toby rise from his favorite spot on the kitchen rug and head to her side. Gemma reached a hand down to pet the dog, a gesture he sensed was more for her own comfort than for the dog.

"There it goes," Josh said ruefully. "I was pretty sure that would happen eventually. The power goes out every time the wind blows too hard. Don't worry. I have a backup generator if we need it and plenty of lanterns. Why don't you sit by the fire and I'll find some light?"

He gathered up all the lanterns and emergency candles he could find and lit them all.

"Sorry about that," he said again.

"Do you think it will come back again soon?"

"Hard to say. Sometimes it's only out an hour, sometimes all night. I'll keep my fingers crossed it's a short outage."

"Why do you live out here, instead of closer to your shop in town?"

He considered his reasons. "The horses, mostly. I can ride into the mountains right after work without having to hitch up a trailer. And I suppose because I like the quiet. I grew up in a large family with two brothers and three sisters. My childhood was *never* quiet."

"How do you fare in the winter? Aren't you stranded up here?"

"There are a half dozen other year-round properties among the vacation cabins. The county plows to the end of the pavement and the rest of us trade off plowing the lower section of the road so we can get out. It's beautiful up here in the winter."

"I'll have to take your word for that."

He wanted to invite her to come back in a month or so but didn't want to scare her off. Anyway, she would see plenty of snow in the morning.

"Can I interest you in dessert? We could make s'mores in front of the fire."

"I've never had a s'more. Is it marshmallows and biscuits?"

"Plus chocolate. You can't forget the chocolate. I have a

special recipe. I use Nutella and sliced strawberries. And I happen to have some of both."

She looked intrigued. "Sure. All right. How can I help?"

"You can help me slice a couple of strawberries, if you want."

By candlelight, they worked together gathering the ingredients.

"Do you always keep these things on hand in case you're entertaining a lady friend?"

He had to laugh. "No. My brother and his kids came up to stay and go for an overnight ride last weekend and we did s'mores over the campfire. You're just fortunate enough to benefit from the extras."

"Lucky me." She smiled and Josh suddenly felt a little breathless.

He was the lucky one. Gemma Summerhill was here, in his house, and he wanted to savor every moment.

CHAPTER THREE

"THAT MIGHT POSSIBLY be the most delicious thing I've ever had in my life." Gemma swallowed the last bite of s'more, the marshmallow, strawberry and Nutella melting on her mouth.

"I've got a couple more strawberries if you want to go for another one."

"I can't. Really. You've stuffed me to the brim."

"Well, I don't want them to go to waste. I'd better have another one."

While Joshua speared a marshmallow on the long-handled fork and turned it to the fire's heat, Gemma sat back, perfectly content.

She should be frightened. She was trapped in a mountain hideaway, possibly for several more hours if not days, with a man she barely knew, in the middle of an October snowstorm.

She wasn't. All her nerves seemed to have disappeared around the time the power went out.

How strange, that something that had starting out so frightening could evolve into an evening she had enjoyed more than any she could remember in a long time.

Joshua Bailey was wonderful company. He was funny, clever, solicitous. And, she had to admit, deliciously good-looking.

After he finished roasting the marshmallow, he slapped

it on a biscuit, spread Nutella from a jar on the other one, added sliced strawberries then took a big bite of the whole concoction.

"There you go. The third one was just as good as the first," he declared after he finished it off.

His dog hopped onto the sofa to curl next to him and Josh absently stroked Toby's ears. She had a feeling this was a routine they were both accustomed to.

He was very different from the somewhat arrogant American cowboy she had taken him for the first time they had met. This version of him was sweet and funny and definitely a man she liked very much and wanted to get to know better.

"So," he said into the conversational lull. "I have a serious question for you."

"Oh?"

"I'm a bit hesitant to ask it."

"Go ahead," she said. "You've told me about your brothers' divorces, your mother's breast cancer scare and breaking up with your girlfriend two years ago. I suppose it's my turn. I can always refuse to answer, if you get too cheeky."

He gave her a careful look that sent alarm bells ringing. When he spoke, his voice was measured and his eyes were solemn. "Does anybody else in town know you're British nobility, Lady Gemma?"

Of all the questions he might have asked her, that was the last one she expected. She felt her breath catch. "I beg your p-pardon?"

"Sorry." He gave her a rueful look. "I shouldn't have just sprung that on you like that. You obviously have your reasons for keeping quiet."

"Yes. I most certainly do. Which begs the question of how you found out and how long you've known."

And why hadn't he said anything before now?

"That's somewhat of a long story and kind of a crazy coincidence."

"Tell me."

"Three years ago, I happened to be in the UK visiting one of our suppliers, a company that makes a phenomenal line of fly-fishing rods we carry at Bailey Outfitters."

"Summer Rods," she said faintly. It had to be. It was one of the smaller of her father's many businesses but one Lord Henry was passionate about.

He nodded. "They have an almost cultlike following among serious anglers and we're fortunate enough to be their exclusive supplier across three states. Which certainly made a buying trip to Dorset to meet the owner worth my while."

"You said you were there...three years ago." The pieces were beginning to fall into place.

He nodded, the good humor fading from his eyes to be replaced by compassion. "The week I was there, all the UK papers were filled with a story about a tragic car accident involving a truck driver who fell asleep and plowed through an intersection, killing both the driver of the truck and a passenger in the car. A passenger who happened to be a viscount, the son of the Earl of Amherst. The same Earl of Amherst who owns Summer Rods and whom I was there to meet."

She should have known the world was too small these days for her to hide away, even in a remote community in the mountains of Idaho.

"Also seriously injured was the earl's only daughter, who was the driver of the vehicle," he went on. "The story in the papers included a picture of you and two brothers from happier times."

She couldn't breathe suddenly and the room seemed too small. No. She wouldn't pass out again. She could talk about the accident without falling apart.

Still, she rose from the easy chair and paced to the fire, trying to gather her thoughts so she could respond without breaking down.

"I'm so sorry," Joshua said, his voice low. "I shouldn't have brought it up. You obviously have your reasons for not using your title here. It's none of my business."

"No. It's not," she said faintly.

She felt a warm, wet pressure against her hand and realized Toby had risen from beside Joshua and had come to her, probably sensing her turmoil.

"I won't say anything. I've known since you came to town and haven't mentioned it to anyone. You can trust me to keep your secrets."

She didn't know how to respond, too busy fighting down the familiar guilt and pain that always hit her when she thought about the accident.

"I'll show you to the guest bedroom. I started a fire in the woodstove so it should be warm, even if the power doesn't come back."

The odd note in his voice finally made her turn from the fire to face him. He was genuinely upset at her distress.

None of it was Joshua's fault. He had only asked a question that set up all kinds of flashbacks.

"The accident that killed my brother was…horrific. I was in hospital for a month and nearly lost my leg."

"Oh, Gemma."

"I would have gladly let them take both legs and my arms too, if I could have brought David back. He was a shining light in the world and in my family and I… I took that away."

To her horror, she felt tears begin to leak out, as if she hadn't cried enough over the past three years.

Her tears only intensified his distress. He cursed under his breath. "I'm sorry. So sorry. I shouldn't have said anything."

Somehow, the compassion in his voice made everything feel more acute and fresh. She could feel more tears escape and tried to tell herself it was a combination of exhaustion and stress.

"I'm the one who's sorry. I don't know what's wrong with me. Do you have a tissue?"

He rushed to the kitchen and returned a moment later with an entire box. "Here," he said. But instead of handing her the box, he took one out and dabbed at her eyes, completely disarming her.

She couldn't hold back the tears now and let out a sob. He looked helpless and uncertain for only a moment before he wrapped his arms around her.

Gemma froze for a moment, not sure what to do, but he was solid and strong and offered comfort beyond measure. She finally wrapped her arms around him and let herself cry.

Her family was so careful around her, so solicitous. Margaret and Henry didn't bring up the accident unless she did. They rarely even mentioned David's name, though he was a constant presence at every family gathering.

She tried to be strong most of the time but it felt heavenly to lean on Joshua's strength for a moment.

Still, she couldn't stand here all night blubbering.

"I'm sorry," she said after a moment and wiped at her eyes with a clean tissue. "I don't know what came over me."

"My mom says that sometimes a woman just needs a good, hard cry to clean out the cobwebs in her tear ducts."

"Your mother sounds very smart."

"She is. And she'll be the first one to tell you so."

To her surprise, she could feel some of the sadness leave her. She even managed a small smile. While she loved being held by him, Gemma had a feeling a little distance would make her story easier to share.

She wanted to share it with Joshua Bailey, though she couldn't have said exactly why. She hadn't even told any of her coworkers or new girlfriends in Haven Point the truth, but she wanted to talk about it with Joshua.

She returned to the easy chair and was grateful beyond words when Toby came with her and settled at her feet.

"David's death devastated my family, as I'm sure you can imagine."

Josh nodded. "I can. My youngest sister died during surgery for a congenital heart problem when she was a year old. My family never really recovered."

"Oh. I'm so sorry." It was an important reminder to her that everyone, no matter how good-natured and charming on the surface, could have deep pain in the past.

"Then you understand. In our case, it wasn't only that my parents lost their son. As I'm sure you can imagine, when a title is involved, things can get messy. As the eldest, David was set to become the next Earl of Amherst when my father dies. David's death means that responsibility automatically passes to my second brother, Ian, who already had a thriving career he loved and never wanted anything to do with the earldom."

"And you blame yourself because Ian now has to give up his career."

She should have expected he would cut straight to the heart of matters. "In a nutshell, yes."

"Balderdash."

The word was so unexpected coming from him—more like something her maiden aunt might have said—that Gemma had to laugh.

"Pardon?"

"I'd like to say something a little stronger but I'll wait to use the full creative range of my vocabulary until we know each other a little better."

His words sparked a little flare of anticipation inside her. She wanted a chance to get to know him better. Wanted it very much.

"My point is," Joshua said, "you can't possibly blame yourself for something that wasn't your fault. Even the accounts in the newspapers I read back then said so. The truck driver fell asleep at the wheel. How could you possibly be responsible for that?"

Yes, she had heard that argument before. "I know that, intellectually. It's hard to reconcile that with my heart, which can't help but feel that my brother would be here today if only I had made different choices. If I had taken a different route home from the holiday party, if we had left ten minutes earlier or later. Or if I hadn't been such a coward that I needed him to go to my company party with me in the first place."

There it was, the thing she blamed herself for the most. Her own weakness.

In the flickering light from the fire, she didn't miss the steady, probing look Joshua aimed at her. "I sense there's more to that particular part of the story."

So much more. She had never shared that with anyone else. Not even her parents. "You don't want to hear it."

"We're trapped here together for at least the next twelve hours. The s'mores are all gone. You might as well tell me."

Before the night was over, she had a feeling he would wring every single story from her.

She sighed, memories flooding back. "At the time, I was head of Programming for a startup in London. It was an exciting place to work. The owner of the company was ambitious and creative but…he had no boundaries."

His gaze sharpened. "In what way?"

"In every way. He was interested in me, I wasn't interested in him. I told him no but he continued to be…inappropriate with me. I should have quit. I was building up to that, actually. I loved the work but was so tired of his pestering. Meanwhile I had the obligatory holiday party to get through so I asked David to go with me. For once, I thought having Viscount Summersby along to have a word with my boss might help clear the air and make my situation more bearable so I could stay."

Her leg throbbed with pain suddenly and she tried to force her muscles to relax their sudden tension. "I should have simply handled the matter myself. If I had been stronger, if I had stood up for myself firmly and decisively, Colin would have had to back down. There was no need for me to drag my brother into it. No need at all."

"Did your brother mind helping you?"

"No. He was glad to do it, actually. He pulled Colin aside and subtly gave him a talking-to at the party about proper behavior in the workplace." Despite her pain, she had to smile a little, thinking of her protective brother standing up for her.

"As a brother myself, I can tell you I love when my sisters or brothers ask me to help them with something. I think David would have minded more if you *hadn't* turned to him for help."

Despite his quiet tone, his words seemed to resonate

straight to her heart. He was so right. David had been thrilled when she reached out to him.

She thought of how happy he had been, almost giddy, after talking to Colin. He didn't go full viscount very often but when he did, David could be formidable.

"I also don't think he would like the idea of you spending even a moment blaming yourself for what happened. I imagine he would want you to go ahead and embrace your life and all the adventures to come."

She could almost hear those very words coming out of David's mouth. Tears threatened again but this time she managed to blink them away.

"How did you know I've been needing to hear that?"

He smiled. "Lucky guess. Am I wrong?"

"No. I guess I needed the reminder."

"Good. Which still doesn't explain why you're traveling incognito, your Ladyship."

Oh, she liked him. More with every passing moment. "I have spent my entire twenty-eight years being Lady Gemma Summerhill. There are obviously certain expectations that go along with that. People always treated me differently, from primary school to university to my career. I never knew if people wanted to be my friend because they truly liked me or because my father is the wealthy and powerful Earl of Amherst."

"You are eminently likeable," he said, his voice rather gruff.

She could feel her face flush. "Being Lady Gemma in the technology field was more of a curse than a benefit. Every time I was introduced, people would make a big deal about it. After David died, I became not just Lady Gemma but Poor Lady Gemma, which was only about a thousand times worse. When I decided to take the job with

Caine Tech, I wanted to be done with all of that. To begin somewhere new without history constantly hanging over me. Does that make sense at all?"

He smiled softly, leaving her feeling lit up from the inside. "Perfect sense. There's an incredible freedom in starting over without the expectations of the past, isn't there?"

"Yes. Exactly."

"I won't say anything, I promise."

"Thank you," she said and was astonished at the complete trust she had in him.

Joshua Bailey was a man a woman could count on. She didn't know how she could be so certain, but something told her that when he met the right woman, he would do everything possible to make her know she was loved and appreciated every day of her life.

She wanted to be that woman suddenly, with a ferocity that astonished her.

It would be terribly easy to fall in love with him.

The thought should have scared her. Oddly, it only filled her with a strange, bubbly kind of anticipation.

He was the first to look away, glancing down at his watch. "It's late. Almost two. Toby, I can't believe you let me keep our guest up this late."

His dog cocked his head and whined a little and Gemma was charmed when Josh reached down and rubbed the dog's head.

"You should probably get some rest, especially since we might have to ride Ollie out of here tomorrow."

"Do you really think things might come to that?"

"I'm hoping the crews are at work clearing the slide away right now but we won't know the status until morning."

"If I had to stay another night, I wouldn't mind."

She hadn't meant to say that out loud and could blame it only on her exhaustion and the seductive lassitude stealing through her.

"You wouldn't?"

At his intense look, she shrugged. "I like your house. It's quiet here. Restful. I haven't had nearly enough peace over the past three years."

He gave a bright, broad smile that again stole her breath. "I'm glad. You're welcome anytime."

He led the way holding two of the lanterns through a doorway off the great room. Though most of the room was filled with shadows, a cheery fire burned in the glass-fronted woodstove and the room seemed warm and cozy.

"I need to add another log to the fire so it will burn all night for you."

"Thank you."

He pulled a split half log from a basket next to the stove, opened the door on the woodstove and pushed it inside.

She had to admit, she liked him fussing over her.

After closing the woodstove door, he rose. "The en suite bathroom is through that door. I'll probably sleep out on the sofa so I can keep an eye on the fire out there. Let me know if you need anything."

You. Does that count?

She managed to swallow down the words before she could blurt them out. "Thank you again for rescuing me and feeding me. I enjoyed the evening very much."

"So did I." He paused, looking rather adorably uncertain. "I would really like to kiss you right now. Would that be terribly forward of me?"

Heat flared inside her, a warmth that had nothing to do with the fire crackling inside the stove. She took a step forward. "Not terribly. No."

With a low sound, he wrapped his arms around her and kissed her.

This was no gentle good-night kiss. His mouth was firm, hard, with a fierce intensity that left her knees weak.

His arms felt perfect around her, as if she had finally found a safe shelter she had been seeking for a long time without being fully aware of it. With a contented sigh, she wrapped her arms around his waist and kissed him back. She wanted the kiss to go on forever, until they learned each other's every secret.

How was it possible for a man who had been merely a passing acquaintance eight hours ago to become so very dear to her? She didn't know. She knew only that now she had found him, she never wanted to let him go.

CHAPTER FOUR

ALL EVENING, JOSH kept thinking this whole thing had to be an incredible dream.

This, though. This was beyond a dream. He didn't have the imagination to make up something so perfectly *right*.

Gemma Summerhill was actually in his arms, soft, sweet-smelling, delicious.

He was the luckiest guy in the world right now.

It was crazy, how much an accident that had happened to strangers in another country could impact him. Josh's meeting with Lord Amherst had been canceled because of the death of the man's son and the injuries to his daughter. He had still met with company officials, still managed to seal the deal to carry their fly rods at Bailey Outfitters, so the trip hadn't been wasted.

For three years, he had wondered about Gemma Summerhill, that lovely, laughing woman whose image in a newspaper had so impacted him. At random moments, he would wonder how she was and hope she had recovered.

He thought he would never see her again and then fate had played a weird trick on him by entwining their paths together here in Haven Point and then dumping her practically on his doorstep.

She was the one for him.

He didn't know how he could possibly know that after

only one evening spent with her but Josh didn't question it for a moment.

While he wanted to push her back against that bed and spend the rest of the night learning everything she loved, he knew there would be time for that, once they knew each other better and she was as certain as he was that they were meant for each other.

Somehow, he managed to ease his mouth away. Her eyes were dazed, half closed, and the arousal in them made him want to forget all his good intentions and take what he wanted.

"I should go or I won't be able to walk through that door," he murmured.

"Do you have to?"

He groaned a little and rested his forehead on hers. "Yes. When I make love to you, I don't want you to have any regrets."

"Who says I would have regrets now?"

Her throaty question made him want to throw all caution out the window and start working his way through the layers they both wore.

But he was playing the long game here. He suddenly knew he wanted forever, not just tonight. He eased away from her so she could see him in the firelight and could know he meant every word.

"I want this to be real between us, Gemma. Full warning, I am well on the way to being crazy about you. I have been since you moved to town—longer, if you want the truth. This is going to sound strange but I've never forgotten you, since learning about your accident and seeing that picture of you and your brothers in the UK papers."

She stared at him, mouth swollen from his kiss and her eyes huge and shocked. "You have not."

"You were wearing a green dress. There was a boat behind you, a sailboat of some kind. You were holding a wineglass, as I recall. Your brothers were both smiling at you as if you'd made a joke."

She looked as if she didn't know what to say and Josh hoped he hadn't moved too quickly, overplayed his hand.

He reached for her fingers. "I was drawn to that woman for reasons I can't explain and felt so sad about the accident. It haunted me, if you want the truth. Every time I talked to people at Summer Rods, I tried to drop your name into the conversation and ask how you were. I figured I would never meet you in person but I always hoped you had recovered and were going on with your life."

"You...did?"

"When I walked into that party at Bowie and Kat's place and was introduced to you as the new programmer in Bowie's department, I just about fell over. Something led you here, Gemma. Admit it. You didn't move here on a whim."

She swallowed hard and shook her head. "I didn't understand it, but when Aidan offered it to me, I knew I had to take the job. Everyone tried to talk me out of it but it felt more right than anything else I've ever done."

He reached for her hand, again feeling like the luckiest damn man in the world. She was his. He didn't know how he knew they were meant to be together. That they *would* be together. He knew only that now he had found her, he couldn't imagine a world without her in it.

"I'm looking for something real and lasting. Just so you know where I stand."

"What if that's not what I want right now?" She still looked dazed, as if everything she thought she knew about her world had just been shaken up and put back together in a different way.

He shrugged. "Then I'll wait around until you change your mind. And you should know, I'm a very patient man."

He smiled and after a moment, she smiled back, though she still looked thunderstruck.

"Good night, Lady Gemma. Sweet dreams."

She gave a short laugh. "You impossible man. How am I supposed to sleep now, after you drop a bombshell like that on me?"

He kissed her one more time. He couldn't help it.

"Easy," he murmured against her mouth. "You can sleep well knowing tomorrow is the day we wake up and start building a future together."

A future that would be wonderful, filled with laughter and dogs, horseback rides into the mountains and long, delicious kisses that would always leave him wanting more.

Josh couldn't wait.

* * * * *